UNNATURAL CAUSES

ALSO AVAILABLE BY DAWN EASTMAN

The Family Fortune Mysteries

Pall in the Family

Be Careful What You Witch For

A Fright to the Death

An Unhappy Medium

UNNATURAL CAUSES

A Dr. Katie LeClair Mystery

Dawn Eastman

CROOKED
LANE

NEW YORK

Published in the United States by Crooked Lane Books, an imprint of The Quick Brown Fox & Company LLC.

Crooked Lane Books and its logo are trademarks of The Quick Brown Fox & Company LLC.

Library of Congress Catalog-in-Publication data available upon request.

ISBN (paperback): 978-1-68331-777-7
ISBN (hardcover): 978-1-68331-313-7
ISBN (ePub): 978-1-68331-314-4
ISBN (ePDF): 978-1-68331-316-8

Cover design by Melanie Sun
Book design by Jennifer Canzone

Printed in the United States.

www.crookedlanebooks.com

Crooked Lane Books
34 West 27th St., 10th Floor
New York, NY 10001

Hardcover Edition: December 2017
Paperback Edition: November 2018

10 9 8 7 6 5 4 3 2 1

To Brent,
My favorite brother

1

Although Dr. Katie LeClair knew her racing heartbeat was due to a surge of adrenaline, she couldn't calm the fear and anxiety that fueled it as she strode through the sliding emergency room doors and into Baxter Community Hospital. A whoosh of cool September air followed her inside and blew her long auburn hair into her eyes and mouth. She pulled it back into a tight ponytail and kept walking. During medical school, she'd imagined running down a hospital corridor—hair flying out behind her, stethoscope around her neck, racing to save a life. She'd since discovered that it was hard to run with a stethoscope around her neck—even painful. And at least in residency, by the time she arrived at any emergency, there was already a whole crew working on the patient.

She slowed her pace when she saw that the ER waiting room was empty on this late Wednesday evening. Brightly colored plastic and metal chairs sat empty along the walls. No one to witness her arrival in paint-spattered jeans and an

1

old men's oxford shirt. Three months into a full-time job, in a small private practice, with a real emergency, and she'd been caught off guard. Nick Hawkins, one of her new partners, was on call but couldn't be reached. When the answering service had called, she'd been on a ladder painting her new dining room. She'd dropped everything when she heard the patient's name and driven to the ER. It was only when she noticed the empty waiting room that she realized she probably should have called first. Maybe the answering service had gotten it wrong. Maybe she was too late. She took a deep breath, adjusted her messenger bag on her shoulder, and approached the door leading to the exam rooms.

"Can I help you?" A bored voice emanated from under the reception desk.

Katie stopped and looked over the divider.

An older woman wearing pink hospital scrubs decorated with fairies climbed up from the floor with difficulty. By the time she was standing, she was breathing heavily. She brushed dust off the fairies and removed a fuzz-covered piece of surgical tape from her knee.

"Had to reboot the computer again," she said. She must have seen the question on Katie's face. She glanced angrily at the ancient plastic box and continued: "These things are so old, we have to crawl around underneath and unplug them."

"I'm here to see a patient," Katie said. She turned to go through the door.

The woman sat in her wheeled desk chair and rolled to the computer screen. "Patient's name and your relationship."

"No, I'm her doctor." Katie pulled her jacket across her paint-splotched shirt and hoped the desk covered her ripped jeans.

"Oh, sorry." The woman and her fairies looked Katie up and down as if *she* were the last word on fashion. She *knew* she should have changed before she left her house. "I didn't recognize you. Dr. LeClair, right?"

After nodding to the receptionist, she stood taller and turned toward the door. She pushed the metal plate on the wall, and the frosted glass doors slid open to reveal the treatment area.

Baxter, Michigan, half an hour west of Ann Arbor, had a very small emergency room. It was no more than three cubicles with curtains for privacy and usually one doctor and one nurse.

"Hey, Doc! I thought they said Nick was on tonight."

Katie turned toward the familiar gravelly voice and saw the chief of police, John Carlson, leaning against the wall by the door. He was stocky and balding and would soon have more belly weight than was healthy. But his eyes were kind, and Katie was happy to see him. His usual affable smile was missing this evening, replaced by a grim line.

"They couldn't reach him, so they called me."

Carlson lowered his voice. "It doesn't look good."

"What happened?"

"Beth Wixom, Ellen Riley's daughter, couldn't reach her on the phone. She went to the house and used her key to get in and found her mother unconscious. She called nine-one-one, and we got there just before the ambulance."

"Poor Beth." Katie scanned the ER. "Where is she?"

"They took her to a conference room back there." Carlson pointed to a hallway off the main room.

He patted her shoulder and bestowed a kind smile. A month into her new life in Baxter, Katie had witnessed an accident that had left John's dog, Bubba, bloody and scared. She'd scooped up the black lab and driven him to the emergency vet clinic, which had been closed. She'd taken him to her own clinic, patched him up, and stitched his wounds. Only afterward did she realize it was the chief of police's dog. She had hoped that he wouldn't arrest her for treating Bubba without consent or a veterinary license.

Instead of arresting her, John Carlson treated her like a hero. By the next morning, everyone in Baxter knew that she had pulled Bubba from a ditch and carried him over her shoulder two miles to her clinic, where she wrested him from the brink of death. The gossip mill was nothing if not inventive.

Their brief conversation had alerted the staff to her presence. A nurse approached with her hands up like a traffic cop.

"No family back here right now; we're dealing with an emer—oh, Dr. LeClair. I didn't recognize you."

A curtain whisked open, and a gurney emerged. There were several people working around it. One adjusted an IV drip, one pushed the bed, and another barked orders. They were intensive care nurses and therapists, who must have been called from the ICU to assist.

"Get her settled and call Hawkins again; I can't babysit his patient all night," a man in a white coat said to a nurse.

He turned quickly and almost knocked Katie over.

"Sorry," he said. He put his hand under her elbow to steady her. "Can I help you?" He was tall, at least six feet to Katie's five and a half, and she had to tilt her head back to look him in the eye. Matt Gregor.

Flustered, she took a step back and stuck out her hand. "Katie LeClair. I'm covering for Dr. Hawkins. The answering service couldn't reach him."

His dark hair was long and fell forward as he looked down at her. He took her hand. "Matt Gregor. Aren't you a resident? I've seen you before."

"I just joined the family medicine practice in town," Katie said, "but yes, I was a resident here and at University Hospital." She couldn't believe that he recognized her. He'd been chief resident when she was an intern, and their paths had rarely crossed. University Hospital was the teaching hospital in Ann Arbor. It was a behemoth compared to Baxter's tiny community hospital. Katie looked forward to working in a place where she could get to know everyone from the physical therapists to the ICU nurses. Her constant rotation through the different areas of the hospital in residency had meant that she'd felt like she was starting a new job every month.

Matt Gregor was a good doctor, and Katie was happy that he had been taking care of Ellen even though she wondered why he was working the ER here in Baxter.

"I thought you were in private practice in Ann Arbor," Katie said.

Gregor nodded. "I am, but I'm doing some moonlighting out here since they're short staffed." He grabbed a clipboard off a nearby counter. "Okay. It's not good news. Frankly, I'll be surprised if she makes it through the night." The gurney had disappeared through another set of doors, and he started walking in that direction.

Katie ran to catch up to him.

"That was Ellen Riley?" She gestured toward the end of the hall.

He nodded. "Overdose, we think. We coded her for fifteen minutes after she got here. The EMTs found her unresponsive at home, barely breathing but with a heartbeat. They had to shock her once on the way here, and by the time she hit the ER, she had a weak pulse. While we were assessing, she flatlined. We coded her again and finally got her tubed. I've already pumped her stomach, but there wasn't much there. Her daughter found her, so we have no idea when she took the drugs."

Katie's mind was spinning. Ellen taking drugs? It was unbelievable.

She cleared her throat. "What did she take?"

"The EMTs grabbed everything from the scene. Looks like she took a bunch of diazepam. The bottle was empty, and she only filled the prescription a few days ago." He glanced at her and then quickly looked away. "Diazepam can be a dangerous drug in the wrong patient."

Katie felt her shoulders stiffen. Diazepam was also known as Valium and could be very sedating. "I know that. Where did she get it?"

Dr. Gregor stopped walking. "From you. Your name was on the bottle. That's why we called your practice."

Katie didn't say anything. She sensed that he was studying her the way an attending studies a new intern, but she didn't like those questions in his eyes: *Can this person be trusted with my patient? Do I have to watch everything they do?*

She had thought the need to prove herself would be over once she finished residency, but apparently it just went on and on.

He turned away from her and walked quickly down the hall. Katie hurried to keep up with him as he rushed after the gurney.

The ICU was chaotic. Usually a quiet area with beeping machines and hushed voices, the entire staff gathered in one section to work on a patient. The only patient—Ellen Riley.

Respiratory therapists barked orders at the nurses, and the nurses spoke over one another. It was all a babble of coded instructions about vitals and medicines, but it conveyed two things: fear and urgency. A young pharmacy tech hovered outside the room, obviously afraid to go in.

Dr. Gregor strode forward. He spoke very softly and calmed the room with his voice. "Vitals?" Katie had to lean forward to catch it, and the rest of the team quieted in order to hear his questions and to answer.

"BP sixty over palp. Heart rate thirty-five."

"Atropine ready, Doctor," said a nurse.

Katie hung back. Ellen was technically her patient now that she was here in the ICU, but Gregor had been working on the situation for an hour. It made no sense to step in and take over when she only knew the outlines of the case. She stayed to the periphery, trying not to get in the way.

A respiratory therapist bumped into her when he moved to the head of the bed. Katie stepped back and felt like a student again, watching the action but not participating.

While she watched, the frantic movements slowed and finally stopped.

Dr. Gregor looked at the clock on the wall. "Time of death 11:16."

A silence fell over the room as it always did when a patient died during a code. The battle had been lost.

It felt like a kick to the gut. Katie had seen many deaths, but Ellen's felt personal. She had known and liked Ellen Riley. The tentative friendship that they'd begun had made Katie feel like she might actually fit in in Baxter.

In the quiet, they heard the door swoosh open.

"Where's Ellen? Where's my wife?"

Christopher Riley looked wildly around the ICU. His usual elegant businessman image had faded. He wore jeans and a Michigan sweat shirt. His salt-and-pepper hair stuck up in odd places as if he had just woken or had been running his hands through it. And as he got closer, he looked every one of his fifty-odd years.

The nurses and therapists began to quietly clean up the area. Matt Gregor stepped forward to block Christopher's view.

"Mr. Riley?" Dr. Gregor put his hand out. "I'm Dr. Gregor."

Christopher looked past him and saw Katie.

"Dr. LeClair? What happened?"

Katie cleared her throat and pulled her shoulders back. She needed to be a doctor now, not a friend. She glanced at the entrance to the ICU and saw John Carlson standing there. She met his eyes and then looked away. He studied his shoes, and she could see his sigh of resignation from across the room.

"Mr. Riley, let's go sit over here for a moment." Dr. Gregor turned him away from Ellen's room.

Katie followed them to a small room with a table and a few chairs. The family conference room. The room where people decided to remove life support or send a loved one for rehabilitation or where they learned that they had narrowly dodged a tragedy—or not.

After they sat, Dr. Gregor said, "Your wife came to us unconscious with a very weak heart rate. We did everything we could, but we were not able to save her. I'm very sorry for your loss."

It was the standard bad-news speech. As medical students and residents, Katie and her colleagues had been coached in the best way to deliver bad news. For Katie, the hardest cases were the ones where she barely knew the patient or the family.

Emergency room physicians had to do it all the time. Sudden death through accident or illness, no relationship with the patient or the family, and then saddled with the job of shattering someone's life with a few words.

Christopher let his head fall into his hands. "This can't be happening. She was so healthy." He looked at them with red eyes, pleading with them to tell him something, anything else. "What happened?"

"We'll have to do some more tests, but there was an empty bottle of Valium at the scene. We assume it was an overdose," Gregor said.

"Overdose? Ellen?" Christopher looked at Katie. "She hated taking any medicine. I didn't even know she was taking Valium."

Christopher had echoed her thoughts. She frantically searched for something to say that wasn't "I didn't know either." Instead, she stood and said, "I'll go find Beth. She probably hasn't heard."

Katie breathed deeply for the first time as she left the ICU. There was something stifling about a closed space holding so much fear and sadness. She squared her shoulders and walked in the direction of the ER, bracing herself to give the same speech to Beth that Gregor had given to Christopher.

It hadn't gotten easier as time passed, and she doubted it ever would.

She found Beth sitting alone in the ER conference room. She was petite with dark spiky hair. She reminded Katie of a brunette Tinkerbell. Beth leapt to her feet as soon as she spotted Katie.

"Dr. LeClair, is my mom okay?" Beth rushed toward Katie. "The nurses won't tell me anything." Her eyes were red and swollen, and she clutched a crumpled tissue.

Katie gestured to the chairs, and both women sat.

Katie took a deep breath.

"Beth, as you know, your mom was unconscious when you found her. Her pulse was weak, and her heart failed on the way to the ER. They worked for over an hour and couldn't stabilize her. I'm so sorry for your loss."

Beth sat completely still, as if she hadn't heard Katie. Then one tear tracked its way down her cheek.

"What happened?" Beth's voice was hoarse.

"They think she overdosed on diazepam. They found an empty bottle at the scene."

Beth shook her head. "She hated taking medicine. I'm sure you knew that." She looked at Katie. "You aren't saying this was suicide? There's no way my mom would kill herself."

"We don't know yet. They'll do an autopsy, and we should have some more information then."

"Dr. LeClair, she was happy. Maybe a little stressed, but happy."

"That was my impression too. But we don't always know when people are struggling." This was so hard. Katie focused on staying calm and helping Beth, not dredging up her own issues.

Beth shook her head. "No, that's not my mom. It was just the two of us for years after my dad died and before she married Christopher." Beth took a breath, and she blinked back tears. "She was my best friend."

"What was she stressed about?"

Beth shrugged. "She was doing some sort of research and was worried about what she'd found. She never had a chance to tell me about it. We kept rescheduling our dinner plans." Beth's voice cracked, and she began crying.

Katie sat with her and offered tissues. She felt like an imposter when Beth thanked her for her kindness.

As she led Beth back to be with her stepfather, her mind drifted. There was one thing that bothered her about Ellen's death. Katie had no memory of writing that prescription.

2

Katie drove home slowly, trying to make sense of the evening. How could she have missed the signs? And where had Ellen gotten diazepam?

Katie had met Ellen over a year ago while doing a residency rotation with her current partners. She'd learned that Ellen and Christopher were newly married and had relocated from Chicago to Baxter after Christopher's mother died. There was certainly more to the story if a son only moves home after his parents are dead, but Katie had never pursued it. She understood the need for parental distance.

Ellen had switched her care to Katie three months ago when Katie started working with Emmett and Nick Hawkins. And now the police were suggesting suicide. Katie agreed with Beth. She couldn't accept it.

But what was the alternative? Ellen had *accidentally* swallowed an entire bottle of diazepam?

Katie pulled into her driveway and killed the engine. The lights were still on in the dining room. Caleb was awake.

She took a moment to breathe in the comforting smell of wood smoke and autumn leaves. She let herself in the side door and dropped her bag on the kitchen counter. Her brother, Caleb, sat at the paper-strewn dining room table, hunched over his laptop. His hair was long, and he hadn't shaved in a couple of days. She'd grown used to his pirate look when he was involved in a large software-coding project. He looked up and smiled as she entered the room.

"You're back earlier than I expected. Is your patient doing better?"

Katie pressed her lips together and shook her head. She wavered between the desire to go straight to bed and the desire to tell Caleb about her evening. Knowing she wouldn't be able to sleep, talking won. She pulled out a chair and sat.

It was always a struggle to convey her concerns without violating privacy laws. In the past, not ever saying the patient's name had been good enough. But in a small town like Baxter, the news would be in the public domain before morning.

She focused on the two things that bothered her the most: the idea of the suicide itself and the fact that she didn't remember writing the prescription that led to Ellen's death.

When she finished her brief recap, Caleb said, "I'm so sorry, Katie."

"I don't know if I can do this, Caleb." Katie pressed the heels of her hands to her eyebrows. "I can't believe I didn't see this coming—again."

"Katie"—Caleb pushed his laptop away and touched her hand—"none of this is your fault." He leaned forward and held her gaze. "Just like Mom wasn't your fault."

Tears pricked at the back of Katie's eyes, and she looked away. Why did he always see right through her?

She had only been thirteen. Their mother had been sick for a year, the chemo and surgery draining the life right out of her. But Katie never stopped hoping that a miracle might occur.

She'd known her mother was in horrible pain, but when she started to refuse her pain meds, Katie had thought that maybe things were getting better.

She ran home from school each day hoping her mother would meet her at the door. Every day she let herself in with her key and raced up the stairs to her mother's bedroom. They couldn't afford a full-time nurse, but a visiting nurse came every day at lunchtime to check in.

Katie sat with her mom every afternoon and did her homework, chatting about her day and watching for any sign of improvement. But in those last weeks, her mother became silent.

"I'm sorry, Katie-girl," her mother said. "I don't think I can hang on any longer. You're too young to understand, but I can't take the pain anymore."

Katie rummaged on her mother's table and found the bottle of pain medicine. There were only a few tablets left.

"Don't these work anymore?"

"I think they'll work just fine, love."

"Do you want one now?" Katie heard the urgency in her own voice. She wanted her mom back. The healthy mom who used to sing and dance while she cooked dinner. The one who read bedtime stories and did *all* the voices, even when Katie was too old for bedtime stories.

"No, not yet." She took the bottle from Katie and set it gently back on the table.

Katie heard nine-year-old Caleb thundering up the stairs. He stayed at a friend's house every afternoon until their dad brought him home after work. Katie always went to make dinner when Caleb came home.

"Dad brought pizza!" Caleb exclaimed. "Hi, Mom. How are you today? Do you want to have some pizza with us?"

"No, thank you, sweetie. I'm not hungry."

Caleb's face fell.

"Why don't you sit here with me for a minute?"

He pulled up a chair near the bed.

"Tell me about your day." Her voice was hoarse and quiet. "What did you do at recess?"

Katie slipped out and went downstairs. Her dad had just opened a Coors—the first of what would likely be many for the night. She'd never seen her dad drink more than one beer—except on Sunday while watching football—until her mom got sick. Now he sat and drank like his life depended on it. Katie was grateful that he usually just fell asleep; she knew from her friends that sometimes people got loud, or mean, or silly when they drank. Katie's dad just checked out.

"How's your mom?" he asked.

"The same. She says she's not hungry. I know she's in pain, but she doesn't want any medicine right now. I think she needs more."

Her dad held up a medicine bottle. "I picked up a refill on my way home. I'll bring it up to her in a minute and talk her into taking some." He drained the beer bottle. Katie had noticed that he never went to see her mom without at least one beer in his stomach.

15

Caleb came into the kitchen. He glanced at the beer bottle on the counter, looked at Katie, and hung his head. "I'm gonna watch *SpongeBob* and eat my pizza."

"I'll watch with you," Katie said.

She heard her dad's heavy, slow tread on the stairs.

She wished, later, that she remembered more about that night. What she had watched, what she and Caleb had laughed at, and what time her dad had passed out. But it all became a blur the next morning when she went to say good-bye to her mom on the way to school.

She knew the minute she walked into the room. It was too still, as if all her mother's items were holding their breath, waiting for someone to discover their dead owner. The smell in the room was stronger this morning. Katie had gotten used to the faint odor of decay and medicine that lingered around her mother. She walked slowly to the bed. Her mom's face was gray. She lay still and quiet, not breathing.

Katie glanced at her mother's bedside table and saw three empty bottles of medicine. They hadn't been there the last time Katie was in the room. She grabbed all three and read the labels. And then she started to cry.

"Katie?" Caleb moved his hand in front of her face, breaking the spell of memory.

She would never come right out and say it, but she was grateful for Caleb. They had stuck together as their father fell deeper into his grief and alcohol. Shuttled from one relative to another while in school, they ended up living all over Michigan. And they had only been separated for the four years that Katie was in college. He knew her better than anyone. He knew about the guilt that she could never quite shake.

In medical school interviews, they always asked, "Why do you want to be a doctor?" Katie's answer was that her mother died of cancer, which would elicit a sympathetic face and rapid progression to the next question. But that wasn't really the whole story. Her mother didn't actually *die* of cancer, and Katie had so far spent her adult life in a daily do-over. She never wanted to miss a cry for help or a subtle sign of illness again. And now she had.

She gave him a small, reassuring smile. "I know. Sometimes people don't want to be helped."

Caleb relaxed into his chair. He'd heard what he was hoping to hear.

Katie said good-night and went to her room. After a quick trip to the bathroom to brush her teeth, she climbed into bed. She knew that she wouldn't be able to sleep right away. She picked up the photo of her mother that she kept by her bed. It had been taken a year or so before the diagnosis, and her mom still had her beautiful strawberry-blonde curls and perfect skin. Katie shared her mom's deep-blue eyes and upturned nose. Katie's hair was just as curly, but darker. She missed her every day. And felt guilty every day.

Caleb might know her better than anyone, but he didn't know everything.

3

"Did you hear about Ellen Riley? It's alarming!" exclaimed Mrs. Winchester.

"I *did* hear about it, Mrs. Winchester," Katie said. "But what is equally alarming is your blood pressure."

Mrs. Winchester was normally one of her favorite patients, but Katie's lack of sleep had made her cranky. Katie turned to wash her hands in the sink and wondered yet again how she'd gotten through her residency. It had been routine in the beginning to get only moments of sleep in a thirty-six-hour period, but now that she was on a more normal schedule, it was as if her brain refused to go back to functioning on so little sleep ever again. Even her hair was tired. It hadn't put up any fight when she twisted it into a clip that morning and not one curl had sprung loose. Mrs. Winchester was only the fourth patient of the morning, and Katie was already running almost an hour late.

At eighty-four years old, Mrs. Winchester took care of Mr. Winchester, her dying sister-in-law Gladys, and a gang of cats. Her blood pressure was frequently out of control, particularly on housecleaning days. Fighting the dust and dirt that accumulated over one week's time—an alarming amount—got her worked up.

Each of Katie's patients had heard a version of Ellen Riley's death. Those that had been out of the loop due to the lack of a phone or the appropriate gossip contacts got all the information they needed by sitting in Katie's waiting room. Katie tried to steer Mrs. Winchester back to the matter of her blood pressure, but she was already plowing ahead.

"Such a nice woman—although probably too *city* for Baxter," she mused. "She may have done better in Ann Arbor. There's more traffic there, you know." She looked at Katie over the rim of her glasses as if the traffic were her fault. "How you young people can drive with all those other cars on the road is beyond me. Why, when we had to go to the University Hospital in Ann Arbor for those tests, I thought we'd never make it back. Even driving here today, we must have passed fifteen cars! Right here in Baxter! What is the world coming to?" She tilted her head so Katie could look in her ears. "And driving so fast, it's alarming! But poor Mrs. Riley, I just can't believe it. Why anyone married to Christopher Riley would want to die I just can't understand. Such a handsome man, like my Henry when he was young . . ." She stopped talking while Katie listened to her heart. "What's the verdict, dear?"

"You're just as healthy as last time, but your blood pressure is still too high," Katie said. "I'm going to change your dosage and see you back in three months."

"All right, dear." Mrs. Winchester cocked her head. "You look tired today. I hope you aren't working too hard. And you're too thin. I'll drop off a casserole."

Katie smiled at her and held out a hand to help her off the exam table. "I'm fine, Mrs. Winchester. I don't think I work nearly as hard as you do. Say hello to Gladys and Mr. Winchester for me. I'll see you in a few months, okay?"

Katie quickly stepped into the hall before Mrs. Winchester could continue her diatribe against all things modern. Or question Katie's health and lifestyle choices.

She closed the door, turned, and saw Nick Hawkins standing behind the nurse's desk watching her. He was tall with slicked-back blond hair and a penetrating stare.

"I've been looking for you," he said. "Every time I'm out of a room, you're in one." He came around the desk and lowered his voice. "I'm really sorry about the call last night. I don't know what happened. I must have been in a dead zone." He winced, realizing his poor choice of words. Katie knew that he and Christopher Riley had been friends for years. It was probably just as well that she had been the one to take the call.

"It's fine. Ellen was my patient anyway." Katie took a step back. "I'm sorry; I know you were friends."

Nick nodded. He ran a hand over his face and Katie noticed the purple smudges beneath his eyes. She wondered if he'd been up all night too.

"Thanks," he said. "Christopher is devastated." He looked like he was about to say more, but his nurse peeked around the corner and held up three fingers. Nick ran a pain clinic three days a week as well as a regular family medicine clinic. He specialized in palliative care and treating chronic pain. It seemed to Katie that he managed to see twice as many patients as she did.

"I'm falling behind," he said. "Better get back to work." And he disappeared around the corner.

Katie walked down the hall to her office and shut the door. She gulped down her third cup of coffee and pulled her schedule up on the computer. What a day this was going to be. Her already full calendar had been crammed with add-ons. Scanning the list of ailments, Katie suspected word had gotten out that she had information on Ellen. Debra Gallagher, the receptionist, was less than discreet and was probably passing out information in the waiting room. With any luck, some of her appointments would get the gossip they needed and have miraculous recoveries.

Thinking about her clinic as compared to Nick's, Katie got an idea. He turned over almost all the paperwork to his nurse. They had preprinted prescription pads, and all he did was sign them. Katie wrote most of her own prescriptions, but she realized that she didn't know if prescriptions were logged somewhere when the nurses called them in to the pharmacies. They must be. A doctor would need to sign off on them.

She took the back hall to Angie's office. Angie Moon was the head nurse and office manager. Katie peeked around the door and saw that Angie was scribbling notes on a yellow legal pad. Her straight dark hair fell forward as she worked. She startled when Katie knocked on the doorframe.

"Oh, Dr. LeClair, you surprised me," she said. She slid the pad under a pile of charts on the corner of her desk.

"Sorry, Angie." Katie leaned into the office. "I was hoping you could help me understand some of the charting."

Angie nodded and gestured toward a chair in front of her desk.

Katie entered and sat, suddenly feeling unsure. She didn't want to focus attention on the prescription until she knew more. However, she needed to know how Ellen had gotten the medication that had killed her. Curiosity won over discretion. She clasped her hands tightly in her lap and jumped in. "If I make a note to call in a prescription to the pharmacy, is there a separate place where that gets recorded, or does it go directly into the patient's chart?"

"Did something not get called in?" Angie pulled out a different note pad and prepared to take notes on this breach of protocol.

"No, everything is fine. I just wondered . . ." Katie hadn't thought this through. But then she had an idea. "If I call in a refill while I'm on call, do I just make a note in the chart, or do I have to enter it somewhere else?"

"Oh, I see." Angie put her pen down. "You can write it in the chart, but if you don't want to bother, you can fill out a call sheet, and Pauline will file it in the chart—eventually. However, if you prescribe something new, it would be better if you put it in the chart itself so that you're sure it gets recorded properly—especially if it's Dr. Emmett's or Dr. Nick's patient so they know what you've changed."

Katie nodded. "And if I ask my nurse to call in a prescription, where does it get recorded?"

"Usually, she'll make a note in the chart. But no matter what, we log it into the med book so we have a record of what was called in and when."

"So if a prescription is called in, there is always a note in the med book?"

Angie nodded. "We're especially careful about Dr. Nick's pain patients. Any patient on narcotics is closely monitored."

"And you have the book here in your office?"

"No. It's in the med room." Angie narrowed her eyes. "Are you sure there isn't a problem?"

"No, no problem. Thanks, Angie." Katie stood and went to the door. "I just wanted to be sure I'd checked all the boxes."

"I have no worries about you, Dr. LeClair," Angie said, "and I'm really sorry about Ellen Riley. I heard you were there in the ER."

"I was, but it was too late to do anything for her."

Angie shook her head. "Sometimes this job sucks."

Katie gave a brief nod and returned to her office—she had a plan, but it would have to wait until after she'd seen her patients.

At six o'clock, Katie was finally done with clinic. A few no-shows and cancellations in the afternoon had lightened the load and confirmed her suspicions.

Katie sat at her desk with a stale half sandwich from lunch and a pile of charts. The electronic medical record system hadn't found its way into this small practice just yet, and the doctors still handwrote their clinic notes. Katie was pretty sure the old-est partner, Emmett, hoped to hold out until retirement. He wasn't a fan of computers, and Katie had learned not to bring it up for fear of inviting another rant against the digital age.

An hour passed quickly as she scribbled notes while reliving each patient encounter. In residency, she'd done this with a click of a mouse. The computer saved time, but she found the writing reassuring. She revisited the complicated patients and made sure she'd thought of all the options. Sometimes she found things she'd missed.

Katie put the last chart on top of the "done" pile and sat back, suppressing a yawn. She wanted to go home and get some sleep. But she couldn't let go of the feeling that there was more to Ellen's death than suicide. And the question of where she got the prescription still loomed.

She pushed away from the desk and grabbed the pile of charts. When she opened her office door, she realized that everyone else had left. She'd hoped to have the place to herself so she could discreetly check into Ellen Riley's medical records. She found a sticky note on the door asking her to lock up on the way out.

The receptionist, Debra, left every day at five on the dot. Her kids were in some sort of strict day care that charged her for every minute that she was late picking them up. If there were still patients to be seen, she'd be sure the charts were ready to go, and she'd lock the front door. After five, everyone was shown out the back door to the parking lot. Caleb thought it was a creepy system. It meant the patients still waiting never saw anyone leave. How did they know there wasn't something wrong? Katie had pointed out that most people didn't see conspiracies, evil plots, and zombie apocalypses in every situation the way he did.

Being alone after-hours *was* kind of creepy though. The only lights left on were the ones in the reception area, and the whole office was silent. It was an old building, and as she walked to the chart room, the creaking floor made it sound as if someone was following right behind her. Katie was glad no one was there to see how many times she stopped and turned to check that she was alone.

She flicked on the light in the chart room and set the pile of folders on the cart to be filed. The windowless room was filled with row after row of metal shelves. She walked to the back of the chart room to the small medicine room where they kept all the medications that they used in the office. Katie pulled her key ring out of her pocket and briefly wondered how many keys there were for this room. She hadn't needed to use hers yet. So far, the couple of times she'd needed something during her clinic, one of the nurses had gotten it for her. She found the med book right away and turned to mid-August. She ran her finger down the list of patients. Katie caught her breath when she found Ellen's name in early September. But it was only a refill for her thyroid medication. There were no other entries for Ellen Riley. So no one had called it in from the office. Katie was both relieved and more confused. She had dreaded finding a note reading, "per Dr. LeClair diazepam 5 mg called to such-and-such pharmacy." But not finding a note left her no closer to finding out how Ellen had gotten that prescription.

Katie locked up and turned to face the shelves of charts. She went to the section that held the *R*s and found Ellen's chart easily enough, flipping it open. Ellen had come to the practice right after her marriage two years ago. Emmett had treated her for a sinus infection, and she'd been in for a few other minor ailments until three months ago, when she'd switched her care to Katie.

She remembered Ellen's visit because it had been during her first week in practice with Emmett and Nick. Katie had been nervous and double-checked everything. Which meant that she was painfully slow and looked up every diagnosis in the evenings to be sure she hadn't missed anything. All through medical school and residency, there'd always been someone else in charge. Someone else to check that the correct medication was being prescribed or the right test ordered. Katie knew she was a good doctor. But that first couple of weeks had been a leap of faith.

She skipped ahead in Ellen's chart to the last time she'd seen her. It had been a week before her death, and Ellen had come in complaining of feeling "run down." She hadn't been sleeping, she said. Katie had sensed that she was worried about something, and when she'd asked Ellen about it, she had admitted feeling stressed about something to do with "research" and too many late nights. Katie only vaguely remembered that clinic—Nick had been at the hospital dealing with an emergency, so Emmett and Katie had been seeing his patients plus their own. It had been a crazy, busy day. She scanned to the bottom of the note. There was no mention of diazepam.

No matter how busy her clinics became, she didn't think she would forget to chart a medication. And she was sure that she would remember calling it in herself to the pharmacy.

Katie looked in the other tabs to see if anyone had noted the prescription. She went to the "to be filed" bin and set the chart on the edge of the counter. She'd flipped through half the pile and was into dates from August when a loud crash in the hallway made her jump, and she knocked the chart off the counter. On its way to the floor, she saw that the clips were undone. It hit the ground and scattered papers everywhere. Katie listened at the door, her heart racing.

Then she heard the rattling and clanking of a mop in a bucket. Marilyn Swanson, the office cleaning lady. Katie had only met her once when she had stayed late to finish up notes. She took several deep breaths to calm her panic. She knelt down next to the spilled chart and had almost finished piling all the pages back into the folder when the door opened.

"Oh, hello, Dr. LeClair. I thought I heard someone in here," Marilyn said and looked from the messy pile of papers to Katie. "Can I help?"

She was taller than Katie and very thin with long, straight dark hair and severe bangs. She had an exhausted manner as if she carried too many burdens. Katie felt tired in her presence.

"No, but thank you, Marilyn." Katie crammed the pages into the folder and clutched it to her chest. She'd put it all back together later. "I was just finishing up." Katie moved past Marilyn and stepped toward the door. She hoped Marilyn couldn't see which chart she was holding.

Katie pulled open the door.

"Wait." Marilyn held out a registration sheet. "I think you dropped this."

Katie took the document.

Marilyn nodded at the paper in Katie's hand. "It was sure a shame about Ellen Riley," she said.

"Did you know her?" Katie tried to hide her surprise.

Marilyn nodded. "Christopher Riley and I were in school together, so I've known him all my life. Our parents were friends, and we were like cousins growing up. He's always been very . . . supportive. When I started my cleaning business, he was the first one to sign up and told everyone about it. He helped me get clients all over town."

"You must have known Ellen fairly well then," Katie said.

"Not really." Marilyn shook her head. "I only saw her briefly if she was home when I went to do their house. She was always busy with one thing or another."

Marilyn bent to plug in her vacuum. Katie took the opportunity to say good evening and escape back to her office.

4

Katie tried unsuccessfully to corral all the loose papers and get them back in their proper order. She'd spread them on her desk and was organizing them into piles when her phone chirped with a text message. She glanced at it and sighed. She'd forgotten about her plans with Gabrielle.

She shoved the papers back in the folder and stuck the whole mess in her bottom desk drawer. She sent a quick "on my way" text, grabbed her bag, turned out the light, and headed for the back door.

"See you later, Marilyn," Katie shouted over the vacuum as she passed the file room. Marilyn looked up and waved.

Katie had met Gabrielle Maldova during her first year in residency at University Hospital on her required obstetrics rotation. Gabrielle was a second-year obstetrics and gynecology resident, and she had taken Katie under her wing while the two of them endured thirty-six-hour calls. On their busiest night, they had delivered twenty-five babies. The OB rotation had left little time for anything else, and they'd bonded in their shared misery. Both of them were now beginning real jobs, and scheduling time to see each other was getting more difficult.

Katie steered her ancient Subaru hatchback onto the highway and let herself go on autopilot for the short drive to Ann Arbor. Gabrielle lived in a small bungalow far enough off campus to avoid the noise and hectic energy of students but close enough to enjoy the restaurants and shops that catered to them.

It was mid-September, and the leaves in Gabrielle's neighborhood had just begun to change. The few reds, oranges, and yellows gave a preview of the days to come. Katie felt the energy of the campus coming back to life for the fall semester. Autumn always felt like the New Year to Katie. She had lived on an academic schedule for so long, she made resolutions in September rather than January.

Gabrielle swung the door open before Katie had even turned off the car. "You forgot, didn't you?" she accused from the porch. She was taller than Katie with dark hair and olive skin. Katie thought she looked exotic and beautiful, and based on her active dating life, the male population agreed.

"I made a new curry just for you," she said as Katie climbed the steps. Once a month, they got together for dinner and drinks. They tried something new each time, and eventually the competition had ramped up, with each trying to outdo the other from month to month to win their twice-yearly contest.

"That sounds perfect. I'm starved," Katie said, "and I didn't forget, exactly. I just lost track of time."

Gabrielle's living room was a riot of deep jewel tones. Katie sank into the chocolate-brown velvet sofa and watched while Gabrielle dipped the rims of two martini glasses in what looked like melted caramel. She dumped several premeasured shot glasses into a shaker and made a big production of shaking the concoction. She poured it out and garnished each glass with an apple slice.

Katie accepted hers with enthusiasm. If caramel was involved, did it really matter what else was in the glass? But she asked anyway. "What's this?"

"Taste it, and then I'll tell you."

Katie sipped. As usual Gabrielle had mixed up a winner.

"So good!" The sweetness of the caramel and the tart apple flavor reminded Katie of fall carnivals and apple picking.

"It's a caramel apple martini." Gabrielle held hers up in a toast and then took a sip.

"You're really upping the ante here," Katie said. "You know I'm still painting my living room and have hardly any furniture."

"We can sit on boxes and order pizza next time."

Katie grinned at her over the rim of her glass. "You'd love that, wouldn't you? You could claim the trophy."

"That old thing? I couldn't care less . . ." Gabrielle flapped her hand in dismissal.

But Katie noticed the empty spot on her mantel where it used to sit.

Every six months, they voted on who had hosted the best dinners. Katie was currently in possession of the "trophy"—a plastic model of a gastrointestinal tract that they had liberated from a drug representative.

Katie took another sip and felt warm and happy for the first time since she'd arrived at the hospital for Ellen Riley.

"So what's the news from Baxter? Still loving the small-town country-doctor gig?"

"It's gotten a little tricky," Katie replied and set her drink on the table.

She gave Gabrielle a brief rundown on the visit to the hospital, her concerns about the diazepam prescription, and her recent perusal of Ellen's file. She sipped her drink and sat back, waiting for her friend's response.

"Wow. I thought you'd left all the excitement behind when you joined that practice. Just hypertension and well-child visits." Gabrielle took a hefty swig of her own martini.

Katie narrowed her eyes at Gabrielle. The one thing that they disagreed on was the level of excitement they each needed in their jobs. Gabrielle loved the adrenaline rush of an emergency C-section or a baby presenting in an awkward position. She loved to be in the OR for almost any reason. Katie preferred talking to her patients over cutting into them.

"I could have done without this kind of excitement."

Gabrielle nodded. "You really don't remember writing that script?"

Katie shook her head. "There's no record of it in her chart. That's partly what I was doing so late at the office. I wanted to look over her files after everyone left. Since just requesting it would start the gossip mill turning."

She felt uneasy. The drink that had tasted so delicious a few minutes ago now sat like acid in Katie's stomach.

Gabrielle tilted her head and looked at Katie. "Let's talk about it over dinner. Everything is better with curry."

They moved to Gabrielle's small dining area. She'd set the table with a dark-brown tablecloth and bright napkins that completely coordinated with the rest of the living room. Candles of multiple heights flickered playfully on a reflective tray. This was just what Katie needed.

Gabrielle brought a large bowl out of the kitchen and took the lid off, releasing the delicious aroma of curry, onions, and roast chicken. Katie felt lightheaded from the vodka and hunger.

The only sounds for the next few minutes were forks on plates.

"This is unfair. I'm so hungry, and this is so good," Katie said. "I'm going to have to vote this meal as my favorite. And I was planning all my new decor around the trophy."

Gabrielle grinned.

After she'd cleaned her plate, Katie put her fork down. "I don't know why I can't let this Ellen thing go."

"Which part—the suicide or the diazepam?" Gabrielle pushed the bowl of chicken curry toward Katie.

"Both. But right now I'm thinking about the suicide." Katie picked up her drink and set it back down. "I saw no sign of depression. I know I'd only seen her a few times, and several of them were when I was doing my rotation with Emmett in residency, but still. I think I would have picked up on it. Plus, she's a psychologist. She started a life coach business when she moved to Baxter. She knew all the signs of depression. I think she would have asked for help."

Gabrielle shook her head slowly. "You know the rule about patient histories. Everyone lies. Whether it's about how much they drink, or how often they exercise, or whether they're depressed. They all lie about something. Maybe she thought she could handle it."

Katie nodded. She agreed with Gabrielle in principle, but something still nagged at her. "You're probably right. She's just the first one I've lost since I finished residency. She seemed so happy. It just has me questioning . . ." Katie swallowed and blinked her eyes to clear the burning of tears. She adored Gabrielle, but she wasn't going to cry in front of her.

Gabrielle reached across the table and squeezed Katie's hand. Katie gently pulled her hand away and took a swig of water to clear away the last bits of emotion.

Gabrielle focused on her food for a few minutes.

When it was clear that Katie was back in control, Gabrielle said, "I made your favorite cheesecake."

Katie smiled. "Bring it on."

An hour and another drink later, Katie and Gabrielle sat on the couch gossiping about old friends from residency, the nurses in the ICU who were planning an overthrow of the power-hungry head nurse, and the latest surgeon Gabrielle was dating.

"You skated right past the fact that Dr. Gregor was working in the ER last night," Gabrielle said. A smile threatened to take over, but she was clearly trying to keep it under wraps. Matt Gregor was well known to Katie and Gabrielle. They'd admired him from afar for most of their residency. He was two years ahead of Gabrielle, and the fact that he had been chief resident meant everyone knew *of* him.

Katie felt the betrayal of heat rising in her face. Gabrielle knew that Katie's recent romantic past was littered with incompatible and inappropriate men. She had always been able to blame her work schedule to end things before they got too serious. Gabrielle also knew about Justin.

Justin Wright was part of every happy memory from college and medical school. They had met on the Diag at the center of University of Michigan's campus on a beautiful late September afternoon. Katie had skirted around a group of guys playing Frisbee, but when one of them missed a catch,

Katie had jumped up and snagged the flying disc. As the man who'd missed the catch approached to get it back, Katie had been struck by his intense blue eyes and crooked smile. She'd smiled at him when he was a few feet away and sailed the Frisbee over his head to his friend, who had leaped to catch it.

"Impressive," he said.

"Thank you," said Katie.

"No, I meant Kevin over there. He never jumps for a catch." He looked at her from under his blond fringe. "He must be trying to impress you."

Katie laughed.

"I'm Justin," he said. "You should join us; we could use someone who actually knows how to throw."

They'd been inseparable after that. Following graduation, they had coordinated Justin's law school and Katie's medical school so that they could be together. After five years, Katie had assumed that they would get married eventually. Justin had been talking about having kids, houses, and pets in a way that made Katie nervous, but in a good way.

In the spring of her last year of medical school, they went to their favorite Mexican restaurant. Katie knew he was nervous about something. He'd been distant and quiet for weeks. Match Day was quickly approaching—the day when medical students across the country found out where they would do their residency. Katie had placed Michigan residencies high on her list, but she had also included some in Chicago and one as far away as California. Justin was nine months into his first job as an attorney, and they both knew that between residency for Katie and being low in the hierarchy for Justin, they would never see each other if she didn't match in Michigan.

After the waiter left, Justin cleared his throat. He carefully rearranged his cutlery. Katie's pulse quickened. He was going to propose. She wasn't ready to get married, but they could have a long engagement, right?

"Katie, I think this thing between us has run its course."

Katie opened her mouth to say "Yes" and had to stop and process what he had said. *Run its course?* Like a bad case of the flu or strep throat?

"What—" Katie stopped and took a deep breath. He was always pranking her about things like concert tickets or vacation destinations. He'd say, "Sorry about the concert; I couldn't get tickets," and then he'd hand her an envelope with front-row seats. This was a bizarre way to propose, but maybe not for Justin. "What do you mean?"

Justin sighed and actually rolled his eyes. Katie sat back quickly in her chair. This wasn't a prank. He was breaking up with her. She had put Michigan in her top three spots for choice of residency *for him.* She hadn't even seriously considered anywhere else.

"I mean, I think we should see other people," he said.

"You mean, *date* other people?"

Justin nodded. Katie thought back over the last month or so. Ever since they had talked about where she should do her residency, he'd been asking questions about her work schedule. Justin continued to be shocked that she would have to work twenty-four-hour shifts. During some rotations, she would only get two days off per month. She'd argued that he worked all the time as well. He had seemed to think that that made his point even stronger.

"Exactly," he'd said. "Neither one of us can take care of a house or a kid. We can't even manage to have a dog."

Katie had laughed. She'd truly thought he was joking. "I didn't know you wanted a dog."

But he wasn't joking. It was as if the entire time that they had been together and she had applied for and attended medical school, he had been imagining that she was someone else. As if it had come as a surprise to him that her career would be just as demanding as his own.

"I need a wife, not a roommate who occasionally makes it home for dinner," he said and nodded to the waiter when he placed their margaritas on the table.

Katie had felt dizzy and nauseated. She pushed back from the table and raced out of the restaurant. She had to get away from him. Away from this weird Justin who seemed to be living in another decade, maybe even another century. She started to walk home, then called Caleb to pick her up. Thank God she hadn't moved in with Justin like he had wanted her to when he finished law school. Katie hadn't wanted to leave Caleb in the lurch. She made Caleb go to Justin's apartment to get the few things she had left there and to leave her key behind. She never wanted to see him again, but she couldn't imagine not ever seeing him again.

Katie snapped out of her thoughts about Justin and looked at Gabrielle's impish smile. She'd recently made the mistake of telling Gabrielle that she might be ready to try again. "I wasn't focused on Dr. Gregor when my patient was in critical condition," she said stiffly.

"No, I'm sure you weren't. But we could focus on him now." Gabrielle sipped her drink and watched Katie squirm.

5

Friday morning, Katie was back in clinic. She had seen a hypertensive truck driver, a second grader with strep throat, two diabetics, and a sprained ankle by ten o'clock. And the stack of charts didn't seem any shorter than when she had arrived.

She was standing at the counter outside the patient rooms, writing a quick note to herself about remembering to check the X-rays on the sprained ankle patient, when she looked down the hall and spotted Emmett Hawkins leaving the records room. He was tall and lanky with a full head of white hair that never lay flat. He had a stack of charts in his arms, and there was something about the furtive way he moved that reminded Katie of a shoplifter. Emmett was usually off on Friday mornings. She wondered what had brought him in. He was the reason she'd chosen this practice right out of residency. It was exactly the kind of place where she'd imagined working when she'd decided in high school to pursue medicine. She still felt that her mother would have lived longer if her doctors had paid more attention. Emmett had a gentle way with patients, and his use of practical solutions rather than always running tests and prescribing drugs appealed to Katie. She hoped to learn a lot from him.

Katie took a deep breath and grabbed the chart hanging outside the next exam room. Lynn Swanson. Again.

Katie had seen Lynn multiple times in the few months she'd been working in Baxter. Lynn had headaches, stomachaches, back pain, and recently a sprained wrist. At thirty-two, Lynn was only a couple years older than Katie, but she already had four children and a world-weary manner. She looked ancient. Katie had suspected depression on the first couple of visits, but recently she'd become worried about abuse. Previous attempts to talk about it had led to Lynn getting defensive and quiet.

Katie sighed and knocked on the door.

She walked in to find Lynn hunched over a *People* magazine as if it held the secrets to the universe. Her light-blonde hair was pulled back in a ponytail, and she wore jeans, sneakers, and a red plaid shirt buttoned at the neck and wrists.

"Hello, Lynn. How's the wrist?" Katie sat on the wheeled stool by the small desk.

"I think it's almost better," Lynn said. "I've been taking the brace off for longer and longer every day like you said, and it feels okay. I forgot to bring it with me."

"That's probably a good sign if you don't feel you need it." Katie scooted forward on her stool and took Lynn's hand. She turned it over and felt along her wrist for swelling and tenderness. "Where are the kids today?"

"The oldest ones just started school, and my little one is at my neighbor's house." Lynn flinched a bit when Katie pressed on her wrist. "That part is still sore."

Lynn had always brought at least two of her children to every visit, adding to the chaos and diminishing any chance of confrontation. Katie decided to try again.

"It seems much better, though," Katie said. She scooted back to the desk to give Lynn some space. "I'm glad you came alone today. I'd like to talk about your frequent headaches and injuries."

Lynn looked at the floor. "I'm sorry about last time. I didn't know what to say when you asked me if I felt safe at home."

Katie waited. Silence was often the best way to keep a patient talking.

"That's why I left Austin with my neighbor; I didn't want him to hear. Not that the kids can't see what's happening." She cradled her sore wrist. "My oldest in particular—he's so protective of me. But he's only a boy . . ."

"Are you saying you don't feel safe? I can help you, but I need to know what the problem is."

Lynn looked at Katie then. Her eyes were red and wet.

"I don't know what to do. It's been going on for so long that I started to think it was normal. But after this"—she held her wrist up—"I know I have to do something. For my kids' sakes."

Katie nodded to encourage her to continue.

"I've been with Eric since high school. He was so romantic and kind." A sad smile flickered on her face. "But even then he was real jealous, not just of other boys, but of anyone who took my attention from him. After we got married and had the kids, things stabilized for a while. I had to keep the kids quiet and cater to Eric when he was home, but things were okay. I thought I was lucky to have a husband who wanted me around and didn't want to share me with anyone." One large tear slipped down her cheek. Katie handed her the tissue box.

Lynn took a tissue and wiped away the tear. "Anyway, about a year ago, he lost his job at the garage. So Eric picked up work wherever he could. He was home more, and it was harder to keep the kids out of his way and harder to calm him down when one of them broke something or they started bickering. He started drinking more. It got so I hoped he wouldn't come home and would just sleep it off somewhere. He started picking fights over anything."

Lynn took another tissue and blew her nose. Her hands shook as she dabbed at her eyes.

"The first time he hit me, I thought it was an accident. But then it became a regular thing. He's always careful not to hit me where a bruise would be noticeable. But the kids know."

Lynn took a shaky breath. "I have to do something. Ellen Riley was helping me to make a plan, but now she's . . ."

"Were you seeing Ellen as a client?"

Lynn shook her head vehemently. "No, I couldn't afford to pay her. She volunteered at the women's clinic where I go for my birth control pills. They can usually give them to me for free or for only a few dollars."

Katie scooted forward and put a hand on Lynn's shoulder. "I can help. I'll get in touch with people who can help you." Lynn nodded and tried to blot her tears, which only made her makeup smear.

"I'll be right back," Katie said. "I'm going to contact a women's shelter. I want you to talk to them before you leave." As she stood, Lynn grabbed her wrist.

"Don't tell anyone else in the office, please," Lynn said. "They all know me and Eric. My mother-in-law works here. It has to stay a secret."

Mother-in-law? She must mean Marilyn. Was she worried that Marilyn would find out about the abuse or that she would tell her son what Lynn was planning?

Katie nodded and squeezed Lynn's hand. "I'll be right back."

6

Fortunately, Katie was only in the clinic for a half day on Fridays. She wanted to reach out to Beth Wixom to see how she was doing since her mother's death. She buzzed Debra and asked her to find Beth's phone number. Within seconds, Debra was in her office with a phone message slip. She was short and curvy with bouncy blonde curls and a sweet smile set off by dimples. Despite her propensity for gossip, she was a great receptionist, combining her love for people into a bubbly charm that kept the front office running smoothly.

"She called about ten minutes ago, wants you to call when you get a chance."

"Oh, great. Thanks, Deb."

"Are you okay?" Debra tilted her head to get a better look at Katie. "You don't seem quite yourself today."

"Just tired."

Debra sniffed and went back out front. Katie knew Debra didn't believe her. Debra could usually tell right away what kind of mood Katie was in. At first, it had been almost spooky. She wasn't used to someone paying such close attention to her every move.

Debra had explained once. "If my doc is in a bad mood, the whole office is in a bad mood and nothing gets done right. If my doc is in a good mood, the day flies by and all the patients are happy. I make it my business to know what kind of a day we're going to have. Kind of like a weatherman."

Debra was more accurate than a weatherman. She claimed that she could tell what Emmett was thinking just by the way he hung up his coat. It was an amusing parlor trick when someone else was the target. But Katie was annoyed that she could be read so easily. Especially on a day like today when she just wanted to be left alone to do her work and then go home.

She dialed Beth's number and waited while it rang and rang. She expected voice mail to answer, but it didn't pick up. Katie checked the number and tried again with the same result. She was about to call Debra to check the number when Emmett poked his head around the corner.

"My first patient is tricky," he said. "I could use a second opinion."

Katie knew Emmett didn't need assistance, his grin betraying his desire to cheer her up.

She rolled her eyes at him and followed him down the hall.

Mr. Kazinsky and his daughter, Sheila, sat side by side in the small examining room. Katie had seen Sheila for a routine physical a few weeks before. She remembered Sheila telling her that her father was coming to live with her because the family was worried about him living alone.

"Why don't you explain the problem to Dr. LeClair, Mr. Kazinsky?"

"Well, ma'am, I'm not really sure there is a problem, see. My daughter, Sheila, she wanted me to come in and have my heart checked out, but as far as I can tell, it's just fine. I just need to give it a jump-start in the morning is all."

Katie looked at Emmett. "Jump-start?"

"Show her, Dad," Sheila urged. "He just moved in with me, Dr. LeClair, like I was telling you. But he does this thing in the morning. Says he has to get his heart started."

Mr. Kazinsky sat straight in his chair, crossed his arms over his chest, uncrossed them and slapped his knees, moving back and forth and gaining in speed until he was stopped by a coughing spell.

"I have a little cold right now, but that's all it takes to get it going."

Katie looked at Emmett again. "Chest pain? Angina? Shortness of breath?"

Emmett smiled. "No, he just needs a jump-start."

Katie grinned. "How about a stress test?"

"That's a great idea! What do you think, Sheila? We'll do a stress test and see how he tolerates it. Would you feel more comfortable that way?"

"Whatever you think is necessary." Sheila held her hands up. "But Dad doesn't like to go to Ann Arbor. He thinks there's too much traffic. Can you do a test like that here?"

"Sure, we can do a modified version right here," Emmett said. He turned to his patient and held out his hands. "Mr. Kazinsky, I'll have you stand up and take my hands. Let's just start running in place, okay? Just go at your own pace. Let me know if you feel short of breath or have any pain."

Katie watched as her sixty-five-year-old partner ran in place with his eighty-year-old patient. After about four minutes, Emmett slowed. Mr. Kazinsky kept on jogging.

"Okay, that's pretty good there." Emmett held up his hand and stopped jogging. "I think we better stop before I embarrass myself. Sheila, his heart is in better shape than mine. If he needs to jump-start it in the morning, that's fine. Maybe I'll start to do the same just so I can keep up with him."

Katie excused herself and smiled on the way out the door. She could always rely on Emmett to share the "difficult" medical problems with her.

She glanced into the staff room on her way back to her office and saw Debra sitting alone and scraping the last of her yogurt out of the container. Katie hated to interrupt her during her lunch break, but she decided to take advantage of Debra's vast knowledge of gossip.

Debra smiled as Katie entered the room.

"You look better," Debra said. "What happened?"

"Emmett and Mr. Kazinsky." Katie sat across from Debra.

Debra nodded. "He's a character."

"Emmett or Mr. Kazinsky?"

"Well, both I guess."

How could she turn this conversation in the direction of Ellen without setting off all Debra's alarm bells?

"I couldn't get in touch with Beth Wixom—she didn't answer, and there was no voice mail," Katie said. "Do we have a different number for her? Was there any other family besides her mom?"

Debra shook her head. "I don't think she has anyone else, poor thing. From what I hear, they were very close. I can check the number for you." Debra pushed her chair back.

"Debra, wait," Katie said.

Debra scooted her chair closer and leaned her elbows on the table.

This wasn't going well. She had the same look she got when discussing the latest Hollywood divorce.

"Do you know if Ellen Riley had any close friends in town?"

"Are you trying to figure out if she confided in someone about her suicide plan?"

Katie's shoulders slumped. There was no way to be circumspect with Debra. Her brain automatically jumped to conclusions. Unfortunately, this one was on the nose.

Katie nodded. "Beth doesn't think her mother would have killed herself, and I thought I could talk to some of her friends. Maybe they would be more open with me than with Ellen's daughter."

Debra pursed her lips. "You could be right. Let's see." Debra looked to the ceiling as if the list of friends could be found there. "I didn't want to say anything, because once people are gone, it's best to let their trouble go as well. But she was very close to Cecily Hawkins when they first moved here. Something happened between them." Debra held her hand up. "I don't know what, but they haven't been as close for a few months. Patsy Travers is probably your best bet."

"How can I get in touch with her?"

"She lives across the street from the Rileys. Well, from Mr. Riley now. I can get her phone number if you like."

"Thanks, Debra. That's a good place to start."

Debra leaned forward and lowered her voice even though they were alone in the room.

"She's a bit . . . unusual. Try not to get distracted by the exterior. I've never been able to tell whether it's an act or the real deal, but her woo-woo persona disguises a very smart lady."

Katie returned to her office to finish her charts. Because part of her brain was mulling over what she had learned—or, more accurately, not learned—about Ellen Riley, it took twice as long as usual. At three o'clock, she brought her completed pile of charts to the medical records room, grabbed her bag, and headed out the door. She was on call this weekend, so the elation that usually accompanied a Friday afternoon was dulled a bit.

Katie had one stop to make before she was done for the day. One of her nursing home patients had been transferred to hospice care the evening before with urosepsis. He was ninety-two years old and frail. The urinary tract infection had rapidly led to a much more severe infection, and he wasn't expected to live.

The double doors whooshed open as she approached. She wound her way along the dark, low-ceilinged hallway toward the patient care unit. While an ICU was noisy with the muted beeps and gurgles of the machinery designed to keep the human body alive through any number of assaults to its functioning, a hospice unit was often strangely quiet, a place where the regular routines were allowed to run their course.

Katie greeted the two afternoon-shift nurses who were busily charting vital signs, consciousness, and various indicators of the patients' statuses. They pointed her toward Mr. Foster's room.

He was asleep when she entered and would likely stay that way. Katie briefly examined him, recalling the first time she had seen someone who was about to die. A medical student on rotation in her third year, Katie had been on an overnight call with a junior resident. They had been called to a patient's room to evaluate the reddish-purple blotches appearing on her face and hands.

She had been old. Katie did not remember how old, but she had looked ancient. The only indication of life had been the slight movement of her chest up and down. Her face had been drawn and immobile. This had not been the blissful sleep of a child. This sleep had looked painful and unnatural. The resident had pointed out the blotches. Not that anyone could have missed them. The end of her nose had been bruised-looking and purple. Her fingertips had been dark at the end of her curled fingers. He'd explained that she'd had what was called disseminated intravascular coagulation, or DIC. Tiny blood clots throughout her body had been cutting off the oxygen to vital organs. Her entire system had been shutting down, and there had been no way for them to stop it. Infection combined with age and general frailty, a weak heart, kidney disease, and a litany of other medical problems had contributed to her demise.

He had talked about her as if she was already dead. Perhaps she had been, to him. If there was nothing more to do, you had to move on to help those that could be helped. There was no time in residency to dwell on those who couldn't be saved, no time to even acknowledge their passing sometimes. That was what the nurses were for, she was told. Katie had once been reprimanded for getting a patient a drink of water. It was obviously nurse's work. The teaching physician had been disappointed that she would "waste her time" with such activities. The message was, doctors are too important and too smart to be engaging in such small acts of human kindness. She remembered the lesson, but not in the way it was intended. After visiting the dying woman, they had had lunch and never mentioned her again.

She pulled up a chair and took Mr. Foster's hand. He was a funny old guy. An incurable flirt, he liked to chase the nurses down the hall in his wheelchair. Katie had once asked him what he planned to do if he ever actually caught up with one.

"The fun is in the chase, Dr. LeClair. I'll never catch one."

He loved jazz, and there was an unsubstantiated rumor that he had played in his own band when he was a young man. He referred to it all as "ancient history" and refused to talk about it. But he and Katie had bonded over their shared love of big band music.

The night nurses used to bring in all sorts of music for him to listen to. He loved it all and always wanted to hear whatever had been released that week.

"I like to hear the new stuff almost as much as I love the old stuff."

Katie stood up. "I'll miss you, Mr. Foster."

She thought she felt him squeeze her hand, but it was probably just a reflex.

7

Katie was almost home when she decided on a detour. She still hadn't been able to reach Beth Wixom, but she knew that Ellen Riley had lived just a couple of blocks from the downtown area. She turned onto Ellen's street and parked in front of the large white colonial that she had shared with Christopher. Directly across the street was a bright-yellow Craftsman bungalow with red-trimmed windows and door. The porch overflowed with yellow, red, and orange mums in containers. There was an old blue Toyota in the driveway with "Coexist" and "My other car is a broom" bumper stickers.

Katie walked up the front steps and knocked on the door. There were two cozy-looking chairs with thick cushions on the porch. Katie filed the idea away to consider for her own porch. She heard rustling inside and the sliding of a metal chain.

"Hello?" Only one eye peeked out through the small opening. It was pale gray, and Katie saw long, curly gray hair.

"Mrs. Travers?" Katie smiled. "I'm Dr. LeClair. I work with Dr. Hawkins."

"I know who you are. I've been waiting for you." The door slammed shut, and Katie heard the sliding metal sound again. When the door swung open, Katie took a step back.

Mrs. Travers wore a flowing purple tunic over bright-orange leggings. Her hair fell halfway down her back in silver waves. She'd layered more necklaces than Katie owned around her neck, and every finger wore at least one ring.

Patsy Travers peered out of the door and looked up and down the street. "You'd better come in before anyone sees you."

She gestured to a small sitting room that was even more colorful than Gabrielle's living room, mostly owing to the knickknacks on every flat surface and the tie-dye rainbow canvas hanging behind the couch.

"Can I get you anything?" Patsy asked. "I have a lovely chamomile and vanilla tea. It will help you get some rest."

"Thank you, Mrs. Travers, that would be very nice." Katie chose an armchair and sat.

"Call me Patsy. And it's Miss—I never married." Patsy bustled out of the sitting room and began clanking dishes in the kitchen.

Katie surveyed the room and understood what Debra had meant by "woo-woo." An overstuffed bookshelf groaned under the weight of astrology, tarot, rune, and psychic development books. Ellen Riley had been so sensible and no-nonsense. How had these two become friends?

A few minutes later, Patsy entered rattling a tea tray and followed by a white Persian cat who looked down its nose at Katie. It sat in the doorway, tail twitching, watching her.

Katie took the cup offered by Patsy and sipped.

"This is delicious," Katie said.

"I make it myself. I can never find the right mixture in the store-bought kind."

"Patsy, what did you mean when you said you've been waiting for me?"

"You're here about Ellen Riley, right?"

Katie put her cup down on the side table.

"Well, yes."

"I didn't know it would be *you* exactly, but I figured someone would come. Ellen didn't kill herself." Patsy took a sip of her own tea and wrapped her hands around the cup.

Katie sat back in the chair, uncertain how to proceed. This wasn't going the way that she had planned at all. She'd felt wrong-footed from the moment she stepped onto the porch. And the cat had not taken its eyes off her. It was very disconcerting.

"Ellen was my patient, and I was shocked by her death," Katie said. "I heard you two were close and thought you could shed some light on her state of mind."

Patsy turned toward the cat. "Rufus, that's enough." The cat walked to Katie and began rubbing its face on her leg and purring. "He thinks he's guarding me. I have to tell him when to take a break." Patsy watched him, and her eyebrows twitched upward. "He's not usually so friendly with new people."

Katie gave her a weak smile and reached down to pet Rufus.

"Ellen's state of mind was the same as it always had been. She was a very courageous woman, very strong. I don't know if she told you about her first husband, but he died quite young of a heart attack. She raised Beth on her own and put herself through school. All while working two or three jobs just to keep food on the table."

"I didn't know that. She never talked about her first husband, only Christopher. They seemed very happy together."

Patsy pressed her lips together and put down her cup. "I think they were happy. Christopher has a lot of baggage. In fact, if either of them were going to kill themselves, I would have bet on him. His parents were horrible to each other, and his mother was a master manipulator. I think he has a lot of stress with all the restaurants and that son of his. And his aura has become very muddy recently." Patsy shook her head and stared out the window.

Katie sipped her tea and waited.

"I only know that she was stressed about something to do with Christopher's family in those last few weeks. Certainly not depressed or suicidal. In fact, I think she was excited. But I did sense an evil presence over there the last few times I visited. I couldn't put my finger on it, and she never listened to my warnings anyway, so I let it go." Patsy dug a tissue out of her pocket and dabbed at her eyes. "I wish now that I had warned her and made her listen to me."

Katie leaned forward. "You aren't saying that you think someone killed her?"

Patsy shrugged and stuffed the crumpled tissue back in her pocket. "I don't know what happened. Maybe it was an accident, but I know she wouldn't have done it on purpose."

"Did she give you any hint about why she was stressed?"

Patsy shook her head. "Not really. But if it had anything to do with Sylvia Riley, she probably should have left it alone. The whole neighborhood breathed a sigh of relief when *that* woman died." Patsy waggled a finger at Katie. "Don't look so shocked; some people just suck the energy out of every place they go."

Katie tried for a neutral expression. "And Sylvia Riley was like that."

Patsy nodded. "She liked to collect secrets. Her favorite thing was to wheedle confidences out of people and then use them later to manipulate."

Katie sat back in her chair. She had never heard much about old Mrs. Riley, even from Ellen. "She was a blackmailer?"

"Not in the usual sense. I don't think she ever asked for money—just favors. And sometimes she only held it over people and made them worry."

Katie frowned, taking in this new information. "How do you know this?"

Patsy swept her arm in the direction of her bookcases. "People come to me to help them understand their problems. It's one of the things Ellen and I had in common."

Katie left that statement alone. If Patsy thought her fortune telling was the same as Ellen's therapy sessions, Katie wasn't going to argue about it now. "How *did* you become friends?" she asked.

"She took one of my meditation classes at the library." Patsy sniffed and poured more tea in both of their cups. "She wanted to be able to teach it to her clients. We just hit it off and started having a cup of tea together in the afternoons. I'll miss her."

Katie glanced out the window. The unobstructed view of Ellen's house gave Katie another hunch.

"Patsy, did you see anything the day she died?"

Patsy shook her head. "Nothing unusual. Your partner was over there that afternoon, but he was there quite a bit."

"Emmett?"

"No, the son, Nick. Ellen and Cecily spent a lot of time together as well. I think Nick and Christopher were friends, although Nick was quite a bit younger . . ."

"You saw Nick Hawkins at Ellen's house the day she died?"

Patsy nodded. "Oh, and Wednesday is the cleaning lady's day. But I don't remember seeing her."

"I thought Christopher was out of town that day," Katie said.

"I think he was. Nick was there to see Ellen."

Why would Nick be visiting Ellen? He could have faked a prescription easily. Was that why he didn't answer his phone the night she died?

Katie waited for more. Rufus purred.

"I think they were friends as well." Patsy shrugged, unaware that Katie's mind was spinning a scenario where her partner was a murderer. "I suppose he could have been a client. She never said, and I never asked."

Twenty minutes later, Katie had declined Patsy's offer of a tarot reading and managed to get out the door with only a small stack of books on psychic healing. Patsy thought that she could supplement her medical practice with aura cleansings. Rufus sat in the doorway, twitching his tail and watching her as she climbed into her car.

She glanced at Ellen's house, which appeared closed up, abandoned, and cold on this bright fall day. Katie was sure that she was imagining things after spending time with Patsy. Houses didn't have feelings. She started the engine and pulled away from the curb. At the end of the street, she turned and headed home. She pulled into her driveway and heard loud voices. Well, one loud voice.

Caleb had commandeered the dining room table. Paper, pens, books, and wires littered its surface. Caleb sat hunched over his laptop and shouted into his headset. He was deep into an online world involving knights and kings or soldiers and war. Katie couldn't keep it straight.

She shook her head, feeling old. All the years of med school and residency had whittled her leisure time to only allow for an occasional novel or television comedy. Gone were the days of whiling away an afternoon drawing in her sketchbook or listening to music. There were large chunks of pop culture and news events that she'd never know, as if she'd been on an isolated island for the past seven years.

Caleb must have sensed Katie standing there and swiveled in his seat.

"Hey, sis!" He pulled off his headset and shut his laptop.

"Saving the world again?" Katie asked.

"I had to take a break from coding this app," he said. "I was seeing double and couldn't find the bug that makes it crash midload."

Katie nodded and tried to look as if she knew what Caleb was talking about.

"I saved some dinner for you." He tilted his head in the direction of the kitchen.

Katie stepped into the kitchen as Caleb began scribbling notes and sighing.

Caleb had made his specialty—vegetable stir-fry. Even though he made it a lot, Katie loved it. He had a secret ingredient that gave it just a touch of spicy heat. But she especially loved that she didn't have to cook.

Katie walked back out to the dining room to grab her messenger bag from the table.

Caleb snapped his laptop shut again.

"Working on a top-secret app?" Katie nodded at his computer and tried to meet his eyes. He studiously avoided her gaze. "I promise I won't steal your idea." She held her hands up. "Just getting my notebook." She pulled it out of her bag and held it up.

A mumbled "No problem" was his only response. He opened the laptop again and glared at the screen while scribbling notes.

Katie sighed and went back into the kitchen. She never knew when she should worry about Caleb, and so, by default, she worried all the time. He was a genius with computers, and she knew he'd messed around with hacking into computer systems in college. It was more the fun of the chase than any real desire to obtain information, but she knew the courts wouldn't see it that way if he was ever caught. He'd promised he was done with all that, but Katie wondered if it was true.

She warmed up her plate in the microwave and poured a glass of pinot noir. Sipping the wine, she watched the breeze blow more colored leaves into the yard outside the window. Usually this after-work ritual was calming, but this time the wine made her jumpy, and the pleasant breeze seemed to be blowing in unwelcome changes. She couldn't shake the thoughts of Ellen Riley and what might have gone wrong. The ding from the microwave startled her out of her contemplation. Bringing her plate to the kitchen table, she glared at the stack of medical journals awaiting her. She sometimes felt crushed by the sheer volume of information that came to her mailbox each week. There had been a time when she read the journals cover to cover in a mad desire to know everything she could. Now she chose only the articles she knew would apply to her practice. And she often only read the conclusions. Her former teachers would have been scandalized.

She pushed the journals aside and instead pulled out a spiral notebook. She liked to jot down questions and new treatment options in her notebook. This time she turned to a clean page and wrote, "Ellen Riley."

The practice of medicine was mostly detective work. The physician had to collect clues and piece together the identity of the culprit based on the patient's symptoms. Katie decided to apply her medical thought process to the mystery of Ellen Riley.

Using a modified history and physical template, she began to list what she knew and what she still needed to know.

She started her note with the chief complaint. For patients, that was the reason they came to see a doctor.

CC: patient dead from apparent overdose of diazepam.

History of Present Illness: Happy, healthy psychologist and small business owner found unconscious by daughter. Daughter reports that her mother had been "stressed" recently and doing research. Good friend also reports a change in mood over the past couple of weeks, but neither one believes it was depression or that she was suicidal.

Social History: Married to second husband for two years. One daughter from previous marriage. Recent falling out with good friend Cecily Hawkins.

Family History: Unknown. Husband's mother was a known social blackmailer.

Review of ~~systems~~ suspicions:

1. maybe Ellen uncovered one of the secrets Sylvia Riley had been hoarding when she died.
2. maybe Ellen knew something about a client that they regretted sharing with her.
3. The prescription for diazepam was probably obtained illegally—there is no record of it coming from my office.

Differential Diagnosis (list of suspects):

Nick?
Christopher?
Unknown clients of Ellen
Unknown victims of Sylvia

Assessment: Death due to diazepam overdose. Likely not suicide or accident. Therefore, the only possibility is murder.

Plan/questions to answer:

1. Find out where she got the diazepam. No record in chart or med book.
2. Find out what research she was working on.
3. Why was Nick at her house the day she died?
4. Who were her clients?
5. What secrets did Sylvia Riley leave behind?
6. Talk to Chief Carlson about the prescription. Suicide seems unlikely.
7. Talk to Emmett.

Katie sighed. She felt that there were more questions than facts. Selfishly, she was most worried about the first question. According to the label on the bottle, Katie had written the prescription that Ellen had used to kill herself.

No matter how hard she tried, she couldn't remember writing that script. The possibility of early memory loss aside, the other explanations were even more worrisome. Did one of her partners—likely Nick, since she couldn't imagine Emmett doing it—write it and not chart it? Nick was at Ellen's house that day, and the two couples were friends. Would he have prescribed diazepam for Ellen using Katie's name? If Ellen hadn't died, Katie never would have known. Did Ellen somehow manage to write it for herself? Could it have been one of Katie's staff?

She wasn't even sure *where* it had been filled. And some inner instinct warned her to tread lightly. She couldn't just accuse Nick. If she was wrong, they'd never be able to work together. If she was right, she had an even bigger problem. She would have to try to find more information to get to the truth. She flipped the notebook shut and ate her now-cold vegetable stir-fry.

8

Saturday morning, Katie rounded on the two floor patients first. In a hospital, the "floor" patients were the ones on a regular nursing floor, as opposed to those in one of the intensive care units. Neither of the patients were Katie's, but she was on call for the practice and had to visit anyone in the hospital. Katie first visited one of Emmett's long-time diabetics, who was only partially compliant with his insulin regimen. He was admitted a few times a year, usually after another illness had disrupted his blood sugar control.

"Hello, Mr. Walsh. How are you feeling today?" Katie asked as she entered the room.

"Much better now that you're here," Mr. Walsh said. He winked at her and smoothed the four white strands of hair across his head.

Katie smiled at him and flipped open his chart.

"Looks like your blood sugar has stabilized. Do you feel well enough to go home this afternoon?"

"I don't know, Doctor." Mr. Walsh shook his head slowly. "My wife's sister is visiting. It might be better if I just stayed here for a couple of days."

"I think you should give it a try," Katie said. "Don't you get along with your sister-in-law?"

Mr. Walsh sighed. "She's fine. It's just that when she and my wife aren't arguing, they're laughing. It makes for a loud and unsettling visit."

"Would you like me to talk to your wife?"

"No! No, that will make it worse, Doc." Mr. Walsh held up his hands to fend off her offer.

"What if I send home a prescription for quiet rest? Would that work?"

Mr. Walsh sighed. "It's worth a try. And I'd rather eat at home than here."

Katie smiled at him. "I'll get the paperwork ready."

The second patient was a young man with chronic pancreatitis. He was so frequently in the hospital that he probably could have managed his own care. It mostly involved pain control and following labs. Once the excruciating pain had subsided, he would ask the nurse to discharge him.

She wrote brief notes and updated the orders while sitting at the nurse's station.

"I think the whole thing is fishy," a voice said from the supply room. Katie glanced at the door, but it was mostly closed.

"People do kill themselves, Sharon," another voice said. "It's not like every death has to be a murder. You watch too much TV."

Katie's hands went still on the keyboard, and she held her breath. Sharon was one of the nurses who worked weekends.

Katie didn't recognize the other voice. Were they talking about Ellen? Katie stayed very quiet and shamelessly eavesdropped.

"I *don't* think every death is a murder. We have plenty of deaths here—those aren't murder," she said.

"So who do you think killed her?"

"I don't know. Her husband? Cecily Hawkins?"

"What? Dr. Hawkins's wife? Why would she do that?"

Sharon's voice dropped to a low murmur, and Katie stood and stepped closer to the door. "Didn't you hear about Dr. Hawkins and Ellen Riley? They—"

"Hey, Dr. LeClair!"

Katie startled and turned back toward the desk.

"I just want to thank you so much for seeing Jimmy the other day." Layla Price, another nurse who worked mostly weekends, leaned over the high counter and grinned. "He's much better now on that antibiotic."

The voices in the closet had gone silent. Katie dredged up a smile for Layla. "I'm so glad to hear that."

"Of course, now that he's better, he's running me ragged. I had to come to work to get some rest!" Layla laughed at her own joke until her attention was pulled by something down the hall. "I have to go see what four-twenty-three needs. Nice to see you, Doctor." Layla hurried down the hall.

Katie finished her charting with no more gossip emanating from the supply closet. She'd have to find out what they were talking about. Of course, she didn't want to *start* a rumor by asking around about Nick's wife and her feelings toward Ellen Riley. She'd have to be careful.

Katie logged out of the patient chart and grabbed her messenger bag. She had one more stop to make before she was done for the morning. Turning the corner at the end of the hall to enter the ICU, she hesitated at the doorway, remembering the last time she had been there. The doors breezed open on their sliders. Most of Baxter Community Hospital was older and, to Katie's mind, quaint. But the ICU had been completely updated two years ago. It was like stepping off a horse-drawn carriage into a space ship.

Three of the five patient rooms were occupied, but Katie was only here to see one of them. Ethel Blackstone was seventy-six years old and had been brought in two nights ago due to a stroke. She had been in and out of consciousness, making a full neurological exam tricky. Emmett wanted her to stay in the ICU through the weekend to be sure she was well monitored. He had told Katie he didn't always trust the weekend nursing staff on the regular floor to keep a close enough eye on the sicker patients. Plus, Marcy was working in the ICU this weekend, and she was a former neurology nurse. Ethel was in great hands and hardly needed Katie at all. She walked past the large desk that housed the monitors and computers and all the paperwork that went into caring for patients. She glanced at the two people sitting at the desk and did a double take.

Marcy was there as she expected, but sitting at the end, head down and tapping away on a laptop, sat Matt Gregor. He must have sensed her staring and looked up from his screen.

A smile spread slowly across his face, so warm that Katie felt heat rising in her own cheeks.

"Dr. LeClair, we meet again," he said, flipping his laptop shut and leaning back in his chair.

"Dr. Gregor," Katie said and nodded at him.

"Are you here for Mrs. Blackstone?" Matt asked and grabbed a chart from the rack before coming around the desk.

The ICU director didn't trust computer records and insisted on hard copies of all active patient files.

"Yes, I . . . I'm on call this weekend," Katie said.

"I'm moonlighting for Dr. Peters. She's out of town this week," Matt said. "I have the other two." He nodded toward the remaining cubicles in the unit.

"Moonlighting?" Katie mentally smacked her forehead. She sounded like an intern on her first week of residency.

"Well, locums work, really. She shut her office down but wanted me to deal with any hospital stuff or emergencies."

Katie nodded, still wondering why Dr. Gregor, who had been a rising star in the Internal Medicine department at University Hospital, was working ER shifts and doing locums work. It didn't seem like he'd have time, for one thing, and for another, it was usually people in-between jobs or transitioning to another specialty that signed on with locum tenens companies. They were like temp services for doctors. The last she'd heard, Matt was in practice with his father in Ann Arbor.

"Are you . . . not working in Ann Arbor anymore?"

Matt grimaced. "I'm still working with my father, but I'm doing some extra shifts here and there. It's decent money, and the work isn't too demanding."

He lowered his voice and said, "How are you doing after the other night?"

Katie felt her eyebrows shoot upward. "You mean Ellen Riley?"

Matt nodded. "It seemed like maybe she was your first."

Katie took a step back. "I've had plenty of patients die."

Marcy's head snapped up.

Katie held her hand up. "I didn't mean it that way." She hoped her face wasn't as red as it felt.

"But the first one after residency, when it's your own patient, it's different," Matt said. "Doctors have a tendency to blame themselves even if it wasn't their fault."

"I'm fine, thanks," Katie said. Could he sense her feeling of guilt, or did he think she *should* feel guilty for the diazepam? Gabrielle's voice in her head said, "Maybe he's just a nice guy."

"If you ever want to meet for a drink and talk about it, here's my number." He slipped a piece of paper out of his pocket and wrote a number on the back.

Marcy caught her eye and gave her a thumbs-up behind Matt's back.

Her heart was pounding in her chest, and she hoped Matt couldn't sense that as well. Katie took the paper and shoved it in her bag. Gabrielle would tell her to set a date right now, this minute. Instead, she said, "Thank you. I'll think about it."

Ugh! What was wrong with her? It's not like Justin had left her last week. It was years ago. And why did she think of Justin every time she contemplated Matt Gregor? Then Katie realized what it was. She had the same jittery, bubbly feeling that she'd had the first time she met Justin. Well, she wasn't going to tell Gabrielle about this. Maybe if she ignored it, it would go away. And if she was going to run into Matt Gregor all over town, she'd better get control of herself.

She turned to the counter and set the file on top. As she flipped it open, she saw Matt put his computer away and slide the strap of his bag over his shoulder. "See you tomorrow, Marcy," he said. He nodded at Katie and said, "Dr. LeClair."

"Dr. Gregor."

Just as he reached the door, an alarm sounded in one of the patient rooms. Mrs. Blackstone's vitals monitor made a loud shrieking noise. Marcy was out of her chair before Katie had even identified the source of the racket. Katie rushed into the room and felt Matt right behind her. Mrs. Blackstone's EKG had flatlined.

Marcy hit the code button, sending an announcement throughout the hospital that they needed backup to perform cardiac resuscitation and get Mrs. Blackstone's heart beating again.

Katie felt for a pulse while Matt went out in the hall to get the crash cart.

"Ready, Doctor." Marcy was in position to begin chest compressions.

"Wait. She has a pulse," Katie said. "In fact, it's quite strong." She glanced down at Mrs. Blackstone's hand and saw the cord for the monitor sitting loosely in her hand. She must have woken enough to pull on the cord. A good sign neurologically, but one that had thrown her doctors into a tizzy. Katie pushed the button to silence the alarm and plugged the cord back into the machine.

A regular, steady beat began to crawl across the screen.

"She must have pulled the cord out," Marcy said. "I'll make sure it's taped out of the way."

Katie looked at Matt, and they shared a moment of relief. She wished all alarms were dealt with as easily.

"Are you finished with your rounds?" she asked. Still flustered from the near-code, her heart was racing. She reminded herself that Matt wasn't Justin. He wasn't anything like Justin.

Matt nodded.

"Can I buy you a cup of coffee?" she offered. He had been ready to jump right into another medical emergency, no questions asked. And she was being too standoffish, as usual.

"Sure."

Katie examined Mrs. Blackstone and quickly wrote a note in her file. She and Matt stepped out of the shiny ICU into the older part of the hospital.

"I don't think I can stomach the cafeteria coffee," Katie said. "Want to meet at the Purple Parrot?"

Matt's smile transformed his face, and for a moment Katie saw the person behind the white coat.

They were almost out the front door when Chief Carlson stopped them.

"Hey, Doc! Wait." He jogged up to them.

"Hi, John," Katie said. "You remember Dr. Gregor from Wednesday night."

Carlson nodded, and the men shook hands.

"Actually, I was looking for you as well, Dr. Gregor."

Matt's eyebrows rose a fraction, but otherwise he waited for Carlson to continue.

"Beth Wixom is asking for a full investigation into her mother's death," Carlson said. "I'll have to ask you both some questions about that night."

"We were just about to get some coffee at the Purple Parrot," Katie said.

"Great, I'll meet you there," Carlson said.

She thought she heard Matt sigh next to her, but when she looked at him, he appeared unfazed by the unexpected guest.

Katie smiled at John. "Okay, we'll see you in a few minutes."

"Good," Carlson said. "This is just a casual conversation. I'm not sure there will be anything to learn that will change how we pursue this, but I'd appreciate it. The sooner I can tell her we've looked into it, the sooner I can close the case and let the family move on."

Matt pulled his keys out of his pocket and jingled them in his hand. "Want to ride with me? I can drop you back here when we're done."

Katie sensed that he wanted to talk to her before they met with the police chief.

"Okay."

"I'll see you both there in a few minutes." Carlson headed back into the hospital, presumably to get his car out of the visitor lot.

Katie followed Matt to the back doctor lot, and he led her to an older Honda sedan. It was immaculate inside, and Katie settled back in the seat.

When he turned on the ignition, Frank Sinatra's "Come Fly With Me" blasted from the speakers. Matt quickly hit the button to shut it off.

"Sorry," he said.

"I love Sinatra. My mother listened to him all the time when I was a kid."

"Okay then." He smiled and hit the button again but turned down the volume.

When he didn't bring up Chief Carlson's desire for a meeting, Katie finally concluded he'd just wanted to ride with her. She settled back and listened to Sinatra croon.

"People usually give me a strange look when they hear I like Frank Sinatra," Katie said.

Matt steered the car out of the small employee parking lot and onto the treelined drive that led to the hospital. He turned right out of the hospital campus and headed toward downtown.

"Me too. My mother also loves him," Matt said. "I guess he just wormed his way into my brain."

"Is your mom a physician too?" Katie asked. She already knew the answer but didn't want him to know she was fully informed about his background. Better to not seem stalker-ish, especially since it was Gabrielle who had gathered all the intel.

"Yes, she's head of pediatrics at the university. Before she got involved in administration, she was a pediatric gastroenterologist."

They entered the three-block "business" section of town. Antique shops shared space with a few small boutiques, a craft store, and a tiny pharmacy.

He parallel parked a few spots down from the Purple Parrot, the only coffee shop in town. There were two bars, Pete's sandwich shop, Riley's, and the café. Mrs. Peterson and her daughter ran the Purple Parrot together. When Mr. Peterson died, he left just enough money for them to invest in the small sandwich and coffee shop. Most of their business was during the lunch hour, but they did stay open until eight to catch some evening customers. It was a smart move. They were down the block and across the street from Riley's.

Christopher Riley had turned the business around after his father died. He had opened several other locations in the Midwest, and the Riley's in Baxter was always packed on the weekends. Almost all the people who came out to Riley's between six and eight o'clock, only to discover there was more than an hour wait for a table, gravitated over to the Purple Parrot for coffee. Katie didn't know where the shop got the name, but it was one of her favorite places in town.

Matt held the door open for her, and she stepped inside. The café felt like a library reading room with shelves on every wall filled with books and knickknacks. The seating was mostly couches and overstuffed chairs situated around coffee tables. The purple-and-yellow color scheme managed to be cheerful and soothing at the same time. Sandwiches, potpies, and thick soups dominated the menu.

Katie and Matt went to the counter to place their orders.

Bella Peterson was in her midtwenties with blonde hair, blue eyes, and a sweet smile. She blushed as Matt stepped to the counter.

"Hi, Dr. Gregor. What can I get for you?" She fumbled for a pen and dropped it along with her order pad. Her face was even redder when she stood up after retrieving them.

"Just a regular coffee, please."

"Dr. LeClair?" Bella turned to Katie.

"English breakfast tea, please."

"Will do. I'll bring it out in just a minute." Bella gestured at the seating area.

Katie and Matt chose a cluster of comfy chairs with a beat-up wooden table in the center.

"How is it going with the Hawkinses' practice?" Matt asked.

"Pretty well so far. I like the patients."

Matt raised an eyebrow. "But the partners leave something to be desired?"

Katie had learned long ago that medicine was a small community. For all she knew, Matt and Nick Hawkins were the best of friends.

"No, I didn't mean that. Emmett is wonderful. And Nick is a good doctor. The pain clinic is doing really well, and I think it's adding a great service to the area."

Matt waited, a half smile on his lips.

"Nick just takes some getting used to," Katie said. "He's a bit harder to get to know than his father."

Matt snorted. "You're very diplomatic. Nick Hawkins is a prima donna, except his ego is bigger."

So not best friends.

Katie smiled but didn't encourage him. She didn't want to gossip about Nick or talk to Matt about her practice.

"What's it like to be in practice with your father?" Katie asked.

Matt tilted his head side to side in a so-so gesture. "I've been there for about a year, so I know what Nick and Emmett have to navigate. I cut back on my hours a couple months ago and started doing locums work. I like the flexibility, the money is good, and I don't have to deal with my father as much."

Katie had only ever heard good things about Dr. Gregor senior. He was revered at the medical school and had won teacher of the year on several occasions. He was the go-to guy for tough internal medicine cases. But Katie knew very well that the public face could be quite different from the private one. And dealing with a highly regarded parent probably wasn't easy.

Katie was saved from responding by the appearance of Bella bearing a tray of drinks, sugar, and milk. Just as she set down their mugs, John Carlson pushed open the door and walked to their table.

"Hi, Chief," Bella said. "The usual?"

"You know me, Bella." John winked at her and took the remaining empty armchair. He sank down into it and had to lean forward to keep himself from being swallowed by the cushions.

"Thanks for meeting me."

Katie stirred milk and sugar into her tea and nodded. Matt sipped his black coffee and regarded Carlson over the rim of his mug.

"I need to take a statement from both of you about the night Ellen came into the ER."

"Dr. LeClair was hardly there, Chief. I can tell you whatever you want to know."

Chief Carlson nodded. "I remember. I saw her come in that night. But according to the EMTs, the pills Ellen Riley took came from a prescription Dr. LeClair wrote. Mr. Riley is convinced that Ellen would never have taken diazepam. He said she hated taking meds of any kind and certainly wouldn't have taken an antianxiety medicine."

Katie took a deep breath and wondered the best way to tell Chief Carlson that she agreed with Christopher and had no idea how Ellen had gotten the prescription.

"The thing is, the prescription bottle is missing."

"What?" Katie said.

Matt set his mug down and leaned forward.

"The EMTs are very clear that they saw the bottle. It was your name on the label, and it had only been filled on Monday. But they either forgot to grab it when they took her to the hospital or lost it along the way. It's not at the house or among her things that were given back to Mr. Riley."

Katie took a large gulp of tea and tried to appear unconcerned.

"Maybe it was tossed with all the other debris from the code?" Matt asked.

Chief Carlson shrugged. "It's one of the reasons I need to ask you to review what happened that night."

Matt looked around at the other seating areas filling up. Katie exchanged a look with him, and they both turned to Carlson. Katie imagined they wore the same look of disbelief.

Katie lowered her voice and leaned toward John. "I'm sure the entire town knows you're talking to us right now," she said. "It's probably the reason the café is filling up so quickly."

Carlson glanced around, and his shoulders slumped.

"These people are unbelievable," he said with a sigh. "Okay, just a couple of questions and then I'll ask you to stop by the station either later this weekend or on Monday at the latest."

Matt leaned back in his chair and sipped his coffee.

"Did you see this pill bottle in the ER?" Carlson asked Matt.

He shook his head. "I only know what the EMTs told me. I was too busy working to get a heartbeat to worry about where the pill bottle was."

Katie felt her heart racing. She knew the next question was going to be about the prescription. Why did she prescribe it? How long had Ellen been on it? She didn't want to answer at all and especially didn't want to answer in front of Matt.

Carlson turned to Katie. "You said the other night that you weren't on call. Has Nick given an excuse as to why he didn't answer his phone?"

Katie felt herself relax a bit. She could answer this one. "He said he must have been in a dead zone when the service tried to call. But he didn't tell me where he was."

Two older women sat in the chairs closest to their area and quietly sipped their coffee. Katie and Carlson exchanged a look.

Carlson jotted a note in his notebook. "Okay, I'll need to talk to you both alone. Just call my cell, and I can meet you."

He struggled out of the cushy armchair and lumbered to the door of the café. Katie noticed several people whispering and watching him leave.

Matt let out a breath. "I hate answering those kind of questions. I want to help, but I also feel a little bit like I'm on trial."

Katie nodded. She finished the last bit of cold tea and set her cup on its saucer.

"Do you buy Nick Hawkins's excuse?"

Startled, Katie turned to look at him. "Why wouldn't I?"

Matt shrugged. "Seems pretty weak. It's one of those excuses that, even if it is true, you'd think you'd try to dress it up a bit if your partner had to cover for you."

At first, Nick had apologized, and she'd moved on. But now she reconsidered. Patsy Travers's report of seeing him at Ellen's house the day she died already had her suspicious of Nick. Katie couldn't help but wonder what he had been doing there. Now she wondered whether he had purposely ignored the emergency call.

9

S everal hours later, Katie was undergoing an intense
interrogation of a different kind.

She had returned home after rounds and her tea
with Matt to find Gabrielle and Caleb painting the kitchen.
She could have just said she was returning from rounds,
but she had an annoying honest streak and admitted she'd
been at the Purple Parrot with Matt Gregor.

Gabrielle launched into a meticulous dissection of every
word, look, and gesture. Caleb had deserted them to go work
on his app, and Katie felt like she was stuck being grilled by a
rabid government agent.

"So when he asked you to have a drink, was it like a 'Let's
grab a drink as doctors and talk about patients,' or was it 'I
don't have the guts to ask you out, so let's go get a drink'?"

Katie sighed and then started to laugh. This was the fifth
iteration of the same question. Gabrielle's look of annoyance
made her laugh harder until she had to step off the ladder and

set her paint roller down before she hurt herself or got paint all over the floor.

Gabrielle stood with her hands on her hips, glowering. "You aren't taking this seriously."

That made Katie laugh even more. When she finally caught her breath, she nodded and then shook her head. She had to look away from Gabrielle to control the giggles that kept bubbling up.

"You're right. I'm not." She took some deep breaths. "Sorry."

"Hmph." Gabrielle turned to the wall and began rolling the paint hard enough that it splattered on her arm. "You've been talking about him since we were residents, and now that he's finally noticed you exist, you won't give me anything to go on."

"I'm just distracted by this suicide and the weird prescription." Katie pushed her hair back with her arm and picked up her roller again. "I don't want to read too much into it because maybe he's just being nice. He guessed she was the first patient I had lost since finishing residency, and I think he feels bad for making it sound like I shouldn't have prescribed the diazepam."

"Well, that's not very encouraging." Gabrielle set her roller in the paint tray and turned to face Katie. "Listen, I did some snooping at the hospital. My scrub nurse told me Matt Gregor's one of those I-won't-date-a-medical-person types. I was hoping she was wrong, but maybe he's already written off any relationship because you're a doctor."

"Oh, I guess you could be right," Katie said. She was surprised at her own disappointment. She squared her shoulders and moved to another section of wall. She swallowed and made her voice more businesslike. "Now that we've exhausted the Matt Gregor issue, let's turn your inquiring mind to another problem."

Gabrielle looked like a cat that had just seen a mouse dart across the room. "Ooh, is there another handsome stranger in the mix?"

Katie smiled and shook her head. "No. This is serious."

"Handsome strangers *are* serious."

"This is about my patient. The one who died Wednesday." Katie bent to roll her brush in the paint and saw Gabrielle's smile fade.

"The suicide? What about her?" Gabrielle picked up a brush and began cutting in along the baseboard.

"I'm worried it may not have been suicide."

"Why? Even if you didn't write that prescription, she could have gotten the medicine in any number of ways."

"I know," Katie said. "It's just that everyone close to her says she was happy. She had no reason to harm herself."

"You think it was an accident?" Gabrielle set her brush down and swiveled from her spot on the floor to face Katie.

"She thinks it was murder," Caleb said from the doorway.

Katie glanced at Caleb and nodded. How long had he been standing there? He generally made himself scarce when Gabrielle was on a matchmaking jag.

"What?" Gabrielle looked from Caleb to Katie. "In this tiny little town?"

"People are the same wherever you go," Katie said.

"Yes, but you never expect to know someone . . ."

"But let's say it was murder," Caleb said and walked farther into the room. "How do you force someone to take a bunch of pills?"

Katie shrugged. "I don't know. As far as I know, there was no sign of a struggle, but if the police assumed suicide, would they even process the room as if it were a crime scene?"

"Probably not," Gabrielle said. "They might not think that way. I would imagine the worst they deal with around here is bar brawls and domestic violence."

"This has to stay here in this room," Katie said. She held Gabrielle's gaze until she nodded. There was no need to check with Caleb; his brain was like a vault. "I'm worried it could be Nick Hawkins."

"Your partner? Why?"

"I've been doing my own checking around, and he was at her house that day. He never answered his phone when she went in to the hospital, and apparently Ellen and Nick's wife *used* to be friends."

"So you think there was an affair," Gabrielle said. Katie wasn't surprised that she had gone in that direction; Gabrielle always suspected an affair.

"Or something," Katie said. "As far as I know, Ellen was happy with Christopher."

"It sounds like we need to do some more nosing around," Caleb said.

"We?" Katie looked at Caleb.

"Well, whatever I can do to help," Caleb said. "But I guess mostly *you* need to nose around."

Katie's shoulders slumped. "I'd really like to know how that prescription came to be. And whether Ellen had any enemies. From what everyone says, she was well liked."

Caleb went back to his laptop, leaving Katie to fill Gabrielle in on what little they knew.

The two of them batted the few pieces of information around until they had exhausted the possibilities and almost finished painting.

"We've been working at this for a couple of hours. What if we each finish our wall and then I take you to Riley's for dinner?"

"Race you!" Gabrielle began rapidly spreading Sunshine Gold.

* * *

Riley's was all steel and glass and brick with a large open dining room that felt like it belonged in a big city rather than a small town.

The noise level on a Saturday night made it almost impossible to hear what your tablemates were saying. Gabrielle and Katie had come early enough that they scored a table at the back in a relatively quiet corner.

They ordered drinks and then sat back to people watch. A favorite pastime of theirs was to make up stories about the people at the other tables. Doctors began every encounter with a patient by taking a history—usually limited to the reason for the visit, but often it was much more comprehensive. But the exam started from the moment they walked in the room. By evaluating body language, clothing, and appearance, they could get a few clues to the patient's condition. Gabrielle's stories tended toward the illicit affair, and Katie saw spies and secret meetings.

"That guy over there." Gabrielle nodded to a table where a man sat alone checking his watch every minute or so. "His mistress has finally gotten sick of waiting for him to leave his wife, and she's standing him up."

Katie choked on her drink. "That's the minister at the Methodist church," she said.

Gabrielle lifted an eyebrow. "So I'm right?"

Katie laughed. "I doubt it. Look. Here's his daughter."

A pretty dark-haired young woman sat down in the chair opposite the minister, and his face blossomed with a warm smile.

"Hmm, okay, your turn," Gabrielle said. "It's kind of unfair that you know most of these people."

Katie shook her head. "I only recognize a couple of people from town. I'll bet a lot of them are from Ann Arbor."

She surveyed the room until she found someone who looked suspicious. "Over there," she said. She tilted her head in the direction of a woman sitting at a table with a man who was studying the menu. The woman was applying lipstick and using her phone as a mirror. "She's a private investigator staking out that group of young women."

"Them?" Gabrielle gestured with one finger while keeping her hand on the table.

Katie thought that she and Gabrielle were probably the most suspicious people in the restaurant.

"Yup. She's not really looking at herself. She's snapping pictures."

"Why?"

"Umm, the father thinks she's meeting her ex-boyfriend and hired the PI to follow her."

"Ooh, that's good," Gabrielle said. "Is the boyfriend cheating on her, and the father knows it?"

"No, the boyfriend wants to move to New York to pursue his musical career, and the father doesn't want her to move away."

"Why don't the people in your stories ever just talk to each other?"

Katie made a face. "How come all your stories involve sex?"

"I'm an obstetrician. I'd be out of business if people didn't have sex."

Katie laughed and sipped her drink. This was what she needed—to take a break from worrying about Ellen, rogue prescriptions, and murder.

"What can I get you tonight?" The waitress had sneaked up behind them as they talked about their fellow diners.

Katie hadn't even looked at the menu, but she didn't need to. "I'll have the lamb and quinoa stew, please."

Gabrielle ordered the chicken special and another round of drinks.

Katie held up a hand. "Just water for me, please."

Gabrielle made a face.

"I'm on call—one-drink limit," Katie said.

"Right," Gabrielle said. "I forgot."

After the waitress left, Gabrielle leaned forward. "Behind your left shoulder—don't look now!" Gabrielle said. "Isn't that your new partner?"

Katie turned in an exaggeratedly slow manner. "Yup. That's Nick and his wife."

"They don't look very happy."

Katie turned again and tried to evaluate the mood at the table across the room with the peripheral vision in her left eye.

"I can't really see them. What are they doing?"

"Eating in silence. Not looking at each other."

"Hmm. I don't know her very well, and Nick *has* been grumpy lately." Katie fingered the rim of her glass and looked around the room.

"Is it still going well at the practice?"

Katie nodded. "I love the patients and the location. The staff is really good."

"But . . ."

"Besides the question of whether he was having an affair with Ellen, there's something weird going on with Nick and Emmett. I don't know if it's a father-son thing or if there's more to it than that."

"Are they arguing?"

"No, nothing like that. It's hard to define. When I worked with them a year ago on my rotation, Emmett was a real talker. He clearly loved what he was doing and wanted to share it with anyone who would listen. He's still sort of like that, but it's like he's been dialed down. I'm not sure if it's the practice, or me, or just that I don't know them that well."

"You've only been there a few months. It'll take a while to get the sense of all those undercurrents."

Katie looked down at her drink and swirled the contents with the tiny straw.

"Dr. LeClair?"

Katie looked up to see Todd Talbot, the manager of the restaurant, standing at the table.

"Hi, Todd! I'm back again for my usual," Katie said. She gestured across the table at Gabrielle. "This is my friend, Dr. Gabrielle Maldova." She turned to Gabrielle. "Todd manages the restaurant and is personally responsible for my favorite meal."

Gabrielle and Todd exchanged greetings.

"Could I join you for a moment?"

"Of course." Katie gestured at the empty chair.

"I'm sorry to interrupt your dinner, and Beth likely won't speak to me for days, but I saw you and thought I would give it a try."

"Beth?"

"Beth Wixom and I are engaged," Todd said.

"I remember Ellen mentioning that," Katie said. "I'm sorry for your loss."

"Thank you." Todd drummed his fingers on the table and didn't meet her eye. "The thing is, Beth doesn't think it was a suicide."

Katie sat back in her chair, and Gabrielle feigned interest in the bread basket.

"She mentioned that to me at the hospital."

"I think she'd really like to talk to you about her mother." He finally met her gaze with a pleading look. "I don't know what the rules are about privacy and all, but if you could meet with her and . . . I don't know, just hear her out?"

"I'd be happy to talk to her, Todd." Katie didn't mention that she'd already tried to contact Beth. She didn't want to get his hopes up that she agreed that Ellen's death was suspicious. "But I heard the police are investigating."

Todd snorted. "For whatever good that will do."

Katie felt a surge of irritation. She liked John Carlson, and she knew he was looking into it.

Todd must have noticed her change in expression. He held up his hands as if to calm her. "It's not that they aren't listening; I just don't think they really believe her. They think she's just being overly emotional."

She briefly wondered if she should mention that Chief Carlson had already talked to her but decided to keep that to herself as well.

"I'd be happy to talk to her, Todd." Katie gave him her cell number.

"Thank you, Dr. LeClair. Maybe you can help her feel some closure on this whole thing."

Katie wondered how she would manage that when *she* was questioning the circumstances of Ellen's death as well.

"Wow, no pressure there." Gabrielle whistled when Todd was out of earshot.

Katie grimaced and took a big gulp of her drink.

10

Sunday morning, Katie drove to the clinic. She'd taken a phone call for the practice the night before and wanted to look at the patient's chart. There was something about the patient that struck her as odd, and she was hoping the chart would shed some light on it.

She also wanted some time alone in the office.

She unlocked and pushed open the door. The alarm pad flashed and beeped, and she quickly entered the code to disarm it. The hallway of exam rooms was dark. Natural light spilled from the doctors' offices—the only rooms with windows at this end of the hall.

Without making a conscious decision, she walked toward Emmett's office and stepped inside. She felt weird being in his private space, but the patient she'd talked to was his, and she thought the chart might be in his office. That's what she told herself at least. Emmett had been acting strangely since she'd started with him at the beginning of the summer. She'd shrugged it off at first, but now she was convinced something was bothering him. She'd noticed that Angie had been bringing stacks of charts into his office.

Katie wondered if he was checking up on her. Not that she would really mind. In residency, she'd become used to people double-checking everything she did. But the idea that he was doing it in secret made her think that he didn't trust her.

His office was in its usual state of disarray. She had yet to see a doctor's private office that didn't have journals piled in a corner and charts stacked on most flat surfaces. He had a corkboard on one wall with pictures of all the babies he'd delivered when he was still doing obstetrics. It was a rare family doctor who still delivered babies in Katie's generation, but Emmett had done so for the first twenty years of practice. The photos were yellowed with age and filled the board, newer pictures obscuring the old.

She walked to the table by his window and ran her finger down the pile of charts. None of them were her patients. But she recognized a couple of the names as Nick's patients. She quickly flipped through the pile and saw Nick's sloppy scrawl on all of them.

He was checking up on Nick?

She turned to his desk and saw a note—"Missing: 2 v. Dem, 1 v. Fent." Demerol and fentanyl? Both were strong narcotics and often abused.

She reached to pick up the note when she heard the back door click shut.

Her heart began to race. Had she locked the door? She'd heard stories of small clinics being burgled for their drugs. If she *had* locked it, who was here? She didn't want to be caught in Emmett's office. She tiptoed to the doorway and listened.

Whoever it was, he was walking toward the chart room. He wore heavy shoes and had an uneven gait. Nick?

Nick had been in a motorcycle accident a few years ago and still walked with a limp. His experience with recovery was what prompted him to open the pain clinic.

Katie stepped into the hall.

She walked slowly past the break room and the storage room. Just in case it wasn't Nick, she ducked into the cleaning closet and grabbed a broom. Holding it up like a bat, she continued down the hallway. All the exam room doors stood open, and the rooms were empty. She peeked around the doorway to the records room—empty. Then she heard a noise toward the back of the records room in the small medication room.

Katie froze. There was a narrow shaft of light underneath the door to the medication room. It *was* a drug thief! Had someone stolen the Demerol and fentanyl and now come back for more? She crept to the door and put her ear up to it. It didn't sound like a crazed drug seeker. She only heard an occasional soft clinking of glass as if someone was looking through the med cabinet.

Katie turned the knob slowly and pushed the door open.

"Aah!" Nick dropped a vial, and it shattered on the floor.

Katie lowered her broomstick. "What are you doing here? You scared me."

"*I* scared *you*? What are you doing with that?" Nick gestured to the broom that Katie was trying to hide behind her back.

"I heard you come in, but I didn't know who was here."

"And you thought I was a burglar? And you were going to stop me with an old broomstick?"

Katie shrugged. She turned the broom around and handed it to Nick to sweep up the shards of glass.

"Thanks," he said and began sweeping the glass into a small pile.

"What was it?" Katie hoped it wasn't something expensive.

"Just insulin," he said. He kept the broom over the mess so she couldn't see the label.

Katie wondered what he was hiding. It didn't smell like insulin, which had a strange Band-Aidy smell.

"It doesn't smell like insulin," Katie said.

Nick stopped sweeping. "Did my dad ask you to check up on me?"

"I'm just here to look at a chart." Katie held her hands up in surrender. "Sorry to have startled you."

Nick nodded and pulled a paper towel out of the dispenser by the sink. He carefully picked up the larger pieces with the towel and used another one to mop up the liquid.

"No problem. You can report back that I was just checking our supplies. We have to place an order next week."

"I don't know what you're talking about," Katie said.

"Okay, we'll play it your way." Nick turned his back on her and continued to mop up the spill.

Katie backed out of the room. She'd heard from the nurses that he could be grouchy, but she'd never seen it herself. She turned to the shelves of files but kept one eye on the door to the med room. Angie usually took care of ordering the medication for the practice. Why was Nick here on a weekend taking inventory? Maybe she *should* be checking up on him.

She found the chart that she was looking for and went to her office. It only took a few minutes to confirm that the medication dose was correct. She could see that Emmett had tried the usual dose with no effect. She picked up her phone and called the pharmacy the patient used to order the beta-blocker.

She hung up the phone and glanced at her bottom drawer. She'd stashed Ellen's file there and hadn't gotten around to putting it back together properly. Katie pulled the drawer open and reached inside. The file wasn't there.

She sat back in her chair and ran that evening through her mind again. She was sure she had put it in that drawer. It was her "pending" drawer where she put anything she didn't want sitting out but that wasn't ready to file.

She opened the drawer again and flipped through the contents: medical journals, nonurgent mail, a crayon drawing from one of her pediatric patients, but no file.

She looked in every other drawer in her office and still couldn't find it.

Finally, she headed back to the records room. Before she entered the room, she heard Nick's voice.

"I can't," he said in a low voice.

He was on his cell phone and pacing in the medication room. The cabinet was still open.

She wasn't sure why, but Katie stepped back into the hallway before Nick saw her. She didn't want to give his spying theory any more credence.

She raised her voice. "See you later, Nick!"

She heard Nick stop his pacing. "See you tomorrow. I'll lock up when I'm done."

Katie grabbed her bag from her office and let herself out the back door.

She stood in the parking lot, trying to calm the thoughts that swirled in her head. Nick was up to something, and Emmett was checking up on him. He could have called in that prescription for Ellen and put the medication in some food or drink. If they *were* having an affair, she would trust him. So one partner was checking up on the other, *and* he might be a murderer.

Her idea of an idyllic rural practice was rapidly evaporating.

* * *

She had arranged to talk to John Carlson at three o'clock. Now she sat in his office checking her watch and nervously doodling in her notebook. He had just as many files and magazines piled around his office as Emmett. There was a picture of his wife, Linda, on his desk and several pictures of Bubba hanging on the wall. She added another item to her "plan" section: "find out what Nick is up to and why Emmett is monitoring his charts."

She heard footsteps in the hall and quickly stashed the notebook in her bag as she tried to compose a neutral expression.

"Hi, Doc," John said as he hurried into the room. "Sorry you've been waiting. I always forget about the gauntlet of coming in on a weekend. Things that no one wants to call me about pile up, and then when I show up, they're suddenly elevated to emergencies." He sat in the chair behind his desk and swiveled to face her.

Katie smiled, thinking of times she had been met at the door by her nurse or receptionist with a list of "urgent" questions.

"Thanks for coming in," he said. "I just have a couple of questions for you." He pulled a notepad out of the center drawer of his desk and flipped it open.

Katie cleared her throat. "Sure, John. Happy to help."

"You were Mrs. Riley's primary care doctor?"

Katie nodded.

"How long have you been her doctor?"

"I met her a year or so ago when I was doing a month-long rotation with Dr. Hawkins. She switched her care to me when I joined the practice three months ago."

"Have you seen her recently in your clinic?" Carlson kept his eyes on his notes.

"About a week ago. She came in complaining of feeling tired and wondered if she needed a different dose of her thyroid replacement medication. But as we talked further, it seemed more likely she was dealing with mild stress."

Carlson looked up. "What kind of stress?"

Katie consciously loosened her clasped hands and took a deep breath. "She was working on some sort of research project, and she said she hadn't been sleeping."

"Other than the recent stress, what can you tell me about Ellen Riley's state of mind in the past month or so?"

Katie sat up straighter in her chair. "I thought she was basically happy. She'd been a little bit tired and was maybe working too much, but in general, she was the same as always."

John scribbled a note. "You didn't see any signs of depression or a desire to harm herself?"

"No. I had no inkling that anything like that was bothering her," Katie said. She leaned forward and looked him in the eye. "I was very surprised that she killed herself."

John nodded. "That seems to be the consensus from everyone who knew her." He sighed and put his pen down on the desk. "The autopsy report should clear things up for us. There was no indication *other* than suicide at the scene." He spread his hands out, palms up. "Unless it was a terrible accident, I have to conclude that she took the diazepam knowing that she would overdose."

Katie tensed and waited for the next question. If he asked about the diazepam, what should she say? That she suspected that someone had forged the prescription? Would that implicate Ellen or someone in Katie's office? Would it just make it look as if Katie was incompetent?

"Did you prescribe the diazepam due to the stress she reported?" John's hand hovered over his notepad.

Katie swallowed. "I didn't prescribe the diazepam."

John looked up from his notepad. "What do you mean? Did one of your partners prescribe it?"

Katie shook her head. "As far as I can tell, it didn't come from our office. I've looked in all the places where it should have been recorded, and it wasn't."

"Why didn't you tell me this earlier?" Carlson put his pen down again and leaned forward.

Katie looked down at her lap. "I had to be sure that I hadn't just forgotten. It was bad enough that I couldn't remember, but if I checked the chart and it was recorded, then I didn't want to make a big deal out of it. Now I wonder how she got it."

"The paramedics were quite sure your name was on the bottle."

"I know. All I can think of is that maybe she called it in herself." Katie held out her hands palms up. "It's not that far-fetched. Anyone can look up the dose online. She would know how to order it from her work as a psychologist."

"Do you think that's what happened?" Carlson's voice had taken on a hard edge. "Did she ask for medication, and you refused?"

"No. In general she didn't like to take medicine. Even over-the-counter stuff. And I can't imagine her doing that. It's illegal, for one thing, and it was unnecessary. If she had asked for diazepam to help her sleep, I probably would have given her some or another sleeping medicine. But I can't come up with any other explanation for the diazepam that the EMTs found." Except that maybe Nick was dealing drugs. Or someone in her office was writing prescriptions and not recording them. But she didn't want to make that accusation until she knew more. She owed Emmett that much.

"Okay, we'll try to look into that." Carlson sat back in his chair and picked up the pen. "I'll talk to the guys again and see if any of them remember which pharmacy it was from, and we'll try to track it down that way."

Katie relaxed into her chair. She'd been dreading admitting to her concerns about the diazepam, but giving Chief Carlson this piece of information was the right thing to do. And if *she* found out where it came from first, she'd find a way to get the information to him.

Carlson's pen scratched along the paper. He looked up at Katie and changed the subject. "You told me that you weren't on call that night. Did you ever find out where Nick Hawkins was that evening?"

Katie shook her head. He had already asked her this question when they had coffee yesterday. Why the interest in Nick? Did Carlson know something? Maybe her silence wouldn't protect Nick at all. "No. He didn't say. He just said he must have been in an area where his phone didn't work."

Carlson glanced at his papers and flipped a couple of pages. "They tried to reach him for half an hour before they called you. That seems pretty irresponsible of him."

"It happens." Katie shrugged. "Maybe he didn't realize his phone wasn't picking up the calls. Maybe some other glitch prevented the calls from going through. It's why we have a backup plan."

"And you were the backup?"

"Yes. If they can't reach his cell, the answering service is supposed to call his house and maybe his wife's cell phone. If they still can't reach him, they call the next person on the list. On Wednesday night, that was me."

"Cecily Hawkins might have also gotten a call?"

"You'd have to check with the service. I don't know how he has it set up. I have them call my house and then my brother's cell, figuring that he's likely to know where I am and could track me down if needed."

Carlson made more notes.

"John, why does it matter that Nick didn't answer the call?" Katie asked. "She ended up in the ER anyway. He wouldn't have had anything to do with her care initially."

John flipped his pad shut. "Just following all the lines of inquiry."

He stood and held out his hand. "Thanks for coming in, Doc. You need to come out to the house again soon. Bubba misses you."

"I'd be happy to come check on him; he's a sweet dog." Katie clasped his hand.

"Tell my wife that. He dug up her flower bed this week."

John walked her to the front door and waved as she got in her car. She waved back and let out a sigh of relief when he went back inside.

11

Katie had finally contacted Beth that morning, and they'd made a tentative plan to meet at the coffee shop after her meeting with Carlson. She sent a text to Beth telling her that she was on the way. She was close enough to walk, so she got back out of her car and headed down the street. The afternoon had cooled off, and she wished she'd brought a jacket as she strode the two blocks to the Purple Parrot.

Katie ordered tea and a muffin and sank into one of the cushy couches by the window. She felt herself relax and realized how much that mysterious prescription had been weighing on her. She would still try to track it down, but sharing her concerns with Carlson meant she was more likely to get answers. Katie just hoped it hadn't been one of her office staff.

She saw Beth leave Riley's and cross the street. Beth spotted Katie in the window and waved.

She stopped at the counter, ordered, and then came to sit with Katie.

"Thank you for meeting me, Dr. LeClair." Beth set her coffee down on the small table and sat in the armchair closest to Katie.

"Please call me Katie. I'm happy to help, but I'm not sure how."

"I really just wanted to talk to someone who knew my mom." Beth leaned forward and held Katie's gaze. "I sensed the other night that you understood what I was going through."

Katie looked out the window at the purpling sky. She closed her eyes briefly and then looked at Beth. "I lost my mother to suicide as well. I understand some of what you're feeling, but every relationship is different, and everyone grieves in their own way."

Beth blinked back tears. "I'm so sorry. I didn't know."

"It was a long time ago," Katie said. She didn't have the heart to tell Beth that it never really got easier; the sharp edges just got dull from so much handling. "How can I help?"

"I've been thinking more and more about this." Beth pulled a notebook out of her bag. "I made a list of all the things that made me doubt she killed herself. It's not just a vague feeling or a wild hope. I have good, verifiable reasons. First, she didn't leave a note."

Katie put her hand up, but Beth kept talking.

"I know you're going to say that a lot of people don't leave notes. But my mom left a note if she was running out to the grocery store. She put notes in my lunchbox when I was in elementary school. She left notes around the house for herself and for me. I used to tease her that she couldn't think unless she had a pen in her hand. There is no way that she would kill herself without leaving a note."

"Okay, I can understand that," Katie said. "Could she have left a note on a computer or on her phone?"

Beth's face fell. "I didn't think of that. She did have a laptop." Beth leaned forward and put her head in her hands. Her voice was muffled when she said, "I'll have to find the laptop and check, but I doubt she would have done that. She thought computers were for research and shopping. Maybe e-mail."

"It would help to take a look," Katie said. "Maybe there will be some reference to what your mom was working on before she died."

"Yes, you're right. I didn't think of it because I got the impression she had been researching things the old-fashioned way. But she may have left some notes on her computer."

Beth sat up and flipped open her notebook. "Besides the lack of a note, she hated taking medicine. She would have needed to swallow a lot of pills to overdose on diazepam, and not only can I not imagine her taking *one* of them, but she would never take a whole bottle."

Katie sat quietly, not wanting to argue every point with this grieving daughter. She agreed with Beth that things didn't add up.

"Also, she was really happy," Beth continued. "She was thrilled when Todd and I got engaged. She was helping me plan the wedding . . ." Beth stopped. "I just realized she won't be at the wedding." Beth picked up her mug of coffee and held it tight with both hands. She took a big sip and swallowed. Katie watched her regain control of her emotions.

Katie agreed with all of Beth's points. If she promised to help her, it would mean she was in this 100 percent, regardless of what they discovered. She took a deep breath.

"I believe you," Katie said. "I think there are too many things that don't make sense."

Beth smiled at Katie and dabbed her eyes with a napkin. "You have no idea how much that means to me."

Katie took a fortifying swig of tea. She hoped the answers they discovered wouldn't make things worse.

"Okay, let's make a plan. I don't think the police will appreciate us mucking around in their investigation, so we need to keep this relatively quiet for now."

Beth nodded. "I know. But they don't seem to be taking it seriously. They're all quite comfortable with the idea of suicide."

"Chief Carlson told me he's looking into it." Katie didn't think she should talk about the prescription until she knew more. She didn't want to get Beth's hopes up. "Why don't you find the laptop and check it out? We can meet up again in a day or two."

"I'd like that," Beth said. "It's nice to have someone to talk to about this."

"I think we need to be very clear that if we don't believe this was suicide or an accident, the only conclusion is that someone murdered your mother."

Beth nodded solemnly and blinked back tears.

*　　*　　*

That evening Caleb bounded into the living room with all the pent-up energy of someone with big news. Since Caleb was usually secretive about most things, Katie knew there was more than a bit of drama in play.

"Guess what I did today?" He bounced on his toes like a kid.

"Hacked into the NSA?" Katie asked. "Are they coming to get you?"

Caleb's face fell. "How did you know? And no, they aren't coming to get me, because *if* I did that, they'd never know."

"Okay, what did you do?" She closed her notebook. She'd been working on her list of things to do for her unofficial investigation.

"I found your pharmacy."

"What pharmacy?"

"The one where Ellen Riley filled her prescription." Caleb flopped onto the armchair and feigned boredom.

"What? How?" Katie leaned forward, all thoughts of her list gone.

Caleb tapped his temple. "I'm not just a pretty face."

"But I couldn't even find out which pharmacy it was from. How did you track it down?"

"I started thinking that if *you* didn't write it, then maybe someone was trying to fill a fake prescription. If they used any pharmacy nearby, it's likely they would be recognized. So I looked at small pharmacies, ones that aren't part of a chain, that are more than ten miles outside of Baxter. I narrowed it down to five." He held up five fingers.

"That *is* clever."

"I know!" Caleb couldn't have been more pleased with himself.

"What did you find out?"

"Well, it took some doing." Caleb leaned forward, the excitement of his narrative taking over. "The owner of one pharmacy refused to give me any info. I went back after striking out at all the other places, and fortunately, the owner's daughter was working today. She was more forthcoming."

"So you charmed an unsuspecting girl. And?"

"She remembered filling a prescription for diazepam last Monday. She looked it up, and it was made out to Ellen Riley. It was picked up by a woman, and she paid cash." He handed her a piece of paper with the pharmacy name and address on it.

"So it could have been Ellen. Maybe she called in her own script and picked it up."

Caleb shook his head. "I showed her a picture of Ellen. She didn't recognize her."

"Strange. Maybe she had someone pick it up for her?"

"Or someone filled it without her knowledge."

"Where is this place?" Katie held the paper with the address up.

"About fifteen minutes west of here. It's a tiny private pharmacy. They don't have anything computerized. It's all logged in a big book by hand. Whoever chose it was very clever."

"I didn't think anyone still did things that way."

Caleb shrugged. He thought *everything* should be computerized.

"Thank you for doing this, Caleb. Although now I don't know what to think."

"You're welcome. I figured you needed some answers, but now I think there are more questions."

Katie looked at him. "You're right; there are more questions. I was hoping my idea that Ellen was murdered would be proven wrong, but the more I learn, the more likely it seems."

Katie felt a whoosh of relief when she said the words. She hadn't even realized how much she'd been hoping for this to be an accident—or even murder. She just couldn't accept that she had missed all the signs of suicidal ideation. And she didn't want to think she was responsible.

"I think you need to get your buddy Carlson to open a real investigation."

"He already has. I'll let him know about the pharmacy tomorrow. He didn't seem nearly as concerned about where the prescription came from as I was."

Caleb sat back and put his feet on the ottoman. "Maybe I can charge him a consultant's fee."

"I think the less he knows about your involvement, the better," Katie said. "I don't think he's the type of guy who would want help from civilians."

12

Katie was glad that on Mondays she only had an afternoon clinic and was in charge of rounds with the hospital patients in the morning. It freed her up to focus on Ellen's death.

Katie planned to see her patients and then go find John Carlson and figure out a way to steer him in the direction of the pharmacy Caleb had found.

She didn't have to look far. She'd just shut her front door on her way out, heading to the hospital, when his police cruiser pulled into the drive.

"Hey, Doc, do you have a minute?" His face was grim, and Katie felt her mouth go dry. Had he discovered what Caleb had been doing? What was the penalty for weaseling information out of a pharmacist?

"Sure, come in." Katie unlocked the door and gestured him inside. She took deep breaths to steady herself and followed.

John Carlson stood in the entryway looking around like a prospective buyer. "This is nice. I haven't been inside here. It seems like over the years I've been in just about every house in Baxter, but not this one."

"Thank you." Katie showed him into the sparse living room. "Can I get you anything?" She was stalling and trying to sense whether this was a social or business call.

"No, thanks. I have to be on my way soon." John sat on the small loveseat, and Katie took the only other chair in the room.

"What can I do for you?"

"There's been a development in the Ellen Riley case, and I wanted you to hear it from me."

Katie let out a breath. He wasn't here for Caleb. She nodded to encourage him.

"The labs came back, and there was only a low level of diazepam in her system. She didn't kill herself with those pills because she didn't take enough to do any harm."

Again, Katie felt relief, but this time it was followed quickly by questions.

"Then . . . what?"

"The labs showed a high level of Demerol."

"Why would she have—?" Katie stopped. Was there also a prescription for Demerol with her name on it? Then her mind flashed on the note in Emmett's office—"missing: 1 v. Dem and 1 v. Fent." Had the drug come from her own clinic?

"The medical examiner thinks it was injected. And there were no needles or syringes with her when she was found. We're treating it as a homicide."

Her stomach dropped as the reality of what he said sank in. Even though she'd been hoping Ellen hadn't killed herself, the firm knowledge that it was murder was almost worse.

Katie put a shaky hand up to her mouth. "But who would want to hurt her?"

Chief Carlson shook his head. "We'll have to start over with the investigation. The scene was photographed, but there's nothing there. We collected a few things from the scene, but I'll have to go back over the evidence and see if we missed anything. I doubt we'll find anything useful, and the room has likely been cleaned by now. It already feels like a cold case even though it happened less than a week ago."

"I'm so sorry for her family. Can I do anything to help?"

"I don't think so. I only wanted to let you know before you hear any gossip."

"Thank you for telling me."

Katie and Chief Carlson walked to the door. "If you think of anything I should know, give me a call," he said.

"John, wait," Katie said. She went into her room and came out with the piece of paper with the pharmacy address on it. "I think this is where the prescription for diazepam came from."

Carlson took it and glanced at the address. "This is way out of town. How did you find it?"

"Just a bit of minor sleuthing. I don't suppose it matters now."

"Maybe not, but we'll look into it." He tucked the paper into his shirt pocket. "Let us take it from here, Doc."

Katie nodded and shut the door behind him. She would go to the hospital later. Right now she needed to talk to Caleb.

*   *   *

Caleb and Katie had never kept normal hours. After their mom died and their dad disappeared into work and a vodka bottle, they had mostly raised themselves. She had hated to leave him when she went off to college, but the bonds of childhood never weakened: Caleb enrolled at a community college near Katie's medical school, and they had shared an apartment ever since. This was their first house. Technically it was Katie's, but she hoped Caleb would stay for a long time.

It wasn't unusual for either one of them to be awake for the entire night. Katie often kept irregular hours during residency, and Caleb did likewise while working on a coding problem or brainstorming with his fellow computer geeks. They had an unwritten rule to only wake the other person in case of emergency. Surely this was an emergency.

She quietly opened his door and checked to see if he was still asleep. Caleb had installed blackout shades that allowed only a dim gray light into the room. The large lump under the blankets indicated he was in residence.

Katie went to the window and pulled the shade up, hoping that the bright sunlight would wake him, and she wouldn't have to do any more. He didn't even flinch. Katie hesitated. She knew how uncomfortable it was to be awakened from a deep sleep. Maybe she should just leave the shade open and write a note asking him to call her.

She turned to his desk and rummaged for a pen and paper. Both items flew from her hands when a voice emanated from the bed.

"If you're going to search my room, at least wait until I'm out."

She spun toward him. "I'm not searching your room. I'm trying to wake you up."

"By tiptoeing around?" He stayed buried under his blankets and talked into his pillow.

"I felt bad waking you up."

"Not bad enough, apparently." Caleb sat up and rubbed his face. "What time is it?"

"Almost ten."

He swung his legs over the side of the bed. "Okay, six hours is pretty good. I assume you need me?"

Katie nodded and sat in his desk chair.

"Ellen Riley was murdered."

"What? Well, that's great!" He put his hand up. "Not great that she was killed, but at least you're off the hook. Whatever hook you had yourself on, that is. You didn't miss any signs, and you didn't prescribe the murder weapon, and no one in your office prescribed the murder weapon." He ticked the items off on his fingers.

"You're right." She did feel a huge sense of relief and felt guilty about that as well. What kind of a person is glad to hear that a murder was committed? A crazy, sick, selfish kind of person, that's what kind.

"And you shouldn't feel bad that you're a little bit glad it was murder," Caleb said. "You can find a way to feel guilty about almost anything."

She smiled then. Having someone in your life who knew you well enough to call you out on your self-destructive thoughts was a priceless gift.

"Right again, Dr. Freud."

Caleb stood and pulled a sweat shirt over the T-shirt and sweats he'd slept in. "Come on. You can make me some pancakes while we talk." He headed toward the door.

She grabbed a pillow from the bed and threw it at his retreating back.

When she got to the kitchen, Caleb was already ensconced at the table and tapping away at his keyboard.

She whisked the eggs, oil, and pancake mix together with milk in her plastic pancake bowl. Caleb knew it was *the* pancake bowl and so she often found popcorn kernels or potato chip crumbs in it. It was his way of teasing her and pointing out her type A tendencies. Brothers.

"What will you do now?" He flipped his laptop shut and turned to face her.

The pan sizzled when Katie flicked water onto it. She scooped out some batter with a measuring cup and poured it onto the pan.

"I don't know," she said. "I still don't understand how my name got onto that prescription bottle or how Ellen got the prescription in the first place." She waited a minute and checked the pancakes—perfect. She flipped them and waited again.

"It seems strange that someone would go to the trouble of faking a prescription and then use something else entirely to actually kill her," Caleb said.

"We're assuming that the killer is the one who put the prescription there," Katie said. "For all we know, Ellen sent someone to get the diazepam. Maybe she was more stressed than I realized, and she decided to take matters into her own hands. She would certainly know how to write a prescription with her career as a therapist."

Katie put a plate of pancakes in front of Caleb. He dumped syrup on them and dug in.

"I s'pose you're right," he said around a mouthful.

Katie poured more batter. She couldn't resist the smell of syrup and pancakes, even though it would be her second breakfast.

"But if she didn't have much diazepam in her bloodstream, where did all the other pills go?"

"The whole situation is sketchy," Caleb said.

"I still want to know how it happened. It makes me nervous to think that someone could be out there using my name to write prescriptions." Katie flipped the pancakes and stood watching them brown.

She turned toward Caleb. "What if it wasn't her? What if she purchased them from someone on my staff?"

"I can go back to the pharmacy with pictures of more people," Caleb offered, "but we don't know whether the prescription bottle had anything to do with the murder."

Katie sat across from him and poured syrup on her stack. "What if the killer did leave the bottle there? That means the killer used *my* name to obtain the decoy drug. I probably know that person."

Caleb looked up from his food. "In a town this size, it's almost certain that you know the killer. The question is, how well?"

Katie put her fork down and pushed the plate away. The pancakes sat like a hard lump in her stomach. Caleb was right.

"I guess I'd better figure that out."

13

Katie finished rounding at twelve thirty. She hadn't even started until almost noon because of her impromptu pancakes and planning session with Caleb. She was lucky that she knew all three patients and they were all stable.

Her afternoon clinic started at one, and she was too full to think about lunch. So with a half hour to spare, she decided to take a walk through the woods surrounding the hospital. There was a pathway through the grounds with a small garden not far from the back door. A family who'd lost their father after a long battle with heart failure had donated the benches and paid for the landscaping.

Katie wandered the familiar path, lost in thought. She loved walking in these woods, especially in the fall when the leaves were just starting to turn. During her residency rotation at Baxter Community Hospital, every time she got a chance to escape the hospital even for ten minutes, it had been like a minivacation. Most of her rotations had been at University

Hospital in Ann Arbor, but she had managed to schedule a few here. Just being outside away from the noises and smells and sounds of the hospital had saved her mental health.

She tried to stop thinking about Ellen's death, Nick secretly inventorying the drug cabinet, and the mysterious prescription. *Just focus on the trees and birds and the sound of a fall breeze through the leaves.*

She stopped short when she got to the garden. Sometimes she would find a family sitting there, but usually it was deserted. This time Matt Gregor was there. He hadn't seen her yet. He'd draped his white coat over the back of the bench, and the remains of his lunch sat next to him. He was hunched over a notebook, scribbling madly.

She wasn't sure whether to interrupt. She realized she was happy to see him. Then she remembered what Gabrielle had said. Well, regardless of whether he'd want to date her, she still liked talking to him. During this dithering, she took a step backward and snapped a branch. Matt looked up and scanned the area. He shut the book and slipped it into the canvas messenger bag that sat at his feet. When his eyes fell on her, his face broke into a warm smile.

"Dr. LeClair! How nice to see you again." He gestured at the seat next to him.

"Dr. Gregor," Katie said. She walked to the bench and sat, feeling awkward that she had interrupted his break. "I was just out for a quick nature fix. I didn't mean to intrude." She slipped her messenger bag strap over her head and dropped the bag on the ground next to Matt's.

Matt waved off her apology. "No worries. I have to head back in a couple of minutes anyway. I'm in the ER again this afternoon."

"Oh, more locums work?"

"The regular guy is on a two-week fishing trip," he said. He leaned over and lowered his voice. "The rumor is that the nursing staff took up a collection and paid for his cabin in the woods. He was so burned out, none of them could stand to work with him anymore."

Katie remembered a cantankerous older doctor in the ER earlier in the summer. He'd admitted one of her patients for a "rule out MI," which meant he had thought there was a chance the guy was having a heart attack, but none of the tests could confirm it. He had been pleasant enough on the phone, but Katie had overheard the nurses on the floor complaining about his grouchiness.

"Do you think he'll come back?" Katie asked.

Gregor shrugged. "Probably. He's been at it for almost forty years. Hopefully he just needed a break. Or maybe he's ready to retire."

He sat back against the wooden slats of the bench and closed his eyes. "I love this little garden," he said.

Katie grinned at him even though he wasn't looking at her. "Me too. I used to come here during my residency. It was like heaven after a long night on call."

"It does help to put things back in perspective."

"There's a train that comes through around midnight," Katie said. "I used to wait for it before going to sleep—if I was able to go to sleep at all. I liked to think of it traveling far from the worries of being on call. It was reassuring. Reminding me that there is life outside of the hospital."

Katie felt her cheeks growing hot. Why was she telling him this?

He sat forward and looked at her, smiling. "I know that train! I listen for it every time I'm working in the ER. I have this idea that if I hear it go by, I won't have any major disasters come through the doors that night. If I don't hear it, and I realize it later, I get this nervous anxiety that doesn't stop until my shift is over."

Katie laughed. "It seems every doc I know has some kind of superstition."

"Of course. How else can we control the uncontrollable?"

They fell silent for a moment, listening to the woodpeckers tap-tapping deeper in the woods and the squirrels and chipmunks rustling through the leaves.

"You seem more relaxed today than when I saw you over the weekend."

"I suppose I am, somewhat." Katie met his gaze. "I found out this morning that Ellen Riley was likely murdered."

"What?" Matt sat up straight. "I hadn't heard. And why would that make you relaxed?"

"I didn't write the prescription for diazepam," Katie said. "I don't know how she got it, and I've been worried about it since she died. At first I thought I'd forgotten, which was concerning enough. Then I thought maybe someone had called it in from my office. But now that I know she didn't die from the diazepam, it's like a weight has been lifted."

"I'm sorry you were so worried," Matt said quietly. "You know that even if you had prescribed it, it wouldn't have been your fault. We can't control everything."

Katie sighed. "I understand the theory, but it's hard to put it into practice—I like to imagine that if I just try hard enough, I can keep my patients safe and healthy."

Matt turned and looked up into the trees. "That's a pretty heavy burden you've chosen."

"I know."

"How did she die? If it wasn't the diazepam?"

"The chief said it was a Demerol overdose. It was injected, and since there were no vials or syringes at the scene, he's treating it as a homicide."

Matt nodded. "That makes sense. I was surprised that there was so little in her stomach when we were treating her. But murder? That's not something you see every day in Baxter."

"You don't think it would have made any difference if you knew you were dealing with something other than diazepam?"

Matt shrugged. "Maybe. We would have used different meds to counteract the Demerol. I was surprised that she crashed so quickly, but now it makes sense. I think by the time she was found, she was already pretty far gone, but maybe we could have saved her if we knew. Actually, I knew Ellen, and I didn't think she was depressed either. She was such a nice person, I don't know why anyone would want to hurt her."

"How did you know her?"

"You know, small town and all . . ." Matt glanced at his watch. "I'd better head back. I was supposed to be there twenty minutes ago."

"Me too. I have clinic starting in five minutes, and it's a ten minute walk."

Katie reached for her bag at the same time Matt reached for his. The straps got tangled, and they sat laughing with their heads together while undoing the mess. It seemed the more they pulled or threaded the straps, the worse it got. Katie's heart was racing, and she knew it wasn't because of the tangled messenger bags. Sitting this close, he smelled like fresh laundry and the breeze through the woods. She would have been happy to sit there all day.

"Here, wait," Matt said. "The buckles are stuck." He deftly unclipped the buckles, and the bags separated.

Slightly disappointed, Katie stood and put her bag over her shoulder.

They walked back along the path, crunching the few leaves that had fallen.

"How did it go when Chief Carlson had you in for questions?" Matt asked.

"Terrible," Katie said. "He put me in an empty gray room and shined a light in my eyes. But I didn't tell him a thing."

"Okay, Bourne. I didn't realize you were so tough," Matt said. "I had the impression he was more likely to offer you tea and cookies."

"He thinks I saved his dog's life," Katie said, "so he owes me."

"That was you?" Gregor stopped and turned toward her. "I heard about a doctor who rescued Carlson's dog from a burning building, carried him on her shoulders several miles to a clinic, and resuscitated him using a suture kit and IV fluids."

Katie laughed. "It gets better every time I hear it." They started walking again. "There was no burning building, and I only carried him about ten feet to my car."

"That's not a very exciting story." Matt frowned dramatically. "I'll stick with the one *I* heard."

When they came to the fork in the path that led to the hospital and Katie's clinic, Matt slowed.

"It was nice to be interrupted by you," he said.

Katie looked at her feet and felt herself blush again. "It was nice to barge in on your solitude."

She headed down the path and turned just before the bend that would take her past the hospital and toward her clinic. Matt still stood just where she'd left him. He raised his hand, turned, and walked toward the ER.

14

Katie arrived at the clinic feeling calm after her walk in the woods. The serenity lasted all of fifteen seconds. Angie approached with a pile of charts and a worried look.

"Hi, Dr. LeClair. I assume you've heard the news about Ellen Riley. Chief Carlson is treating it like a murder."

Katie nodded. "I heard."

"So has most of Baxter. The phones are ringing off the hook. For some reason, they think we might know something."

Katie and Angie both knew why the patients thought they would get some information at the clinic. *Debra*. Debra was married to Sean, who was an officer in the Baxter police department. *And* her best friend owned the hair salon. Between those two sources, she knew as much about the town as anyone.

Katie didn't say anything, but Angie held up her hand.

"I'll talk to Debra again and tell her not to gossip. It's like she can't help herself."

Angie juggled the pile of charts and pulled a couple out of the middle. "Your first two arrived together—fifteen minutes early. They're in rooms five and seven." She handed Katie the charts. "I'm trying to fend off a stack of 'urgent' visits that have asked to be seen today. I'll do some triage and see if any of them really need to come in. Maybe I'll just tell them we don't know anything and see if they suddenly feel better."

Katie took a deep breath. She hated to accuse anyone at the office, but this had gone too far for her to stay silent. Ever since she'd heard the word "Demerol," she'd been thinking about that note that she'd seen on Emmett's desk. "Angie, did you hear how Ellen died?"

Angie nodded. "I heard it was an overdose."

Katie lowered her voice. "This is confidential, but they got the path report back, and it was an overdose of Demerol, not diazepam as they originally thought."

Angie swallowed. "Demerol?"

"Yes, she was *injected* with Demerol. That's why they're treating it as a murder."

"Oh, poor Mrs. Riley," Angie said. She put her hand to her mouth. "I hadn't heard that part."

"I need to know . . . have any meds gone missing from the med cabinet recently?"

Angie stepped away from Katie and glanced up and down the hallway. "You'll have to talk to Emmett about that."

"*Is* there something to talk to him about?"

Angie sighed. "There might be." She held her hand up when Katie started to speak. "I'm sorry, but that's all I'm saying. Emmett asked me to keep it to myself, and that's what I'm doing."

Angie flipped through the charts in her hands and continued muttering to herself as she walked down the hall to her office.

"Thanks," Katie said quietly, knowing Angie wouldn't hear her.

Katie glanced at the charts in her hands. Mrs. Peabody and Miss Simms. They were both in their eighties, but they didn't realize that yet. Former schoolteachers, they were involved in a synchronized roller skating club and terrorized the streets with their Vespas. They went everywhere together.

Katie had seen them multiple times during her residency and then twice since she'd started with the practice. She had learned her lesson the first time. She wouldn't get any information about either woman without first talking to her friend.

Mrs. Peabody's chart was on top, so Katie knocked on the door to room five.

"Hello, Mrs. Peabody." Katie walked in the room and shook Mrs. Peabody's hand.

"Hello, my dear." Mrs. Peabody's short silver hair sported a hot-pink streak on the right side, and she wore a matching tracksuit. She was thin and taller than Katie by an inch or so.

"Is Miss Simms doing okay?" Katie asked.

"No, she's not." Mrs. Peabody sat tall in her chair and wore a put-upon expression. "She hasn't been sleeping well, and she's very tired. She doesn't even want to go on our daily walk. You should check her over, even if she denies it." Mrs. Peabody nodded to punctuate her order.

"And how are you doing?"

"Fit as a fiddle. Nothing wrong with me." Mrs. Peabody crossed her arms and dared Katie to argue with her steely expression.

"Why don't I just step next door and see what I can do for Miss Simms."

"Thank you, Doctor." Mrs. Peabody opened her book and began to read.

Katie stepped into the hallway and took a deep breath.

She walked down the hall and knocked on room seven's door.

She opened the door and stepped inside. Before she had even shut the door behind her, Miss Simms began talking.

"I'm so worried about Mrs. Peabody!" Miss Simms paced in the small room. She was shorter than Katie and pleasantly round, with white hair pulled into a bun. "She hasn't been well."

"What seems to be the problem?"

"She stopped eating completely, that's the problem!" Miss Simms allowed Katie to lead her to a chair, and she sat.

Katie glanced at Mrs. Peabody's chart. Her weight was stable; she'd even gained two pounds since her last visit. This visit must be about Miss Simms then. But she didn't seem tired. She seemed agitated.

"And how have you been, Miss Simms?"

"I'm just fine, except for worrying, of course." She smoothed her hair, leaned forward, and lowered her voice. "I haven't been sleeping very well. But it's because I've been so worried about her!"

"I have a record here, Miss Simms, and Mrs. Peabody has not lost any weight. Maybe her appetite has changed a little, but it's not affecting her health. I'll talk to her about this. Don't worry, okay?" Katie had needed to have both ladies sign HIPAA waivers to allow her to discuss each woman's health with the other when she first took over their cases.

Miss Simms pulled a tissue out of her pocket and dabbed at her eyes. "Not Mrs. Peabody, Ellen Riley!"

Katie was having difficulty keeping up with Miss Simms as she jumped from one concern to another. She sat back in her chair and narrowed her eyes. "What?"

"Ellen Riley." Miss Simms sniffed and one lone tear fell. "I've been worried about her for weeks, and now she's dead!" Miss Simms began crying in earnest.

Katie placed a hand on Miss Simms's shoulder. "Why were you worried about Ellen Riley?"

Miss Simms looked up at her from red, wet eyes. "She was such a lovely person. I live next door to the Rileys, you know." She blew her nose loudly and mopped her eyes. "She always stopped for a chat if I was in my yard."

Katie waited for her to continue.

Miss Simms took a shaky breath. "She and her husband had begun arguing. Not that I was eavesdropping or anything, you understand." Miss Simms fixed Katie with a forceful stare that would have quelled any classroom jokes and high jinks. "I've known Christopher all his life, so I was surprised when I heard them."

"All married couples fight sometimes."

Miss Simms shrugged. "I wouldn't know myself, but this seemed out of character for both of them. After that, I saw her in her kitchen on the computer at all hours—as long as her husband wasn't home."

"Have you told Chief Carlson about this?"

She shook her head. "No, I didn't think I had anything to tell him. It's just gossip, really. And I don't want to tell Mrs. Peabody. She thinks I have too much imagination. No, I don't think I *will* tell anyone. I feel better already, talking to you." She patted Katie's hand.

Katie went back to room five.

"Well?" Mrs. Peabody snapped her book shut. "Are the labs back already?"

"No, we don't need lab work today," Katie said. Miss Simms had had normal labs just two weeks earlier. "But I think she'll be better from now on."

"Well, that's a relief." Mrs. Peabody stood to leave. "I've been worried since that Ellen Riley killed herself. Miss Simms is very sensitive."

"Yes, you've mentioned that before."

Mrs. Peabody leaned closer to Katie and lowered her voice. "I was with Miss Simms the night Mrs. Riley died. I haven't said anything to her, but I do wonder why Mrs. Riley wasn't found earlier. I saw her husband come home hours before the ambulance showed up."

Katie caught her breath and tried to keep a bland expression on her face. "Excuse me?"

"Christopher Riley. He came home and went inside around seven o'clock. I think he must have been out running. He had on one of those jogging suits with the hood pulled up. Although why he would need a hood on such a pleasant evening is beyond me. Maybe he's doing one of those sweat diets?"

"Are you sure you saw Christopher Riley?"

"Well, of course I'm sure." Mrs. Peabody scowled. "He had a key. Miss Simms seems to think he left again around seven-thirty. She says she heard a car. Of course, she can't see their driveway from the kitchen, but she's sure she heard a car."

"Mrs. Peabody, I really think you should talk to the police about what you saw and heard."

"No." Mrs. Peabody crossed her arms. "That John Carlson has always been a troublemaker. He was in detention more than he was in class. All the practical jokes and shenanigans." She shook her head and glared at Katie over the top of her glasses. "I'm sure he wouldn't believe a word I said. And don't forget this is all confidential. I signed a paper." She tapped the chart in Katie's hand as if Katie may have forgotten where the paper was stored.

Katie wasn't sure the HIPAA regulations applied to gossip and supposition about non-health-related issues, but she let it slide for now.

Katie opened the door for Mrs. Peabody, and she sailed out of the room. Mrs. Peabody knocked on door seven and opened it. A few moments later, the two ladies emerged and made their way to the front desk.

Katie pulled her notebook out of her pocket and added this new information to her ever-growing "plan." She added a note about Ellen and Christopher fighting recently and her suspicions that the Demerol had come from her own office. She would have to look at everyone who had access to the med room and try to find out why Christopher was home hours before he said he was.

Katie would think about how to get the information to Chief Carlson later. Maybe she could convince the ladies to talk to him in spite of his shenanigan-filled youth.

15

Katie moved to the next room and pulled the chart out of the holder, only glancing at the name. Before she knocked, she stopped and looked at the chart again. She flipped open the folder to see why Christopher Riley would be there to see her. He usually went to Emmett. Under "reason for visit," Angie had written, "insomnia."

Katie took a deep breath and knocked on the door.

"Hello, Mr. Riley." Katie held out her hand to him, and they shook.

"Dr. LeClair."

Katie sat on the wheeled stool and flipped his chart open on the counter. "What can I do for you today? Angie says you're having trouble sleeping."

"No, I'm fine. I just wanted to talk to you. I work evenings, and you work during the day, so I thought the easiest way would be to just make an appointment."

"I see." Katie closed the folder and turned to face him. "How can I help?"

Christopher looked at the floor and fiddled with his wedding ring. "I know Ellen really liked you, and I wondered if she told you about anything that might have been bothering her."

Katie chose her words carefully. "Not really. She said she was having trouble sleeping, but that was all."

Christopher nodded. "I know she was worried."

"Have you talked to Chief Carlson today?"

He looked up and met her eyes. "Yes, he told me this morning that they are treating her death . . ." He stopped and swallowed. "Treating it like a homicide. It was bad enough imagining she had killed herself, but murder is worse."

He sat forward and put his face in his hands. Then he ran his fingers across his hair and looked at the ceiling.

Katie sat very still and waited.

"I can't think of anyone who would want to hurt her. Everyone loved her."

"Is there any chance that one of her clients might have had an issue?"

Christopher shook his head. "All her clients see her for career or lifestyle advice. She helps them to figure out what they want to do and then helps them make a plan. She doesn't—didn't—see anyone for any serious psychiatric problems anymore."

Christopher hesitated and then continued. "So she never said what was causing her sleeping trouble?"

Katie shook her head. "No." Of course, she didn't tell him that other people had shared their ideas of what might have been stressing Ellen. She wasn't sure whether Christopher really wanted information or was just fishing to see if she knew anything. The second thought had her on alert.

"I wish I had come home early that night," he said. "I was going to, and then I got hung up in a meeting until after six. I was halfway home when Beth called to say Ellen was being taken to the ER."

Katie studied him carefully. He didn't seem to be lying. She had developed an ability to suss out lies during her training. Gabrielle was right; everybody lied, and a doctor needed to be a good lie detector. But she wasn't picking up on any signals that he wasn't telling the truth. Katie wondered if John had checked his alibi. And whether he would share that information with her. If Christopher was telling the truth, who had Mrs. Peabody seen that night?

And why was he here? To find out what was bothering Ellen or to find out how much she, Katie, knew?

"I'm sorry I can't shed any more light on this for you. Her last visit was pretty routine."

He nodded. "Thank you for listening. I just feel like my whole life has been upended. I guess I hadn't realized how much I relied on her."

He stood, and Katie shook his hand. He left the room, but Katie lingered for a moment, clutching his chart.

She went out into the hall to see that every room had a flag signaling a patient ready and waiting. She took a deep breath and went to the next room.

She grabbed the chart and smiled. A well-baby visit. Six months; pretty much the best age for a doctor visit. Babies were smiling by then but not yet afraid of strangers. Katie rapped on the door and stepped inside.

Three hours later, Katie sat in her office with a stack of charts to write notes in and another list of phone calls to make. She knew she wouldn't get through it all without some coffee. Her mind kept drifting to Ellen's murder and all the unanswered questions in her notebook.

She headed for the break room. As she turned the corner in the back hall, she saw Angie slip quietly into Emmett's office. It wasn't unusual for the nurses to be in and out of doctor's offices to leave messages or charts. But the way Angie glanced up and down the hall and clicked the door shut behind her caused Katie to walk past the break room and tiptoe toward Emmett's office door.

She stopped when she heard voices inside. She looked down the hallway to be sure no one was witnessing her brazen eavesdropping.

"I can't figure it . . ." Angie's voice said, but Katie couldn't hear the rest.

Emmett's response was a low mumble. *Why didn't they speak up?*

"We have to do . . ."

There was silence, and then Emmett's voice again—too quiet to hear.

Katie, worried she would be caught eavesdropping and with nothing to show for it, turned to head back to the break room. She had just stepped inside when she heard Emmett's door click open again.

"Just let me know what you want to do," Angie said. Katie heard her walk down the hall and turn toward the front desk.

Katie saw her opportunity and marched back down the hall to Emmett's office. Something was going on with the practice, and she had a right to know what it was.

She knocked on Emmett's door.

"Come in," Emmett said.

Katie swung the door open, stepped inside, and shut it again.

Emmett smiled warmly at Katie. "Katie, how are you? I heard the news about Ellen Riley—such a shock. I can't remember the last time there was a murder in Baxter."

Emmett gestured to the chair in front of his desk, and Katie sat.

"It's been quite a roller coaster this past week," Katie said, "but I wanted to ask you about something else."

"Oh, yes? Everything going okay in the office?"

Katie nodded. "Yes, everything is fine. It's just . . ." Katie took a deep breath. "I was wondering if any medications had gone missing recently. From the drug cabinet."

Emmett sat back in his chair, and his smile faded.

"What have you heard?"

Katie shook her head. "I haven't heard anything. I was here yesterday to look at a chart, and I found Nick in the med room. He said he was doing inventory."

She noticed Emmett's shoulders stiffen at the mention of Nick.

"I just figured he wouldn't be checking drug supplies unless something was up."

Emmett relaxed again and then nodded. "There have been a couple of discrepancies, and we've been looking into it. You don't need to worry about it."

"You do know that Ellen Riley was killed with a Demerol overdose?"

"What? No. I hadn't heard that part." Emmett swiveled his chair and looked out the window for a moment. "I'm sure it has nothing to do with us."

"I think it might have something to do with the practice," Katie said.

Emmett swung his chair around. "What do you mean?"

"The police originally thought Ellen had killed herself with an overdose of diazepam. A prescription with my name on it."

Emmett looked down at his desk. "I had heard something about that. I should have talked to you earlier. You can't blame yourself, Katie. We can't control everything."

"I don't blame myself." Katie heard the edge in her voice and took a moment to calm down. "First of all, she wasn't killed with diazepam, and secondly, I didn't write the prescription."

Emmett glanced up sharply and met her eyes. "What are you saying?"

"Someone wrote a prescription using our prescription pads and my name," Katie said. "I've looked through all the records, and it's not listed anywhere."

"This *is* troubling," Emmett said. "I'll talk to Angie, and we'll try to get to the bottom of it as well as the . . . other discrepancies."

"Is there anything I can do to help?"

"Thank you, but I think Angie and I have it well in hand."

Katie doubted that was true, but she didn't want to push him just yet.

"Well, I'd better get back to my office. Those notes aren't going to write themselves."

"Wouldn't that be nice?" Emmett smiled briefly.

Katie left his office wondering how he planned to "get to the bottom" of it.

She still felt the need for caffeine and stopped at the break room on her way to her office. It smelled of burned toast and stale coffee. She approached the coffeepot with trepidation. At this time of day, there was no telling how thick the brew had become. She dumped the pot and rinsed everything. Then she loaded a new filter and coffee grounds into the basket, filled the water tank, and pushed the button. While she waited, she glanced out the window toward the parking lot. It was mostly empty this late in the day; the front desk staff had gone home and only Katie's, Angie's, and Emmett's cars sat in the lot. As she watched, an old white van pulled in and parked. Marilyn climbed out and went to the back to remove her supplies.

A man walked out of the woods along the path and approached her. She set her things down to talk to him. Marilyn stood with arms crossed while he talked. Although his back was to her, Katie sensed something familiar about him. It was just at the edge of her brain when the coffeemaker began hissing. She hadn't put the pot back under the basket, and brown liquid ran everywhere.

She shoved the pot underneath the stream of coffee and yanked a handful of paper towels out of the dispenser. The burned coffee smell permeated the room, and by the time she was done cleaning up the mess, the man was gone and Marilyn was lugging her supplies across the parking lot.

16

Tuesday morning, Katie could barely focus on her patients. Her mind was on Ellen Riley, Nick, and Christopher. Her clinic was overbooked again because they were closing early to attend Ellen's memorial service. Katie ran late all morning, and by the time she'd seen the last patient, everyone but Debra had left for lunch and the memorial.

Debra offered to drive them both, and Katie gratefully accepted. She didn't want to walk into the reception alone. She felt like it was still somehow her fault that Ellen was dead. As if she should have known that Ellen's life was going to be cut short. Logically, she knew she wasn't to blame, but facing a room full of Ellen's friends and family was daunting.

Going to the ceremony with Debra could also support her plan to observe the mourners and gather more information on the people close to Ellen. Debra knew everything about everyone, and for once Katie was hoping to hear some gossip.

Debra led her to a small Ford sedan. The passenger seat was cluttered with takeout bags, magazines, and a worn stuffed dolphin. Katie waited while Debra scooped everything up and dumped it in the back seat, where a toddler's car seat and more childcare clutter awaited. Katie gingerly sat down and buckled her seat belt.

Debra put the car in drive and screeched out of the parking lot. Katie gripped the door handle until her knuckles turned white.

Debra's life was truly an open book. She was more upset when people *didn't* know her business than when they did. She began to fill Katie in on her list of concerns.

"So I said to Sean, 'We have *got* to have more sex.' I mean, we all have needs, right?" Debra turned to Katie for affirmation.

Katie gestured at the road. "Stop sign."

Debra slammed on the brakes and apparently assessed the cross street with her peripheral vision before zipping into the intersection. "So he's mad now and says I'm pressuring him. It's not like I'm asking for multiple times a day. Although there was a time . . ."

Katie coughed.

Debra stopped and looked at Katie again. "Is this one of those things?"

Katie nodded. She had tried to instill the concept of "need to know" in Debra.

"Okay. But do you think I went too far? I mean, medically, I'm just wondering what's normal. He thinks I'm over the top, but I just told him how I felt . . ."

"That's always the best way," Katie interrupted. "Tell him how you feel and try to reach a compromise."

Debra nodded. "I know I'm a bit of an oversharer. I guess it comes from being the youngest in a big family—if I didn't tell my parents I was there, they'd have forgotten all about me."

"If this is something that is really bothering you, I can give you a list of therapists to talk to. It's not something we can solve in a five-minute car ride."

"I don't think I need that!" Debra said. "But I'll let you know if I change my mind."

Thankfully, they arrived at the funeral home, and all conversation stopped as they got out of the car and headed inside.

Soothing watercolor prints adorned the gray walls in the large room. Soft classical music played from speakers mounted to the ceiling. The mourners quietly filed in. Christopher, Beth, and a young man stood at the front of the room accepting condolences.

"That's Dan, Christopher's son," Debra said. "I could tell you a few stories about him . . ." Just then Debra's attention was distracted by her good friend Lois from the Clip 'n' Curl, Baxter's other main source of information distribution.

Katie walked to the front and leaned in to hug Beth. As she did, Beth whispered in her ear. "I need to talk to you. This afternoon, maybe?"

Katie whispered back, "Call me later."

Katie shook hands with Christopher and offered her condolences. She then turned to the young man standing next to Christopher.

"Dr. LeClair, this is my son, Dan. I don't think you've met. He lives in Chicago."

They shook hands and nodded, and Katie moved on. As she walked away, she felt someone watching her, and when she turned, Dan was staring right at her as if he didn't like her. He quickly looked away and greeted the next person in line. It gave Katie a chill. She turned and bumped into Todd. "Sorry," she said. "I wasn't looking where I was going."

"No worries," Todd said. "It's pretty crowded."

Katie looked around for Emmett. He had promised to meet her here.

After saying hello to several patients, she spotted her partner at the back. Making her way over to him wasn't as easy as it seemed. She was stopped several times to acknowledge the people vying for her attention. She wasn't sure where the interest came from and cynically decided that they wanted to talk to anyone who had been closely involved with Ellen. So few of Baxter's residents had accepted Ellen in their midst that—even after two years—she was still considered a newcomer. Katie wondered how long it would take them to accept *her.*

Cecily Hawkins sat next to Emmett and bestowed a frosty smile on Katie as she sat down on his other side. Nick rushed in and took a seat next to Cecily just as the service began. Cecily sat stiffly and stared straight ahead. Katie couldn't decide if she was saddened about Ellen's passing or just upset to be there at all.

The service was brief but appropriate. Christopher's comments were cut short by emotion, which surprised Katie, since he always seemed so controlled. Maybe she was wrong to suspect him. When Christopher left the podium to sit down, Katie glanced down her row. She was shocked to see tears streaming down Cecily's face. Emmett handed her a handkerchief, and Nick tried to hold her hand, but she pulled it away and crossed her arms. Katie remembered that Ellen and

Cecily had been close until just recently. With her suspicions of Nick at the forefront of her mind, she now wondered if Cecily could be involved. Could she have killed her friend out of jealousy? Cecily probably could have gotten into the clinic without much trouble. Katie's fingers were itching to add ideas to her notebook, but she would have to wait.

Beth walked to the podium and said a few words about her mother's work and how close they had always been, and that was the end. Everyone filed into the next room for coffee and dessert.

Katie followed the crowd, hoping to pick up clues about Ellen's life and death. She recognized staff members from Riley's restaurant who were there to support their boss. There was a group of women standing together by the coffee urn, patting each other's backs and weeping quietly into tissues. Neighbors? Colleagues? Katie wasn't sure and wished she knew more of the people in town.

She'd headed in their direction when an overheard line stopped her short.

". . . can't believe she's here after the huge fight they had."

"Cecily only sees things from one point of view—hers," came the catty reply.

"I'm sure you're right. Do you think there's any truth . . ." The two women moved out of earshot and, short of following them around the room, Katie had to let that little tidbit go.

She'd just put a couple of cookies on a plate when someone bumped into her, and the cookies fell to the floor. She turned to see who had knocked into her and saw the whole crowd had scattered to the corners of the room. Todd's nose was bleeding profusely, and he swung wildly at Dan. Christopher pushed his way through the crowd and stood between the two men.

"Both of you, stop it!" Christopher said. His face was red and contorted in anger.

Beth rushed up to Todd with a handful of napkins. Dan shook off his father's hand and pushed his way through the crowd and out the door.

Katie had no wish to linger now that a fight had broken out.

She spotted Emmett across the room and moved through the crowd to tell him that she was leaving.

"What was that about?" she asked when she reached him.

"I have no idea." Emmett shook his head. "Emotions always run high at funerals, but you don't often see fisticuffs."

The crowd began to disperse, and Marilyn appeared at Emmett's elbow. Katie stiffened. This was the first time she had seen Marilyn since Lynn had told her about Eric. She knew it wasn't fair, but some part of her blamed Marilyn. Had she abused Eric, and he perpetuated the violence in his own family?

"Hello, doctors," she said. "Dr. Hawkins, Mrs. Williams was looking for you. It was something about the church dinner."

Emmett hurried off in search of Mrs. Williams. He had been put in charge of the fundraiser again, and he said there were always hundreds of last-minute emergencies to attend to.

Katie turned toward the door just as Marilyn said, "It's interesting that Dan came to the service. He and Ellen never got along. In fact, he and Christopher hardly get along. I think Christopher was in Chicago getting him out of trouble on the night Ellen died."

Mrs. Peabody's claim that she had seen Christopher that night flitted across her mind.

"I thought it was a business meeting for another restaurant opening," Katie corrected her and then realized she should have just stayed mute on the subject. It wouldn't be good for people to think she had any special interest in the Riley family.

"Is that what he said? He'd just been there for the opening the week before. At least, that's what Ellen said when I was there cleaning. I must be mistaken. None of my business anyway." She shrugged and directed a rare smile at Katie.

Katie marveled again at how the daughter of one friend and the son of another could have grown up in the same town with such different results. Maybe Marilyn had not had the same kind of support that Christopher had. Marilyn seemed to carry the whole world on her shoulders and never expected more from life than what it handed her. Christopher took what he could from every opportunity that passed by.

"It looks like Dan has made another enemy after that fight," Katie said.

"Fight?" Marilyn looked at her, surprised.

"Didn't you see the fight? Dan and Todd Talbot just had a brawl. Christopher had to separate them."

"I was in the other room," Marilyn said. "Was Todd all right?" Marilyn stood on tiptoes and scanned the crowd.

Katie nodded. "I think so; he went off to another room with Beth."

"That's good. She'll take care of him."

"I should get back to the office and finish up some paperwork."

"I'm heading that way myself," Marilyn said. "Do you need a ride? I noticed you came here with Debra. She won't want to leave until the last cookie is gone."

"That would be great, thank you."

Marilyn led her to a car that was heavily rusted. Katie figured she must use the van only for cleaning jobs. The passenger door had to be slammed shut from the outside and then quickly locked to keep it closed. The inside was worn but tidy, and Katie settled back for the ride.

After their conversation at the funeral home, Marilyn didn't have much to say, and Katie didn't feel like making an effort. The ride was short, and she thanked Marilyn as she turned to open the door.

"Dr. LeClair, I don't mean to speak out of turn, but . . ."

"What is it, Marilyn? You can tell me."

"I know Mrs. Riley really liked you. She told me it was hard to move to such a closed community, and you were very kind to her. It takes people here a while to trust newcomers. And no one likes to dredge up old issues."

"Old issues? What do you mean?"

"I mean everyone has a skeleton or two in their closet. It doesn't do anyone any good to bring them out into the light." Marilyn shrugged. "Just something to keep in mind. I think Mrs. Riley thought she was being helpful, but some things are better left alone. She didn't mention anything to you?"

Katie shook her head. "I can't really discuss a patient with you. But what do *you* mean?"

Marilyn held up her hand. "Of course, sorry. No worries. I don't mean anything by it." Marilyn put the car in gear.

"Thank you for the ride, Marilyn." Katie wasn't sure what else to say.

Katie stepped out and slammed the door. Marilyn leaned over and pushed the lock button.

Marilyn pulled away, leaving Katie shaking her head in exasperation. Of all the strange conversations. Marilyn had barely said more than hello in the whole time Katie had worked with Emmett, and now she gave her a cryptic message. Katie was still mulling it over as she unlocked the building and then relocked the door.

After her last debacle with the coffeemaker, she heated up some water in the microwave and dunked a tea bag in the mug. She flipped open her notebook to update her note on Ellen. She had crossed out "diazepam overdose" and changed it to "Demerol." She was still concerned about who had written the prescription, but it took a back seat at this point to her list of suspects. Nick and Cecily might both have motives. She wasn't sure whether Dan had a motive, but he certainly had a violent streak. Christopher was seen at the house when he claimed to be in Chicago. But after his emotional speech, Katie moved him lower on the list. She didn't like the idea that one of her partners continued to float to the top of her suspect list. And she added that Marilyn had warned her about old secrets. What old secrets? Katie was now even more curious about Ellen's activities in the weeks leading up to her death. She closed her notebook with a sigh and steeled herself to get her paperwork done.

She took her tea and her leftover lunch back to her office and started writing the morning's charts. This was the mind-numbing boredom part of her job that she hadn't been aware of when she started on this path. All the TV shows depicted lots of action and lifesaving. They almost never showed the hours of paperwork: disability forms, insurance forms, notes, case summaries, procedure notes, and physical forms. Katie was just finishing the last chart when she heard a noise at the front desk.

She walked to the front of the building and looked around. The front door was still locked. She must have been hearing things. She turned to walk back to her office and ran full force into Debra, who was coming out of the file room with a stack of charts.

They both screamed, and Debra dropped the top four or five files as she steadied herself.

"I didn't know anyone was here," Debra said. "You scared me, Dr. LeClair."

"You scared me first," Katie replied. They both laughed.

"I looked for you after the service, but someone said you left with Marilyn. Is she here?"

These people didn't miss a thing, did they?

"No, she just dropped me off. I had to finish charting."

"That's what I came to do too. I didn't get a chance to pull charts for tomorrow."

"Okay, let me know when you leave."

Katie started to walk away and then turned.

"Debra, do you know what happened today between Todd and Dan?"

Debra stepped closer to Katie, her eyes bright. She looked up and down the hallway even though they had just established that they were alone in the building.

"I heard that Christopher just put Todd in charge of the Chicago restaurant as well as the one here. Dan is the acting manager in Chicago, and he's furious. Christopher has always been really supportive of Todd, and Dan thinks Todd is taking advantage."

"Hmm. That doesn't seem like something they need to beat each other up over."

"Apparently, Dan said something about how now that his protector is dead, Todd would have to prove himself."

"Todd threw the first punch?"

Debra nodded. "I saw the whole thing start. I couldn't believe it. One second they were standing there talking, the next Todd had decked Dan, and then there was a full-on fistfight."

"Thanks, Deb. It's going to take me awhile to understand all the relationships in town."

Katie wandered back to her office thinking of all the connections in this small town. It was impossible to stay anonymous, but somehow one of these people had been able to kill Ellen and not get caught—yet. She thought of how so many small decisions could lead to such big changes, good and bad. Katie had picked up a Frisbee and met Justin. Beth came here to be closer to her mother and had met Todd. ER doctors saw the results of small decisions going horribly wrong every day. Ellen, deciding to move from Chicago, certainly never suspected it would lead to her death. She probably thought she would be safer in a relatively rural community as compared to the urban sprawl of Chicago. But she had made a decision that must have threatened someone, and now she was dead.

Debra interrupted Katie's reverie by bouncing into her office to announce that she was headed home for the day.

"I shut off the phones and locked up the front. Just set the alarm at the back door when you leave, okay? You aren't going to be here long, are you?"

Katie glanced at her watch and shook her head. "No, I should be finished soon. See you tomorrow."

17

Beth had called Katie that afternoon after the funeral, and they'd arranged to meet again at the Purple Parrot at six thirty.

Katie arrived just after six. She found a table with two chairs in a corner by the window and sat down with relief. She stared, unseeing, out at the street. She felt she was missing something. The same instinct that sometimes told her to order an unusual test or ask an odd question in a patient interview was asserting itself at the back of her mind. Katie decided to put aside her suspicions of Nick for the moment. Even though she felt he was up to something, she wasn't convinced he had a reason to kill Ellen. *If* they had been having an affair, why would he kill her? And Cecily might have wanted Ellen gone, but her grief at the memorial had seemed genuine. And then there was Christopher. What if he had suspected an affair? His grief also appeared genuine, but had he been at the house that evening, as Mrs. Peabody suggested?

She took out her notebook and flipped to her evolving notes on Ellen. The first two items on her list of possible motives had to do with what Ellen might have known. Maybe Katie had been distracted by Nick's odd behavior, and Ellen's murderer had a secret they were trying to protect. She turned to a blank page and wrote, "What did Ellen know?" The rest was as blank as Katie's mind at the moment. But Beth might have some insight. So far, without knowing what Ellen had discovered, it was hard to imagine who would have wanted to do her any harm.

Beth came through the door and glanced around. Katie waved her over. Beth walked to where Katie sat, dumped her bag on the ground, and sank down into the other chair. Katie noticed her eyes were red and swollen.

"I'm so sorry about your mom," Katie said. "We don't have to talk about all this now."

Beth shook her head. "No, I'm fine. I just had an argument with Todd. I couldn't believe he would start a brawl at my mother's funeral. I was so mad at both of them. It's fine now. Dan knows exactly how to push Todd's buttons."

"Yes, that was quite something. Is Todd okay?"

Beth nodded. "He's fine. Just a bloody nose, and he'll have a nice black eye tomorrow."

"You said you needed to talk?"

Beth had the heightened energy of someone with big news. Katie was spared having to decide how much to tell her as Beth relayed the news of the autopsy report and the associated likelihood that this had not been an accident.

"I don't know if this makes me more or less upset, but at least I know she didn't kill herself. I just don't think I could have ever accepted that."

"I know how you feel, but this has taken on a more serious tone," Katie murmured. They had both lowered their voices. "It means there's someone out there who wanted to harm your mother, possibly based on what she'd discovered in her research. It may be dangerous."

"I need to know what happened," Beth said, "and frankly, I'm not impressed with the Baxter Police Department so far. They never treated it like anything *but* suicide, so now they have no evidence or even a weak lead to go on. Sometimes having lived in a big city makes it very difficult to live in a small one."

She pushed her dark hair out of her eyes. In that moment, Katie saw the resemblance to Ellen. They were both small, with fine features and thick dark hair, though Ellen had worn hers longer. Katie was always amazed to watch family members and to see the mannerisms that immediately marked them as relatives.

"I'm sure John feels terrible about the way things were handled," Katie said. "It's not something they deal with very much in Baxter. Not that that excuses it. Whoever did this counted on the scene looking enough like a suicide to appease the police."

"Which means it was carefully planned by someone dangerous enough to kill," Beth said. "Todd doesn't want me to pursue this. He thinks I should just let it go." Beth sighed and worried her engagement ring. "In fact, I think he expects you to talk me out of it."

"I'd really like to help, Beth. Especially if you don't feel you can talk to Todd about it. Whoever did this needs to be caught."

"I could use the help, if you're sure."

"I'm sure." Katie smiled at her. "But we'd better order before all the pot pies are gone."

They got up to place their order at the counter. One of the local high school kids was working that evening, but the Peterson ladies were never far off. The place ran like clockwork, and any servers who were less than completely solicitous were quickly let go.

They went back to their table with mugs of tea and made plans. Beth had obtained her mother's appointment book and laptop by telling Christopher that she needed to get a sweater from Ellen's closet.

"I thought he was going to follow me up the stairs, but fortunately he got a phone call, and I went up alone. She kept them in her closet, way at the back. I'm not sure he even knew they were there. My mom could be quirky about that kind of thing." She patted her oversized bag. "I put everything in here and slipped out before he had finished with his call."

"Don't you think Christopher would be just as interested in finding out what happened as you are?" Katie asked.

"I don't know," Beth said. "I know he and my mom had a couple of big arguments in those last few weeks. It really bothered her because they'd never argued before. She wouldn't go into detail but said she'd discovered something about Christopher's family, and they didn't agree on what should be done about it."

Katie frowned. Was she too quick to discount Christopher just because he was emotional at the funeral? "You don't think Christopher could have killed your mother, do you?"

"No." Beth hesitated. "No, I can't imagine him hurting my mom. But I don't know what was wrong between them, and I don't want to confide in him before I have the whole picture." Beth leaned forward, her elbows on the table, and rested her chin in her hands. "I've known him for three years. He's always been wonderful to me and my mother, but I don't trust him with this."

"What's Dan like, other than short-tempered?" Katie asked. "I hadn't met him until today at the memorial."

Beth sat back and crossed her arms. "I think Christopher would prefer he didn't have a son sometimes. Dan has been nothing but trouble since I've known him. There was some issue with the restaurants. Todd told me that Christopher suspected Dan was embezzling money from the Riley's he was running in New York. I think Dan got into gambling . . ." Beth trailed off.

"Are they on better terms now?"

"I guess so." She shrugged. "Christopher sent him out to Chicago to open a new restaurant and to get him away from New York. I'm not sure how things are going out there now." Beth sipped her tea.

Katie waited and stirred sugar into her mug.

"But Christopher put Todd in charge of the finances, which is partly what Dan was mad about," Beth said. "He thinks Todd convinced Christopher to do that in order to take over more of the business. Todd doesn't even *want* the extra responsibility, especially since he has to deal with Dan all the time."

"Maybe your mother found out something about him . . ."

"I guess it's possible . . ."

"Could Dan have harmed your mother?"

"I hope not, but I think he's capable of anything."

The food arrived, and they both fell silent for a time, enjoying the homemade chicken potpies and soft crusty bread.

"What did you find in your mother's book?" Katie asked. She nodded toward Beth's bag sitting on the extra chair.

"I'll show you." Beth pulled the book out of her bag and flipped it open. "She had the usual hair appointment, and she saw you the week before she died. She also had a couple of phone numbers written down. One is the historical society office. The other is a lawyer's office in Ann Arbor."

"Did you speak to them yet?"

"I have an appointment with the lawyer tomorrow afternoon. I don't know how much he will be able to tell me. There's probably some sort of confidentiality clause."

"I suppose. I guess it depends on what it was about and whether your mother was a client. Did her laptop have anything useful on it?"

"I was only able to access her web browser. I knew her password to open the desktop, but all the files are locked with a different password. I scanned through her e-mails for the past month or so and didn't find anything that seemed relevant. She was visiting a lot of sites that discussed the genetics of color-blindness."

"Was she interested in genetics?"

Beth shook her head. "Not that I know of. Todd is color-blind. I told her about a funny interaction we had while shopping when he was trying to help me pick out clothes. That was about a month ago."

"Maybe she was just looking to see what the chances of a color-blind grandchild would be."

Beth blushed and shook her head. "Maybe. I wish I could get into the rest of the files. It's unusual for her to lock them with a password like that."

"Even client files?" Katie knew how easy it was to get into trouble with privacy laws. Maybe Ellen had been extra careful.

"It's possible, but *everything* is locked."

"Don't you think you should turn it over to the police?" Katie asked.

"Maybe, but then it will sit in some stranger's in-box," Beth said. "I feel weird turning over my mom's personal computer when we don't even know what's on it."

"If you feel comfortable letting me take the computer, I know someone who can probably get into the password-protected files."

Beth's face lit up. "You do? That would be great. I didn't want to take it to one of those computer repair places. Not knowing what's in there makes me nervous. Your person will keep it confidential?"

Katie nodded. "I'd trust him with my life."

Beth slid the laptop across the table.

18

Katie argued with herself all the way home. She took privacy and confidentiality seriously. Not only because it was drilled into her in training but because she walked around every day holding the secrets of innumerable individuals and families locked in a compartment in her brain. There was no way to hack into that.

She glanced at the laptop sitting like a ticking bomb on her passenger seat.

She sighed and turned onto her street. The cool evening air flowed in through the open windows, and she remembered just a week ago when her biggest worry had been whether to paint the dining room gray or red. She pulled into her driveway and parked. She pushed the button to roll up the windows and turned the key to shut off the engine.

She grabbed the laptop, climbed out, and locked the car. All the way to the house, she told herself that she didn't have to give the computer to Caleb. She could sleep on it and decide in the morning. It was like a Pandora's box, and she knew that once she gave it to him, there was no stopping what would happen next. On the other hand, Ellen Riley deserved justice, and if she had to go through her personal files to get it, then who was to say it wasn't the right thing to do? Katie supposed Chief Carlson would say it wasn't the right thing to do, but she'd have to deal with that problem later.

Caleb was at the dining room table working on his computer. It looked like actual work since he didn't have his headset on and wasn't shouting orders at unseen partners in gaming.

"How was the memorial?"

"About as you'd expect," Katie said. She gripped the computer tightly in her arms, struggling with herself.

"What've you got there?" He tilted his head at the computer. "It looks like you're trying to snap it in half."

Katie stepped forward and quickly set it on the table. She stepped back to control her urge to snatch it back again. This was the right thing to do. "It's Ellen Riley's computer, and there are encrypted files. I was hoping you could open them for me."

Caleb sat back in his chair. He made no move toward the computer, although Katie knew that wouldn't last. He couldn't resist the challenge.

"Where did you get it?"

"Beth, Ellen's daughter, gave it to me." Katie sat at the far end of the table and leaned her head on her hand.

"And you want to get into her computer because . . ."

"Beth thinks her mother was working on something that might have gotten her killed." Katie told him about the arguments with Christopher and the strange questions she'd been asking. "Beth was able to look at her browser history, and the only thing that stood out to her was that her mother had been looking up color-blindness and genetics."

"Why is that interesting? I can't imagine anyone would want to kill someone for discovering they were color-blind. Unless . . ." Caleb raised one finger as if an idea had just occurred to him. "Maybe it was a clothing designer who was stealing his ideas from one of his students, and if people found out he was color-blind, then they would know he was a fake!"

"Yes, that's one possibility," Katie said dryly. "Todd Talbot is color-blind."

"The restaurant guy? Who cares?"

"I don't think it matters *that* he's color-blind, just that Ellen was looking into it. Beth and Todd are engaged."

"Hmm. Seems weak." Caleb pulled the computer toward him and opened it. "Let me take a look at the files and see if I can get into them."

Katie nodded and stood up. "Let me know if you find anything." She turned to go and stopped. "Caleb, you know there might be confidential information in there. She used to be a psychologist, and I think she still did some counseling."

Caleb nodded. "You have no idea the secrets I have hidden up here, Sis." He tapped his temple and winked.

19

Wednesday morning, Katie woke with the sense that something was wrong. Had she forgotten something? She'd stayed up late thinking about Ellen's memorial and hoping Caleb would come up with some information quickly. She'd finally heard him go to bed around two. She was overtired and stressed. That was probably where the general anxiety came from.

The sunlight peeking through the blinds promised another beautiful fall day. Katie would be stuck inside for most of it, as Wednesday was her busiest clinic day. Both Nick and Emmett had half days, so she was the one who picked up all the urgent cases.

She sighed and threw off the comforter. She padded to the bathroom and looked in the mirror, sighing at the dark circles under her eyes. She opened her concealer and got to work.

After a quick breakfast and more coffee than was advisable, she grabbed her messenger bag and slipped out the side door.

She didn't notice it right away. She was busy pawing through receipts, notes, a reflex hammer, and spare change that littered the bottom of her bag where her car keys could usually be found. She finally found them and looked up to put the key in the lock.

The driver's window was smashed, and glass shards sparkled on the driver's seat. There was a folded piece of paper on the dash.

Katie hesitated, wondering if she should call the police before touching anything, but her curiosity got the better of her.

She reached in through the shattered window and picked up the paper by the corner. She let it fall open.

In large block letters, the note read, "MIND YOUR OWN BUSINESS."

Katie looked around her neighborhood. The hair on the back of her neck prickled. Was someone watching her, right now? How had she slept through the window breaking? How had the neighbors slept through it?

She pulled her cell phone out of her jacket pocket and pressed John Carlson's number. He'd given her his cell number after her "heroic" rescue of Bubba. She'd never had cause to use it before.

"Carlson."

"Hi, John, it's Katie LeClair." She blinked back tears as the reality of the threat hit her. "Can you come to my house, please? There's been an incident."

"I'll be right there."

He didn't even ask what the problem was.

Katie's eyes were dry, but her hands still shook when John's car pulled in the driveway ten minutes later.

Caleb stood on the porch with her, wearing sweat pants and the T-shirt he had slept in. His hair stood up in spikes, and he looked just as tired as she felt.

He'd told her to put the note back exactly as she'd found it, so the chief could see what the scene had looked like.

Carlson opened his door and looked up at them. The sun glinted off his aviators, and his mouth was set in a grim line.

"What happened, Doc?"

Katie and Caleb stepped off the porch, and Katie motioned for him to follow them farther down the driveway toward the back of the house.

"I was heading in to work, and I found this." Katie held out her hand toward the driver's side door.

Carlson stepped closer and leaned in to get a better look.

"Anything missing?"

Katie shook her head. "I don't leave anything of value in there. And it doesn't look like anything has been disturbed, other than the window, obviously."

Carlson picked up the paper by the corner and let it fall open just as Katie had done. She saw his jaw tense as he read it. He put the note in a paper bag and shined a penlight around the inside of the car.

"I'll call the station and have the guys come check for fingerprints, but I doubt we'll find anything. It doesn't look like anyone even went inside the car, just smashed the window and left the note."

"Okay, what . . . what do I do now?"

Caleb put his arm across her shoulders. She leaned into him, grateful for his presence.

Carlson stood up from his examination of the car.

"You can come to the station and file a report." He shrugged. "It's not much, but it's a place to start. Do you know who might have left this or what the note refers to?"

Caleb and Katie exchanged a guilty look.

"No, not really. I suppose it could be anyone who didn't care for my medical advice. Sometimes I have to recommend quitting smoking, or losing weight, or any of a number of things that might get someone annoyed."

Even Caleb looked at her in surprise.

Carlson said, "You think this is a disgruntled patient?"

"Not really." Katie crossed her arms over her chest. "I don't know who would have done this."

"What other things have you been doing that might have upset someone?"

Katie sighed and looked up to the sky. She didn't want to tell him about the computer because he'd likely take it away, and they wouldn't ever find out what was on it. Plus, she didn't want to get Caleb in trouble. She figured the less the chief knew about Caleb's talents with a computer, the better.

She held her hands out, palms up. "The only thing I can think of is that Beth Wixom asked me to help her look into her mother's death."

Carlson stood taller and put his hands on his hips. Katie couldn't see his eyes behind the sunglasses, but she felt his glare. "This again? I told Beth I was looking into it. If this note is from someone who wants you to stop investigating a death, one that at this point is being considered suspicious, I think you should listen. With that in mind, we need to treat this like a threat, not just malicious vandalism."

Carlson looked at both of them and held their gazes. "I'm not kidding around now. You need to stop whatever you're doing and let us handle this."

Katie nodded agreement but wouldn't meet his eyes. Caleb studied the ground and kept very still.

"Let's see if anything shows up when they check for fingerprints, and we'll go from there. In the meantime, go to work like normal and keep your head down."

Katie nodded again. "Thanks for coming over so quickly."

His tone softened. "Do you need a ride to the clinic?"

"I can take her," Caleb said. Katie was grateful; she didn't want to be stuck in a car with Carlson and his lectures.

"You can vacuum it and take it to be repaired as soon as the fingerprinting is done. If you want to call Rob Kendrick, he'll do a good job for you. Just tell him I sent you." He handed Katie a card with a phone number on it.

Katie thanked him, and she and Caleb watched him pull out of the driveway.

Caleb turned to her with a mixture of concern and excitement in his eyes. "What have we gotten into?"

20

Katie still felt shaky midway through her clinic. Fortunately, the problems had been routine, and she was moving along much more quickly than she had thought she would. A nasty virus was making its way through the preschool set. Katie's biggest problem was convincing the parents that the kids would get better on their own—without antibiotics.

After three vomiters, a hypertension patient, and a yearly physical, Katie saw a break in her schedule and hurried to her office. She shut the door behind her and slumped into her desk chair. Even though clinic had been easy so far, she wasn't sure she would get through a whole day of it. Her brain was so focused on Ellen's murder that the rest of what she did was on autopilot.

She paged through the notes on her desk to see if anything was urgent. Debra and the nurses wrote phone messages on old-fashioned pink slips of paper and attached them to the patient's chart. Katie identified several that Angie could deal with, but stuck in the middle of the stack was a loose sheet with no chart attached.

"Beth Wixom called, said to call as soon as you can."

Katie fished her cell phone out of her bag and clicked on Beth's name.

Beth answered on the first ring. "Dr. LeClair, thanks for calling back. Have you found anything on the computer yet?"

"No, nothing we didn't already know. It might take a little while."

"Can I come see you sometime today?" Beth asked. "I have something I need to show you."

Katie glanced at her schedule for the day. Her eleven thirty had canceled, so she would have a little time around noon.

"I have some time around lunch. Want to meet me here?"

"Sure. I'll bring sandwiches from Riley's," Beth said. "But is there a place nearby we can go that's private?"

Katie flashed back to the meeting with Matt in the gardens. If that didn't work, they could always go to Katie's house.

"Meet me here at eleven forty-five, and we can walk to the hospital gardens. Hopefully, they'll be deserted as usual."

Just before noon, the women shut the back door of the clinic and found the path around the hospital. Katie was relieved to see that the garden was empty, and they sat on one of the benches facing the pathway.

Beth handed Katie a white bag with a turkey Reuben inside and rummaged in her large tote bag. She pulled out a beat-up spiral notebook and set it on her lap. She sat for a moment with her hands on the cover as if she was protecting it.

"I was going through my mom's things last night. Along with her computer, she had some file folders and this notebook.

The file folders weren't very useful—they were mostly clippings from psychology journals. There was no unifying theme, and I think they were just general research she was doing for her business." Beth tapped the notebook. "This was different."

"Different?"

Beth looked down at the notebook. "She had notes about color-blindness, similar to the information we found with her computer searches. She has a hand-drawn chart that I think is a family tree with circles and squares, *X*s and *Y*s. And a to-do list of people she wanted to talk to. Emmett Hawkins was one, and Chief Carlson's wife."

"Carlson's wife?" Katie asked. "Why?"

"She's been the editor of the weekly Baxter newspaper for years," said Beth. "I think my mom wanted to ask her about the town's history. She has some notes about it here." Beth flipped a page and pointed to printed questions about Baxter and the families that had been living here for more than a generation.

"And you said she had a number for the historical society in her datebook," Katie said. "There must be something from the past she was interested in."

"I can't see what could be dangerous about the past," Beth said. "I mean, it's over, right?"

"Was she looking into Christopher's family?"

Beth raised her shoulders. "I can't tell. Her notes are kind of cryptic. My mom could be like that. If she didn't want anyone to be able to read her notes, she used her own form of shorthand. The problem was, she said sometimes even she couldn't figure out what she meant."

"I hope the computer files are more straightforward if we ever get into them."

Beth flipped to the back of the notebook. "Then I found this tucked in the middle."

She pulled out a folded piece of white paper and handed it to Katie.

Katie took it and unfolded it. It wasn't a surprise, not really, but still she sucked in air when she saw what was written there in block letters: "MIND YOUR OWN BUSINESS."

"I got one of these this morning," Katie said in a shaky voice.

"What?" Beth took the note and shoved it back between the pages as if that would keep it from harming them. "How? Why?"

Katie shook her head. "I don't know why, but I can only assume that someone knows we're looking into what your mom was doing, and they don't like it. The notes are identical. They broke my car window and left it on the dashboard."

"Where is it now? You're sure it's the same writing?"

"It looked the same to me. I called Chief Carlson, and he took it away to examine it."

"I wish my mom had done that." Beth's eyes filled with tears. "Maybe she would still be alive."

Katie put her hand over Beth's, which was gripping the notebook with white knuckles.

"She must have thought it had to do with one of her clients and didn't want to involve the police," Beth said. "She was militant about privacy. And knowing my mom, she would have seen it as more of a cry for help than a threat."

Katie nodded. "I can appreciate that. It's not explicitly threatening, depending on how she received it. Breaking my window and leaving it among shards of glass felt a little more dangerous than if it had been left on the doorstep."

"Dr. LeClair, I think you should stop helping me." Beth turned on the bench to face Katie. "I don't want anything to happen to you. I haven't received any notes, so maybe they don't know what I'm doing. But you should lay low for a while. I'll let you know if I find anything."

"No." Katie shook her head. "I don't like bullies, and I'm not going to just sit back and let this person get away with murder."

Beth smiled and let out a breath. "I'm so glad you said that. I really don't want to do this alone."

Beth stood then and said she was going to be late for her appointment with the lawyer. They agreed to talk later, and Beth walked down the path that led to Katie's office. Katie stayed behind in the pleasant garden to think and grab a few minutes alone before her afternoon clinic.

She was less shaky now than angry. Angry that someone would kill Ellen Riley, a woman who only wanted to help others. And angry that she had doubted herself. She'd ruminated over whether she had written that prescription and questioned her own judgment about Ellen's mental state.

She was startled out of her thoughts by the sound of footsteps approaching. She turned toward the sound, but no one was there. Several birds rose through the trees, squawking and chirping. She heard rustling in the bushes as a small creature ran past, and then all was silent.

It must have been an animal she heard.

Katie glanced at her watch and stood. She needed to get back for her clinic, or she'd run late all day and Angie would sigh heavily and glance at the clock after every patient. She pulled out her phone to check her messages and walked toward the pathway. As she turned to step onto the path, she was surprised to see Matt Gregor, who was also focused on his phone.

They jumped away from each other, both of them starting apologies, and Katie's phone slipped out of her hand. They both bent to pick it up and grabbed it at the same moment. His hand was warm, and Katie jerked away quickly at the sudden contact.

"You've stolen my secret hideaway, I see," Matt said. He handed her the phone.

"Sorry, I didn't see your name on it. Did I miss the sign?" She took the phone and slipped it into her bag.

"It's more of an unwritten thing . . ."

"So you're the only one who knows it's yours?"

"Well, yeah." He smiled. "And you. You know it's mine."

Katie crossed her arms in mock annoyance. "Maybe I was looking for you." She mentally smacked her forehead. No matter that the jittery bubbly feeling was back, she was too busy for a relationship. And if she was honest with herself, she was afraid of her reaction to Matt Gregor. She felt more comfortable with subdued pleasure at seeing someone than this weird teenager-y thing that was happening.

Matt's smile was brilliant and warm. "You were?"

Katie looked at the ground, thinking fast. She remembered what Gabrielle had said about Matt swearing off of anyone in medicine. She wasn't going to try to convince him to date another doctor. But he seemed . . . interested. Didn't he?

"Yes, I wanted to ask you about Ellen Riley." As soon as she said it, she knew she'd blown it.

"Oh, sure." His smile faded to a polite interest. "What did you want to know?"

What *did* she want to know? Besides who killed Ellen and who could be threatening her, Katie, now?

"I just wondered . . . if she said anything when she arrived at the ER the other night."

Matt shook his head. "She never regained consciousness. I thought you knew that." He tilted his head and met her eyes. "She never had a chance. I'm not sure how we even managed to get a heartbeat."

"Right." Leave it to her to turn a perfectly fun interaction into a depressing medical discussion. Maybe he was right about not dating a medical person. She should adopt the same rule—then they could just be friends with no weird subtext. "I'd better head off to clinic—my nurse hates it when I run late."

Matt chuckled. "Don't they all. They're very schedule-conscious, those nurses."

Katie turned and walked slowly down the pathway, mentally berating herself for getting flustered by some guy.

"Dr. LeClair?"

Katie turned. Matt walked slowly toward her down the treelined path. A breeze loosed a handful of colorful leaves from their branches, and they fluttered gently down between them. She felt the good kind of butterflies in her stomach.

"Please, call me Katie," she said when he stopped a couple of feet from where she stood.

He held her gaze for a long moment. "Can I . . . I'd like to . . ." He looked away.

Katie curled her fingers into her hand to keep them steady. Maybe Gabrielle was way off base. He was going to ask her out—what should she do?

"I heard you're looking into Ellen's death. I'd like to help, if I can."

It took Katie a moment to shift gears from imagining a date to feeling paranoid that people knew what she was up to.

"You . . . heard?" Katie's mind raced, trying to figure out who knew and who could be talking about it. Other than Patsy Travers, Beth, and Caleb, there was no one. "How did you hear?"

Matt's cheeks turned deep red, and he ran his hand through his hair. "Let's say I *overheard* that you're looking into her death."

"You were *spying* on me?" Katie took a step back from him.

"No." Matt held his hands out, palms up. "It was an accident. I came to the benches during a break, and I saw you there talking to someone. I was about to say hello, but something about the way you two were sitting made me think it was a serious conversation and I should leave you alone."

"Okaaaaay," Katie said. She waited for him to go on.

"So I was about to head back down the path, but I heard you say that you weren't going to let this person get away with murder. At that point, I did leave and waited until the other person left. I saw that it was Beth Wixom." Matt looked at his shoes. "I wasn't going to say anything, but I really liked Ellen, and if she was murdered, I'll help in any way I can."

Katie considered for a moment. She didn't see a downside. Matt wasn't on her list of suspects. He wasn't even from Baxter. But he had been with Ellen in her last moments and had done all he could to save her. Katie understood the desire for closure.

"Okay, yes." Katie's voice cracked. "I'd really like that."

"Good." He held out his hand. "Let me give you my number, and you can text me when you think I can help."

Katie clicked open her phone and handed it to him.

He punched in some numbers and handed the phone back. His warm fingers brushed against hers as he took it. Their eyes met, and Katie let her hand linger a second longer.

Matt smiled. "See you soon."

Katie nodded and hurried down the path toward her office.

21

Katie entered the back door of the clinic still feeling unsteady from her rapid seesaw of emotions. He hadn't asked her out, and that was good. She definitely didn't want to go out with him. But she felt like something had shifted between them. Maybe they were becoming friends. Her mood plummeted when Angie and Debra, who were clearly in a state of high alert, immediately approached her.

"Dr. Nick can't make his afternoon clinic. He needs you to take over for him," Debra said.

"But I have my own clinic . . ."

Angie nodded. "We've shifted most of them to Emmett's clinic, so you should be fine."

"Why don't we just split Nick's patients like we've done in the past?" Katie didn't wait for an answer as she walked to her office to put her bag away and put on her white coat. She was sensing that she would need roller skates as well if the worry she was picking up from her staff was any indication of the way the clinic would go. Debra and Angie followed on her heels.

"Dr. Nick specifically asked that you do his clinic. He said you'd done a rotation at the pain center in Ann Arbor, and he knew you could handle it," Angie said.

Katie was surprised by this. She'd worked with Emmett during several rotations in residency, and she knew he trusted her clinical instincts, but she had never gotten that impression from Nick. In fact, she had often felt that he resented her addition to the clinic. "It's his pain clinic patients this afternoon?"

Angie nodded. "Don't worry; most of them are return visits, and you just need to evaluate and decide if the plan is working. We shifted all the procedures to tomorrow. Nick didn't want those patients to wait until next week to see him."

"How are we going to run three clinics tomorrow?" Katie asked. The small building only had enough rooms to run two clinics at a time, and on staff they had only Angie and Debra to help keep things running smoothly.

"Emmett said you can take the afternoon off, and he'll take the morning," Angie answered. "We're shifting everyone around now."

"Okay," Katie said. Although it didn't sound like anyone was waiting for her approval. "What's wrong with Nick?"

Angie and Debra exchanged a look.

"He's having one of his bad days," Angie finally replied. "No one wants him here when he's like that."

"We'd better get moving—the first four patients have already checked in." Debra hurried back to the front desk.

Katie turned to ask Angie what she meant about Nick, but she was already down the hall with a chart in her hand to bring the first patient back.

Katie grabbed her stethoscope from her desk and followed.

The first patient had spinal stenosis and ongoing chronic back pain. He had been a forklift operator until an accident had left him in too much pain to work the machinery. Katie saw that he was on disability and needed to come in monthly to have paperwork filled out and get a refill on his narcotic pain medication.

The next patient was trickier. He'd been in a car accident six months earlier, and Katie saw that all his testing had come back normal. As far as she could tell, he should be better by now. She knew that it was often difficult to wean off of pain meds—for a certain type of patient, almost impossible.

"Hello, Mr. Taylor." Katie entered the room and put out her hand.

Mr. Taylor took it in a weak grip and looked past her to the door.

"Hello. Are you working with Dr. Hawkins today?"

"I'm covering for him, yes. He had an emergency and won't be able to see you, but I can take care of your prescriptions."

Mr. Taylor moved uncomfortably in his seat. He wouldn't meet her eyes. "I'd really hoped to see Dr. Hawkins. No offense, but I've been seeing him for a while now, and he knows exactly what I need."

Mr. Taylor stood up to leave.

"Mr. Taylor, I'd be happy to help if you'll let me." Katie had occasionally run into this problem as a student. Patients didn't want to deal with a student or even a resident sometimes, and that was always their right. But she felt offended that this man wouldn't even let her write him a prescription.

He sat back down. "I need a refill on my regular prescription, and Dr. Hawkins sometimes gives me a prescription for the stronger stuff."

"Stronger stuff?" Katie sat on the wheeled stool and flipped through the chart. She saw the prescription for tramadol but no mention of any other meds.

Mr. Taylor seemed to get more nervous the longer she looked through the chart and finally said, "I think I'll just reschedule. Thank you, ma'am."

She watched him walk out the door and then snapped his chart shut. Alarm bells were going off in her brain, but she had no time to focus on them. As she left the room, Angie handed her two more charts, and she continued down the hall to the next room.

Katie saw twenty patients in three hours and felt like she'd run a marathon. She usually saw half that many. Plus, Nick knew all these patients and didn't need to get up to speed on any of them. But still, she wondered how he had such a loyal following when he only allotted about three minutes per patient encounter. She didn't have anyone else walk out on her, but she did have several patients ask if Nick had left her a "note" about their treatment.

Katie marked each of those charts and Mr. Taylor's and put them in a separate pile. After she finished all the notes, she looked at her watch and saw that it was nearly seven o'clock. She was too tired and hungry to go through the charts she'd set aside. She piled them near her bag and took the rest to the chart room. Since her car was still at the repair shop, she called Caleb and asked him to pick her up in ten minutes.

She would examine the charts tonight after she had eaten something. Marilyn was in the records room vacuuming when Katie walked in, and she spun around in surprise when Katie set the charts down.

"Dr. LeClair, I didn't realize you were here. You gave me a fright."

"Sorry, Marilyn. Just a crazy day today, and I wanted to finish up all the paperwork. I'm heading out now, so I'll see you later."

"I didn't see your car in the lot. Is everything okay?"

"It just needed a minor repair. My brother is picking me up."

"Sorry to hear that. It seems like when one thing goes wrong, five other things go wrong."

Katie grimaced. Of course Marilyn would get chatty on the one night Katie couldn't wait to get out of the office. "I hope not. See you later, Marilyn."

"Bye, Dr. LeClair."

Katie stood by the back door waiting for Caleb's car. She watched as the sky began to purple and the shadows deepened in the woods at the back of the parking lot.

As she watched, one of the shadows pulled away from a tree and seemed to move farther into the woods. Katie blinked and looked again. She had to be imagining things. She was tired and stressed. There was no one in the woods.

She squinted and watched for movement. A flash of light showed off to her right, and Caleb's car pulled into the lot. As she looked back at the trees, she saw a blink of white and then nothing.

Caleb pulled up close to the door and leaned out the window. "Katie? Are you okay?"

"Yup. Just thought I saw something in the woods, but it's gone now, whatever it was."

Caleb put the car in park and climbed out. "Where?"

"It's nothing, Caleb. I'm just tired. Let's go home."

"Okay. Have you eaten anything?"

"I had a sandwich for lunch."

"Well, that's better than residency. Let's get home and have some dinner."

Katie climbed into Caleb's Jeep and rested her head against the seat back. She closed her eyes and tried to stop thinking for a few minutes. But the day kept replaying in her mind. The patients who only wanted to see Nick, the ones who asked if he had left anything for them. And then the fact that Emmett seemed to be checking up on his son. She was starting to get a bad feeling about his pain clinic.

She jolted awake when Caleb stopped in their driveway.

"You really are tired," Caleb said.

Katie yawned and grabbed her bag and pile of charts.

"What's all that? Do you still need to work tonight?"

Katie shook her head. "I don't need to, but there's something weird going on, and I just wanted to go through a few of these charts."

"Weird how?"

"I can't really say, and I shouldn't even talk about it, but I'm getting worried that Nick Hawkins might be involved in something illegal."

"This move to the country is getting more and more interesting."

They stomped up the front steps and opened the door.

"Oh, no," Katie said when she saw the condition of the house.

Papers littered the floor, the couch cushions sat askew, and Caleb's computer wasn't in its usual spot on the table.

"Caleb, did someone break in? Your stuff is everywhere. And where are the computers?" Had someone stolen Ellen's computer? What would she tell Beth? Her brain was already on the fast track to panic.

Caleb put his hand on her shoulder and looked her in the eye.

"Don't worry. I just got a little frustrated trying to code this app." Caleb stepped into the room and put the cushions back. He tidied the papers and then held his arms out in a "See, it's all fine" gesture.

"Where's your computer?"

"In my room, in my secret hiding place."

"You have a secret hiding place?"

"I have a false bottom in one of my drawers. You can't be a hacker without a healthy dose of paranoia."

"Of course you do."

Katie dumped her bag and the pile of charts on the uncharacteristically empty table. She went to the kitchen and found some leftover chili to reheat. She stuck it in the microwave and hit the button.

Caleb came in with his computer and Ellen's computer under his arm. "Do you want to talk about this now or after you eat?" He gestured at Ellen's laptop.

"Tell me while I'm eating." She took the bowl out and looked over her shoulder at him while she rummaged in the drawer for a spoon. "Did you find anything?"

"Not a lot so far." He set both computers on the countertop and opened Ellen's. "I was able to reconstruct her browsing history and found the color-blindness stuff that Beth mentioned. Also, she was researching some old newspapers from Ann Arbor. She was looking at some stuff from about fifteen years ago."

"What was she looking at?" Katie blew on the chili and took a bite. She leaned against the counter and cradled the bowl in her hand.

"Some guy disappeared, and there was a bit of a search for him before they decided he had just up and left his family. At least, that was the most interesting thing about the dates she searched," Caleb said. "I suppose she could have been interested in the craft show and the Fourth of July parade."

Caleb clicked away on the keyboard and turned the screen so Katie could see. She kept eating and leaned over the counter to take a look.

"She was also searching some names. Jack Riley is the only one that came up with any hits. Is that her husband's father?"

Katie looked at the photo Caleb had found. It was a black-and-white snapshot with the grainy resolution of newsprint.

Katie nodded. "I think so. He's the one that started the restaurant and almost went out of business until Christopher took over and expanded the franchise."

"Let's see, she looked up Lily and Eugene Talbot as well as Sylvia Riley."

"Hmm. Todd's last name is Talbot. He's Beth's fiancé." Katie set down the bowl and scrolled down the browser history. "According to the dates, they would probably be his grandparents. Maybe she was just looking into Todd's family?"

Caleb shrugged and turned the computer back in his direction. "Hopefully the other files will be more helpful. I should be able to access them soon. I have a buddy who could probably get in faster than I can, but I assume you don't want anyone else involved?"

"Let's keep it between us for now," Katie said. "If you don't think you can get in, we'll consider asking someone else for help."

* * *

Katie rinsed her bowl in the sink and set it in the dishwasher. She went back out to the dining room and the stack of charts she'd brought home. Just looking at them made her tired, but she'd never get to sleep tonight if she didn't comb through them.

There were a total of six charts out of the twenty patients she'd seen that afternoon that she had flagged to bring home. Each patient had acted nervous, asked about a "note," or mentioned some sort of unrecorded medication.

She started with Mr. Taylor and went back to his first visit with Nick several years earlier. She saw that he had been in a different, much more serious accident back then and for a time had been using a fentanyl patch. As she scanned through the notes, it showed Mr. Taylor weaning off the strong narcotic to a milder one without trouble. His recent accident had required a short course of narcotics and then weaning to a milder pain medicine. Nick had never recorded any other medication.

Her perusal of the other charts showed the same pattern. A patient with a serious accident or injury, followed by a course of strong narcotics, and then weaning to a mild narcotic or no pain medicine at all. She closed the last chart and drummed her fingers on the table.

She sat back to stretch her shoulders and yawned.

Caleb looked up from his computer screen at the other end of the table.

"You look beat," he said.

Katie nodded. "I can't tell if these charts don't make any sense because I'm so tired or if they don't make sense because Nick hasn't been charting everything. Or if I'm just being overly suspicious."

"Maybe you should look again in the morning," Caleb said. "What's missing from the charts?"

Katie gestured at the stack of file folders. "All these patients used to be on much stronger narcotics but have now tapered off. However, they all acted like Nick gave them 'extra' prescriptions that aren't recorded in the chart."

"Is it illegal to not chart that sort of thing?"

Katie shook her head. "I don't know that it's illegal in the sense that you could go to jail, but the charts wouldn't stand up to any sort of certification scrutiny if he was leaving out a large part of the treatment plan."

"Is there a certification scrutinizer that visits your office?"

Katie laughed at the joke but felt a creeping dread as she looked at the charts.

"No, not really. Not unless there's a reason for the practice to be investigated."

"Wait," Caleb said. "If the practice is investigated, does that mean you could be held responsible for things your partner is doing?"

Katie shook her head. "I really don't know. I know there are limits to what malpractice insurance will cover, but I don't know what happens if there is a criminal investigation. It's not something that comes up in medical school or residency."

"It sounds like you should find yourself a lawyer."

Katie looked at him to see if he was joking, but he was dead serious.

22

On Thursday, Katie had just finished her last patient of the morning and was making plans to use her afternoon off to grab lunch and work on her list of questions when she heard John Carlson's voice in the front reception area. Curiosity winning out over hunger, she headed to the front desk.

Chief Carlson leaned on the counter and spoke quietly to Debra, who, for once, seemed to have nothing to say. She looked at her hands in her lap and nodded solemnly at the chief.

"Hi, John," Katie said. "What brings you here?" She looked from one to the other, hoping for a clue about what was going on.

"Hey, Doc," Carlson said. "I need to talk to Dr. Hawkins."

"He doesn't come in until after lunch on Thursdays," Katie said. "Can I help?"

"The other Dr. Hawkins," Carlson replied. "I need to talk to Nick."

"Oh. Debra, do you know if he's still here?"

Debra nodded. "He's coming."

"I can take you back, John," Katie said. "We'll find him together."

Carlson crossed his arms and shook his head.

"I'd rather not, Doc," he said. "I'll wait here."

Katie tried to read the undercurrents in the room but couldn't place the problem.

Nick appeared from the back hall. He'd taken off his white coat and wore a light jacket.

"Thanks, John," he said. "Let's go."

The two men walked out the front door and climbed into the chief's SUV.

Katie spun toward Debra and narrowed her eyes.

"Spill it."

Debra's already tear-filled eyes overflowed, and she sniffled pathetically.

"It's all my fault," she said. "I told Sean that Nick stuck you with the call the night Ellen Riley died *and* that you had to cover his clinic yesterday."

"I don't understand," Katie said. "John already knew about the call issue. How does my covering Nick's clinic translate into a problem?"

Debra mopped her tears with a handful of tissues. "I also told Sean that Lois said one of her customers at the Clip 'n' Curl had seen Dr. Hawkins at the Riley house on the night she died, and now they've arrested him!"

"What? Chief Carlson didn't arrest him." Katie had simply thought they were going to a very *strained* lunch.

Debra was nodding. "He didn't put handcuffs on him because they're friends, but I'm sure he's under arrest because he doesn't have an alibi for the night Ellen Riley died."

"That's ridiculous," Katie said in a tone meant to convince herself as much as Debra. She really didn't want to believe that her suspicions were correct. She thought back to the charts she had read. What if Ellen had known that Nick was prescribing narcotics and not recording them? What if Cecily had told Ellen, and that's why they hadn't been friends anymore? Katie wasn't even sure Nick had done anything wrong, and it didn't relate at all to Ellen's notes on color-blindness. But if Nick was at the house that evening . . .

"You've told me over and over not to gossip, and now I know why." Debra blew her nose loudly and continued to leak tears. She slumped in her chair. "This is all my fault."

"What? Why?"

"I also told Sean that Dr. Hawkins's wife told her best friend that she thought he was having an affair with Ellen Riley."

"How did you hear *that*?"

"Lois overheard them talking at the salon."

"Oh, Debra." Katie patted her on the shoulder.

"Sean said maybe he killed Ellen to hide his affair. Or maybe Cecily Hawkins killed Ellen, and they need Nick to help them make a case against her."

"Debra, I doubt either one of those scenarios is true. But you shouldn't be talking about those kind of things."

Debra nodded miserably. "I hope Dr. Nick will forgive me. I shouldn't have said anything."

"Does Emmett know?"

Debra sniffed and dabbed at her mascara-smeared eyes. "I don't know."

Katie walked quickly toward the break room to see if Emmett's car was in the lot. Angie came into the room, bringing her anxiety and fear with her. "What's going on, Dr. LeClair?"

"I'm not sure, Angie," Katie said. "Nick just left with Chief Carlson. Debra seems to think he's under arrest."

Angie's hand went to her mouth, and her eyes grew large.

"Is Emmett here yet?" Katie asked. "I don't see his car, and I don't want him hearing about this from a patient."

"I'll call him on his cell and see where he is. He usually stops at the nursing home before coming in on Thursdays." Angie sat at the table in the small room and waited with the phone to her ear. "I don't believe this."

Katie noticed Angie hadn't asked *why* the police had picked up Nick.

"Emmett, it's Angie. Where are you?"

Angie listened and nodded at Katie.

"No, it's not a medical emergency; I'll just talk to you when you get here. See you in a few minutes."

Angie clicked the phone shut. "He's on his way. I don't think he's heard yet. It will be all over town in about fifteen minutes, especially with Debra involved."

"I think Debra has temporarily suspended her news outlet."

"I'd better cancel Nick's patients for tomorrow," Angie said. She stood and walked to the door.

"Wait—don't cancel the clinic yet. I think Chief Carlson just wants to ask him some questions about Ellen Riley."

Angie turned slowly. "Ellen Riley?"

"He was on call that night and didn't answer his phone. I think the chief is trying to piece together what happened."

"Are you sure? It's not about . . ." Angie stopped and chewed on her thumbnail.

"Not about what?"

Angie shook her head. "Nothing, I'd better go wait for Emmett." She hurried out the door before Katie could stop her.

Katie sighed and took her sandwich out of the fridge. She poured a cup of coffee and stood by the window sipping and watching for Emmett. His car pulled into the lot a few minutes later. Angie went out to meet him. Katie couldn't hear what they said, but she could tell by his reaction that Emmett was as shocked as everyone else, and then he looked relieved when Angie said something more.

What were those two up to? Emmett looked over Angie's head toward the window, and Katie stepped back from it. She hurried to the table and was well into her sandwich by the time Emmett and Angie came back inside.

Emmett rushed into the clinic, and Katie heard him stop at her office. Katie went to the door of the break room and peeked down the hall.

Emmett ran his hands through his sparse hair, making it stand on end. He caught sight of Katie and walked toward her.

"Angie says Nick was arrested," Emmett said.

There was something about the nervous way he glanced toward the medication room that made Katie decide to confront him.

"I'm not sure he's been arrested," Katie said. "Debra thinks he was, but it may be that Chief Carlson just wants to talk to him about Ellen Riley."

"About Ellen?"

"He's investigating her murder," Katie said.

Emmett looked confused for a moment. "But that doesn't . . ."

"Emmett, are you worried Nick has been taking drugs out of the med cabinet?"

Emmett slumped into the plastic-and-metal chair that sat near the table.

"I might as well tell you," Emmett said. "I think it's more complicated than that, but yes. I'm almost certain he's selling or trading narcotics prescriptions."

"What? Why?" This confirmed what Katie had already assumed, but it was still surprising to hear Emmett say it.

"I think he's having trouble weaning off the narcotics he was taking after his accident. He had some major injuries from that crash, and it took him a long time to heal. I've been worried about him for some time."

"I'm so sorry, Emmett."

"I'm sorry I kept it from you," Emmett said. "Angie and I didn't want anyone to know until we were sure. He could have his medical license suspended or worse. If this gets out, I could lose my practice."

Katie hadn't thought about how this could affect Emmett. She had been worried about protecting herself—Caleb's recommendation of retaining a lawyer had made an impression. And she'd been so busy pinning a murder on Nick that she hadn't thought much about the impact of a drugs charge on Nick or the practice.

"I don't think this is due to the missing drugs." Katie held up her hands. "I'm sure the chief wanted to ask him some questions about the night Ellen Riley died."

Emmett visibly relaxed and seemed to deflate like an over-stretched balloon.

"That's good." He smiled weakly at Katie. "Thank you. I know he didn't hurt Ellen."

"How do you know?"

Emmett looked away from her, took a deep breath, and let it out. "Because he was with me. I took him to a Narcotics Anonymous meeting in Ann Arbor. He wasn't happy about it, but he sat through the meeting."

"You have to tell the police," Katie said. "They *could* arrest Nick for murder."

Emmett shook his head. "I'll talk to them if I need to, but he didn't do it. I'm sure they'll let him go." Emmett met her eyes and must have read the disappointment there. "Katie, it's his livelihood, his whole life. I have to protect him if I can." He turned toward his office with Angie in his wake.

"Do you want me to see what I can find out?" Katie called after him.

Emmett turned.

"The chief owes me a favor," Katie said. "Maybe he'll tell me what's going on."

Emmett shook his head. "No, thanks; save your favor for something important." He turned away again and Katie thought he said, "We might need it."

Even if Emmett didn't want her help, she couldn't just sit by and wait. She marched to the front desk to see what more she could pry out of Debra.

Debra was speaking in a low voice into her desk phone when Katie entered the empty reception area. She glanced up quickly as Katie approached.

"Call you back," she said and set the receiver in its cradle. "Any news on Nick?"

She shook her head. "They just started his interview about five minutes ago."

"I'm sure it will be okay, Debra. The chief has been talking to everyone who was connected to Mrs. Riley."

And Katie *was* sure—at least she thought she was. If Nick was with Emmett that night, Katie had been way off in her suspicions. Nick *was* up to something, just not murder. She had another thought. What if Nick was covering for Cecily? Maybe he had *told* Emmett not to come forward with his alibi. There were a lot of maybes.

She did wonder why the chief had come to get him like that. She and Matt were more involved in the case, and all he did was ask them to come to the station. Katie mulled over this discrepancy on her way back to her office.

When she entered her office, a stack of charts and more phone messages greeted her. She'd have to deal with it all later. She needed to find out what Ellen had been doing before she was killed. Katie believed Emmett, so if Nick hadn't killed Ellen, who had?

Caleb was in Ann Arbor all day teaching a coding class. Gabrielle was at work. Beth's phone went to voice mail. Katie's car was still at the repair shop. She sighed and decided to take a chance. She knew that the sudden nervousness she felt had nothing to do with asking a near stranger for a huge favor. It had everything to do with wanting to see him again. She pulled out her phone and texted Matt.

23

Twenty minutes later, Katie was waiting in the parking lot for Matt.

She saw his car turn into the lot and walked over to meet him.

She climbed in and said, "I can't thank you enough for doing this."

"Like I said, I really liked Ellen."

"According to Beth, her mom was doing some research on Christopher's family. I think we need to go to the library and see what we can dig up on those people."

"Library?" Matt asked. "Can't you just Google them?"

"I did. There was nothing other than Mrs. Riley's obituary from two years ago. I doubt the Baxter weekly news has been scanned into the web."

"This is getting pretty old school." Matt turned the car in the direction of downtown. "Maybe you should wear a trench coat and a fedora."

Katie smiled. "You want to wear one too, don't you?"

"I wouldn't want to pass up a chance to sit in a dark room scrolling through microfilm. And if I could wear a cool hat, all the better."

Katie laughed. But she was worried there would not be any records at all. Baxter's library was tiny and mostly loaned out popular paperbacks that had been donated over the years.

Five minutes later, they pulled up outside the Baxter Community Library. Katie was surprised to find the place fairly crowded. Who knew that Thursday afternoon was the business rush for the library?

A loud group of kids was alternately singing and screaming in the children's area, which was only a roped-off section of the room. Several elderly men had commandeered a table in the corner and sat quietly reading newspapers. A young man shelved books from a cart with a bored, sullen manner. Katie wondered if any of the books would be seen again. He didn't appear to have any knowledge or respect for the Dewey decimal system.

She and Matt approached the circulation desk to ask about old issues of the Baxter newspaper.

Francine Marshall looked at them over her reading glasses and broke into a warm smile that changed her face from forbidding to almost friendly.

"Hello, Dr. LeClair," she said. "It's so nice to see you out and about."

Katie had recently seen Francine's eight-year-old twin boys in her clinic. Katie was certain they had never been allowed inside the library—they were the kind of kids that climbed on everything, ran everywhere, and never sat down. When they weren't punching each other, they were plotting further mayhem.

Katie introduced Matt to Francine and then leaned over the counter and lowered her voice.

"Do you have any old copies of the *Baxter Gazette*? Maybe on microfilm?"

"Microfilm? How many years ago are you looking for?"

Katie and Matt looked at each other. "Maybe forty or even fifty?" Katie said.

Francine's eyebrows rose, and she pulled off her glasses. "Hmm. Let's go take a look and see what we have."

She led them to a small back room with filing cabinets and began reading the labels. Katie and Matt looked as well, but it didn't take them long to realize that the files only went back twenty years. And even those drawers were filled with yellowed, dusty, cracked microfilm that likely wouldn't survive being loaded into a machine.

Matt looked at the microfilm reader and flicked the switch to turn it on. The bulb inside popped, and the light went out.

"Oh, no," Francine said. "I'll have to see if we have a replacement bulb."

"Thanks, Francine," Katie said, "but I don't think the files go back far enough."

"You might try the historical society," Francine said. "I know they've collected old photos. They might have old newspapers as well."

She followed Matt out to the parking lot, and they climbed back into his car.

"Maybe the newspaper offices keep copies," Matt said.

"That's brilliant!" Katie said. "But there's no way I'll be able to get a look at them."

"Why not?"

"Linda Carlson is the editor. She's married to John Carlson. If I go and ask her about newspapers from forty years ago, she'll tell the chief, and then he'll know what I'm up to."

"How is the chief going to connect Ellen's murder with your interest in the history of Baxter?"

"Well, his wife may have told him that Ellen had been doing some research as well." Katie let her head fall back against the seat. She thought of Ellen's note to herself about contacting Linda. She didn't know that Ellen had ever actually contacted Linda, and Katie needed more information. Between teaching his class and working on his freelance coding job with a looming deadline, Caleb hadn't had time to focus on Ellen's files, so she was left trying to follow in Ellen's tracks and hope she found the same information Ellen had. "But I guess I could tell her I just want to get a sense of the town . . ."

"Let's go," Matt said and started the car. "What's the worst that could happen?"

"Chief Carlson will yell at me," Katie said to the ceiling.

"Yeah, I've seen how scary he is. I'm sure you've held up under worse scrutiny than John Carlson. Just surviving a surgical rotation proves that."

They drove to the small office of the *Baxter Gazette*. The *Gazette* consisted mostly of ads for local businesses and items on sale at the grocery store. The high school dean's list was printed, along with wedding and baby announcements. However, her favorite section was the "Police Blotter," in which the local crimes were listed each week. They never used names, but Debra claimed it wasn't hard to figure out. Much like the stocks in olden days, even if no one threw rotten tomatoes, the whole town knew who was speeding by the school, whose teen had stolen a bike, and where the drug deals were happening.

Matt slowed in front of the office and parallel parked. They glanced into the large window and saw that they were in luck. Lights were on, and it appeared that at least one person was working at a desk toward the back.

They climbed out of the Honda and approached the door. It was locked, but there was a doorbell to the right of the handle. Katie pressed it, and she saw the person at the back peek her head around her laptop.

It was Linda Carlson. She got up and came toward the door, frowning. She was a petite woman, barely making it to five feet, and she wore her silver hair in a sleek pageboy cut. She was dressed in jeans and a Michigan State sweat shirt.

As she drew nearer to the door, she recognized Katie, and her green eyes lit up. The frown was replaced by a warm smile, and she hurried to unlock the door.

"Katie, it's lovely to see you!"

"Hello, Linda." Katie gestured to Matt. "I don't know if you've met Dr. Matt Gregor."

Linda and Matt shook hands. "Come in, please." She stood back and waved them inside. She locked the door after them and led them farther into the office space.

There were three desks, multiple bookcases, and a whole wall of filing cabinets in the small room. Katie was surprised that there was more than one desk. She'd been under the impression that Linda wrote and published the newspaper all on her own.

Linda led them to a small couch and chairs surrounding a low table that held the last few issues of the *Gazette*.

"Can I offer you anything?" Linda asked. "We have tea and water, I think."

"We don't want to take up too much of your time," Katie said.

They had discussed their strategy on the way to the *Gazette* office. To throw Linda off the scent and keep John Carlson from finding out what they were up to, they'd come up with a cover story that they hoped would suffice.

"Matt and I felt like we'd like to get to know Baxter a little better, since we're both practicing here now. It helps to know the community."

"Wonderful!" Linda beamed at them as if this was the best idea she had ever heard. "What would you like from me?"

"Do you have old copies of the *Gazette*?"

Linda waved her arm at the wall of filing cabinets. "Those go back twenty years, but I have the rest in a storage unit a few blocks away. What exactly are you looking for?"

"It's one of those things where we'll know it when we see it," Matt said. "Have there been any major news stories here in Baxter?"

"There was the time the deer crashed into the ICU at Baxter hospital. That was about four years ago." Linda drummed her fingers on the table. "Fortunately, no patients were there at the time. He ran through the window and then escaped into the halls. They had to lock down all the patient rooms and call John. He finally cornered it in the patient lounge. It was part of the reason for the ICU renovation."

"Maybe something a little juicier," Matt said.

Linda held up a finger. "We had a strike at the popcorn factory about ten years ago. It lasted a whole month and was a very big story at the time."

"How about any disappearances . . . or suspicious deaths?" Katie asked.

"Other than Ellen Riley, I can't think of a murder in Baxter in all the time I've lived here." Linda's eyes reddened, and she looked for a moment like she might cry. "Ellen was a really lovely woman."

"I liked her as well," Katie said. "She had a very serene way about her."

"Yes, that's right." Linda held her hand out to Katie, palm up. "She made you feel calmer, just by talking to her. It's probably why she was so good at counseling."

Linda stood and went to the cabinets. "I think there may have been some disappearances, though. Back in the aughts, a teenager went missing but was later found in Ann Arbor." She rummaged in the cabinet and pulled out a stack of old, yellowing newspapers, handing them to Matt.

"And then there was Noah Swanson." Linda pulled open another drawer. "He was never found. According to his wife, he just left one day and never came back. Left behind two teenage boys."

The name instantly struck Katie.

"Is he any relation to Eric Swanson?"

"That's the older son, yes." Linda handed Katie a few newspapers, a much smaller stack than the ones Matt was holding. "It's funny how tragedy sometimes follows a family. I think the wife's father also disappeared, but I'd have to pull those papers from storage. It was during my father's time here at the *Gazette*." Katie hadn't known that Marilyn's husband had disappeared. For some reason, she had assumed she was a widow.

"Can we look through these papers now?" Matt asked.

"Of course. I'll be here for at least another hour. You two can use that desk."

Katie and Matt carefully bundled up the papers and stacked them on the desk. Matt flipped through the stack related to the missing teen, and Katie took the missing husband. The desk was small, and they sat close together. She found she was very aware of his every movement and had to force herself to concentrate on the task at hand. Thinking about the way he had dropped his afternoon plans to help her comb through old newspapers made her wonder again if Gabrielle's information was true. Was he really this nice of a guy, or was he interested in her? Maybe it was both.

The *Gazette* was not a deeply investigative newspaper. The articles consisted mostly of interviews with neighbors and other townspeople who claimed to have seen something or who just had an opinion to share.

Katie read one interview that featured Miss Simms. She was quoted as saying, "Marilyn is better off without him. I'm sure you know what I mean." It sounded like it was a difficult marriage. No wonder Marilyn had such a sad air about her. Katie needed to talk to Miss Simms again.

After half an hour of combing the interviews, gossip, and innuendo that passed for journalism, Katie had found no additional information. But she did know more than when she walked into the office. Noah Swanson had disappeared, he left a good job without notice, he was not well liked, and Miss Simms might be able to tell her more. Katie wondered if there had been abuse. All this time she had conjectured that Marilyn was an abuser, prompting Eric to become the same way with his family. Maybe she'd been a victim as well.

Katie turned to Matt. "Anything?"

He shook his head. "I don't think this is what we're looking for. The girl took off with a boyfriend and came home a week later. Her name was Alicia Stewart."

"I don't recognize the name," Katie said.

Linda had heard them and said, "She's married now. Her new name is Nielsen. She just had a baby."

Katie caught her breath. Her six-month well-baby checkup. The mother was this same teenager.

"I think I know her," Katie said.

Linda smiled. "She's a lovely person. And that baby is adorable. Alicia gave her parents an awful time when she was younger, but she pulled herself together, went to school, and works at one of the smaller university libraries in Ann Arbor."

"Thank you for your help," Matt said. "We've taken enough of your time today."

"I'll swing by the storage unit on my way home this afternoon. I'll call you if I find anything 'juicy.'"

Katie and Matt went back to his car.

"I'm starting to wonder if Ellen died because of her research or something else entirely," Katie said. "We haven't found out anything particularly damaging so far."

"You know what they say on all the cop shows," Matt said.

"No. What do they say?"

"Follow the money," Matt said and put the car in gear.

Matt was right. She needed to figure out who benefited from Ellen's death.

He drove her to the auto body shop where her car was waiting. She'd be glad to have it back. She'd been feeling like a preteen again, relying on other people for rides everywhere.

She climbed out of Matt's car and leaned in the window.

"Thank you for helping today."

"I don't feel like we accomplished much," Matt said.

"Maybe not, but we learned a couple of things about Baxter."

"I guess that's true," Matt said. "It was fun, playing detective."

Katie smiled. "It was." She turned away to walk into the office.

"Katie?" Matt called.

Katie turned and waited.

"Would you like to have dinner with me tomorrow night?"

Katie felt heat in her cheeks. It was just dinner, after all. She'd never forgive herself if she took the safe way out. "Yes, I *would* like that."

"Really? Great!" Matt smiled. "I'll call you tomorrow."

Katie waved and walked into the garage. She noticed Matt was still there when she came out with the keys. He beeped the horn and pulled out of the lot as she climbed into her car.

As she watched him drive away, she pulled out her phone and texted Gabrielle.

I have news, and it's not about a murder.

The answer came back: *I have ten minutes between patients—don't call unless it's about a man.*

Katie grinned and pressed Gabrielle's phone number.

"Oh, my God!" Gabrielle said when she answered. "Tell me everything."

Katie gave her the thirty-second version of her afternoon of sleuthing with Matt.

"Yeah, yeah, very Nancy Drew and whatever the boyfriend's name was," said Gabrielle. "I hope you have more to tell me than that."

"He asked me out to dinner tomorrow night."

"Yes! I knew it," Gabrielle said. "You two are perfect for each other."

"You told me he wouldn't date another medical person," Katie said.

"That was some bad intel. I'll have to check my source—she may not know as much as she claims. Maybe she made it up because he's not interested in her."

"Also, you hardly know him—how do you know we'd be perfect for each other?"

"Because you blush every time his name comes up, and I've never seen you do that in all the time I've known you."

"That's not—"

"Oops, gotta go! I want all the details as soon as you get home." Gabrielle disconnected the call.

Katie sat in the parking lot shaking her head. She pulled down the mirror and looked at her face. She hated when Gabrielle was right.

* * *

Katie had just pulled into her driveway when her cell phone buzzed. She picked it up and saw the text was from Beth.

Saw that you called. Can we meet? I have something to show you.

Katie sent her address and told her to stop by anytime.

On my way.

Katie dumped her bag and jacket in the kitchen and put some water on to boil. She had just poured it over tea in two mugs when she heard Beth's car in the driveway. She went to the door to let her in.

"I'm so glad you were home," Beth said. She stepped inside and glanced around the sparse living room.

"I just made some tea," Katie said. "Let's sit in the kitchen."

Beth followed her through the dining room and into the kitchen, where they sat at the small table.

Beth dispensed with the small talk and got straight to the point.

"I went to see the lawyer yesterday," she began. "He was actually very helpful, and I've been mulling over what to do ever since."

"What did he tell you?"

Beth reached into her bag and pulled out a small yellow mailing envelope. Beth's name was scrawled on the front.

"What's that?"

"Apparently, my mother left this for me. The instructions were to turn it over to me *if* I came asking questions," Beth said. She looked up to the ceiling and blinked several times. She looked back down at the table and took a sip of tea.

"What's in there?"

Beth tilted her head toward the envelope, and Katie reached out to pick it up. The package felt bulky, like there was a small notebook inside. She opened the string clasp and reached in. She pulled out an old leather-bound notebook and opened it to the front page.

"Property of: Sylvia Riley" was written in perfect cursive. Katie looked at Beth. "What is this?"

"I think it's part of what my mom was researching," Beth said. "I read some of it, and it seems to be a collection of secrets or rumors about people in town. I only recognized a few names, but I looked them up, and they all live or lived in Baxter."

Katie put her hand over the book as if that could keep it in check. She remembered what Patsy Travers had said about Sylvia collecting secrets. She had never imagined they were written down somewhere.

"How did your mom get this book?"

Beth gave a half shrug. "The lawyer didn't know. He said he was told to give it to me if I came looking for it. Mom must have felt she was in danger, and she knew I would try to find out what happened." Beth's voice got thick, and she rubbed at her eyes. "I just wish she had told me what was going on before she died."

Katie put her hand over Beth's and waited while she quietly cried. She pushed a tissue box toward Beth. After a minute or two, Beth sniffled and looked at Katie.

"I know my mom was going through the house a little at a time. She had done the most important rooms when they first moved in after Mrs. Riley died. She told me a couple months ago that she was finally going to tackle the upstairs office. I assume she found it in there."

Katie turned to the first entry. The ink was faded. It read, "Mabel Quarton and Reverend Sykes seen together in Ann Arbor," followed by a list of church committees. Sylvia was in charge of all of them. The last entry on the page read, "deceased."

Katie flipped rapidly through the book and saw similar entries for bribery, affairs, and secret pregnancies.

"Wow, this is really something," Katie said.

Beth nodded. "I had to stop reading it. It felt like I was snooping in Sylvia's diary, except all the secrets belonged to other people."

"Can I keep this overnight?" Katie asked.

"You can keep it as long as you want," Beth said. "Maybe when we get into the computer files, we can figure out which of these secrets my mom was researching. It has to be what she meant, don't you think?"

Katie nodded.

"She must have found the book, recognized someone, and started looking into their secret," Beth said. "It makes me sick to my stomach to think about it. I can't imagine my mom blackmailing anyone, but that seems to be what Sylvia was doing. Why would my mom want to keep this thing? Why didn't she just burn it?"

"I don't know, Beth." Katie shook her head. She knew where to find answers. The last entry would presumably be the most recent, so Katie would start there and see if she could come up with some names of people who might have been relieved by Sylvia's death and scared when Ellen started asking questions.

She walked Beth to the front door with promises to call as soon as she knew anything. Katie returned to the small table, took out her own notebook, and mentally rolled up her sleeves.

Two hours later, Katie leaned back in her chair and stretched her arms over her head. Her neck was sore from bending over the book and trying to decipher the handwriting. The entries at the beginning were faded, and the ones at the end were hard to read because Sylvia had developed a tremor, which translated her beautiful cursive into hieroglyphics.

Katie had made some notes in her own notebook and added a couple of names to her list of suspects. According to Sylvia's book, Cecily had been a stripper before she met Nick. Katie assumed Nick didn't know, since Sylvia had written it down. Katie thought she remembered Nick saying that Cecily was from the East Coast but that all of her family had died. Katie wondered if that was why she and Ellen had fallen out. Would Ellen have confronted her friend? And would that be enough reason for Cecily to want her dead?

Reverend Fultz, the Methodist minister, really was having an affair. Gabrielle had been right that night at Riley's. Katie decided not to tell her, but his name went on the list. It was always best not to rule out anything as too farfetched, even though a bad cough was usually from a cold and not tuberculosis.

Partway through the book, a page had been ripped out. Whether Sylvia had done it or Ellen, Katie couldn't tell. She yawned and stood up. It had grown dark outside while she sat immersed in the town's secrets. She called for pizza delivery and sat at the table again to go over her notes looking for something she may have missed.

24

The office on Friday morning was nothing short of chaotic. Debra was overwhelmed with the schedule changes, and Angie stepped in to help where she could.

Nick had definitely been arrested.

Katie leaned over the counter in the reception area and spoke quietly to Debra.

"Do you have any news about Nick?"

Debra pressed her lips into a grim line and shook her head.

"Sean can't tell you anything?"

Debra stabbed the buttons on her desk phone to place a call on hold and set the receiver in its cradle.

"Sean says Chief Carlson threatened to fire him if any information leaked out about Dr. Hawkins." She narrowed her eyes. "I'm just concerned about my doc; there was no need for him to get all threaten-y."

Katie nodded and made reassuring noises but privately wondered why it had taken John so long to plug the leak in his department. She went back to her office to prepare for the onslaught.

Emmett showed up looking as if he'd been up all night with a terminal patient. He said he'd cover Nick's clinic, but Katie was worried he was too distracted to see patients. Emmett was definitely old school and came from the generation of male doctors who saw it as a badge of honor that they'd never been to their children's births, school events, or emergency room visits. Too busy saving the lives of their patients, they'd ceded all domestic chores to their wives. If they were still married.

When Katie suggested that Emmett might want to cancel Nick's clinic and let Katie deal with all the patients for the day, Emmett calmly told her that the best way to help Nick would be to ensure his patients didn't suffer while he was gone.

Angie told her that half of Nick's regular patients had canceled when they were told that Nick was unavailable. She was shuffling in "urgent" appointments to keep Emmett's schedule full.

Angie knew Emmett much better than Katie, and she must have realized that he needed to stay busy. Katie was relieved she'd only have to do a half-day clinic. She wanted to go to the police station and talk to John. And she wanted to follow up on some of the names that were in Sylvia's book. If she couldn't track them down on the Internet, she'd have to visit the library again.

Two hours later, Katie was halfway through a full but relatively easy clinic. Most of the appointments were for sick visits, and since only a few of them were actually sick, it moved along quickly. She picked up the next file and read the name: Eric Swanson. Lynn's abusive husband.

She had met Eric one time when she was a resident following Nick in his pain clinic. Now that she knew more about him, she had to take a moment to prepare herself. It was always difficult to take care of patients that she didn't like. In those moments, she fell back on her training and her oath to do no harm. Even though she'd love to do some harm to this man. This urge was tempered only slightly by the new information about his own childhood.

She took a deep breath and pushed the door open.

He sat in the patient chair, leaning forward with his elbows on his knees. He looked smaller than Katie remembered. Maybe her new knowledge of him had inflated his stature in her mind. He was likely not much taller than Katie, but he had a taut, wiry energy about him that put her on guard.

"Hello, Mr. Swanson." Katie put her hand out to shake. "I'm Dr. LeClair. I think we met a while back when I was a resident."

He took her hand and held onto it longer than necessary. "I remember you."

After extricating her hand and situating herself on the wheeled stool with a clear path to the door, she opened his chart.

"How can I help you today?"

"I need more of the pain medicine Dr. Nick gives me." He gestured at the chart.

Katie looked at the med sheet. Vicodin. She was surprised to see that he wasn't taking a lot of the medication. Even though it had been prescribed on an as-needed basis, he hadn't been in for a refill in six weeks. She was relieved. She hadn't wanted to engage in a battle over how much of the medicine to give him. She had incorrectly assumed that because he beat his wife, he probably also was a prescription drug abuser.

"I see you had an accident at work and have had back pain ever since?"

He nodded. "It only flares up every once in a while, but when it does, I can hardly move." He turned in his chair to show her where it hurt.

"Are you in pain today?"

"No, just a bit of aching, but that's usually how it starts. By Sunday, I'll be in bed with the pain."

"Okay, can you sit up on the table? I just want to do a quick exam."

He climbed onto the table, and Katie ran through a brief neuro exam and felt for trigger points along his back—areas that might have spasmed muscles causing pain. Sometimes those could be massaged or injected with lidocaine to relieve the pain before it got worse.

His nervous system was intact, and she didn't find any significant trigger points. She knew she wouldn't be able to solve his long-term pain problems in one visit and wrote him the prescription.

Eric took the prescription from her and winked. "Thanks, doc. I'll tell Lynn I saw you today."

Katie felt a cold discomfort settle in her gut.

Before her next patient, she called Debra and asked why one of Nick's patients had been added to her schedule instead of Emmett's.

"He asked for you," Debra said. "When I told him Nick was out of the office, he said he wanted to be scheduled with you. Is everything all right?"

"Yup," Katie said. "Thanks, Debra." Why would he ask for her? She had an uneasy feeling about it, knowing that Lynn was actively arranging to leave him. It was well known that abusers became more volatile when they felt they were losing control. She hoped that Lynn hadn't slipped and let on that she was planning to leave. She replaced the phone in its cradle and glanced up and down the hall to see which room was next.

The rest of the morning passed quickly as Katie moved from room to room without pausing to think about anything but the next patient in line. When she finally finished, she had a stack of charts to write in and a burgeoning headache. She escaped to the break room to load up on caffeine before tackling her charts. She didn't want to let them sit over the weekend.

She breezed into the room intent on the coffeepot and didn't notice Emmett standing at the window until she turned around and took her first sip.

"Emmett, I didn't see you there."

Emmett turned slowly and nodded at her.

"Was your morning as hectic as mine?" he asked.

Katie nodded. "It was pretty crazy."

"I'm sorry you've been thrown into this situation. You shouldn't have to keep covering for Nick. And now I don't even know when he'll be coming back. The police won't tell me anything."

Katie set her coffee cup down and went to stand with him. They both stared out at the back parking lot and the woods beyond.

* * *

Ten minutes later, Katie was on her way to the police station. She had left her charts stacked in her office with a promise to herself that she would return that afternoon to finish them. She didn't believe it.

The police department was wedged between an antique store and a yarn shop. Its bright-yellow door blended with the rest of the vibrantly colored shop windows and doors.

She pulled the door open and stepped inside to a utilitarian office space with a large desk blocking a narrow hallway.

"Hello, how can I help you?" a chirpy young woman asked as Katie approached the desk.

"Is Chief Carlson in?"

"Nope." The woman showed a toothy grin. "He just went to lunch."

Katie's stomach grumbled at the mention of lunch.

"Do you know where he went?"

"Probably Pete's, just down the street. It's where he usually goes."

Katie thanked her and headed back outside toward Pete's sandwich shop. She walked into the small, casual restaurant and spotted John at the back. There was a long deli counter down the left side of the room with sandwiches named and described on huge chalkboards. Pete's was a mostly self-serve type of establishment. They made the sandwich, but the rest was up to the customer. She ordered a grilled roast beef and cheddar and grabbed a plastic cup.

She wove through the tables toward John Carlson. He was lost in thought and sifting through some papers that covered his small table.

"Mind some company?" Katie asked and, not waiting for a reply, set her drink on the few uncovered inches of the table.

He startled, then smiled.

"Well, if it isn't my favorite doc!" He gathered his papers to make room for Katie's lunch. "You look like you've had a rough morning."

Katie nodded. "As you know, we're down one doctor, and we've had to see extra patients *and* fend off gossip seekers."

Carlson gave her a sympathetic smile but didn't seem inclined to engage in her conversational gambit. So Katie settled in for a test of wills. She knew she looked kind and somewhat naïve, but no one got through medical school without a steel spine and a hefty dose of stubborn.

Pete signaled that Katie's food was ready, and John hopped up to get it for her. She hoped he didn't think she would be swayed from her mission by a sandwich and some chips.

"Thanks, John. You didn't have to do that."

"It's partly my fault you had such a rough morning." He set the basket of food next to a precariously tilting pile of papers. And Katie thought *she* had to deal with a lot of paperwork.

"I suppose you're right," Katie said.

The chief stacked his files and papers and set them on an extra chair near their table. He glanced nervously at Katie. "Aren't you going to eat?"

"John, why are you keeping Nick?" Katie knew why. Because Nick looked guilty; she had suspected him herself. But she trusted Emmett, and he said he was with Nick.

He started shaking his head at the word "why." "I can't talk about an active case, Doc."

"I have a stressed-out and devastated father back at the clinic. He needs to know what's going on. I know Nick is an adult, but can you tell me anything that I can share with Emmett?"

John blew out air and looked everywhere in the restaurant except at Katie.

"He's a person of interest, and we're trying to either clear him or get enough evidence to keep him. He'll probably be out on bail later today *if* we find enough reason to officially charge him."

"What would you be charging him with?"

"Murder, of course."

"What? What do you mean, 'of course'?"

"How much crime do you think we have here in Baxter? Besides some drunk and disorderly on the weekends and a few domestic calls, we aren't exactly a hotbed of criminal activity. Ellen Riley's murder is about the only thing we're working on."

"You can't possibly think he would kill Ellen. He and Christopher were friends. I know the couples used to go out together."

"He has a lousy alibi, he didn't answer his service that night, and he's been seen visiting the house when Christopher was out."

Katie shook her head. "You think he was having an affair with her and then killed her?"

John spread his hands out on the table. "It's a theory."

"I think you're off track on this."

"He's been acting guilty since he came into the station. He has access to Demerol. He knows how to administer it." Carlson ticked his points off on his fingers.

"So do I. So does Emmett. You aren't questioning us." Katie shoved the memory of Nick standing by the drug cabinet when the clinic was empty aside. Carlson was right. Nick had easy access to any drug he'd want. And he'd know the dose and the method.

"You both have alibis. Your brother was with you all evening, and Emmett was at a meeting for the church fund-raiser."

Katie took a deep breath. "I was a suspect?" She was surprised at how hurt she was that John could have suspected her even for a moment. Then she realized what John had said. *Emmett was at a church fundraiser.* So had Emmett lied to her or to John? And if he lied to John, what was the penalty when he finally did have to tell the truth?

"No, of course not." He scowled at her. "You brought it up."

"What can I tell Emmett?"

"Tell him Nick will likely be out by this evening. But I'd appreciate it if you would keep the rest of this to yourself."

"Of course. Can I help?"

"Do you have a time machine? I'd like to go back to Wednesday night and do things differently. We've been treating it like suicide all along. The rescue workers contaminated her room. The medicine bottle is missing. And there was no sign of a syringe or any narcotic at the scene. I was so certain . . ."

"It's what everyone thought, John."

"That's what everyone was supposed to think. You didn't buy it, though, and I wish I'd listened to you." He hunched forward and lowered his voice as some people sat down near them. "Now I might have a very clever killer out there, or I just have an accident that I can't explain."

Katie glanced at the papers on the table and saw it was the autopsy report.

"Can I look?" Maybe there was something in the report that would exonerate Nick once and for all.

Carlson frowned and then pushed the pages toward her. "Sure, but only in the capacity of medical consultant. I can't have civilians seeing this kind of stuff."

She scanned the report. Bruising to her neck and arms. The coroner couldn't say whether it was from her time in the

ER or earlier. Stomach contents consisted of brownies and milk consumed about two hours before death. After the labs had come back with high levels of narcotic, they'd found the puncture wound on her arm where the drug must have been injected.

There was nothing in it that could rule Nick in or out as the murderer.

When she was done flipping through the report, John gathered his papers and left her to finish her lunch. She barely touched it. She picked at her sandwich and stared off into space. She had many questions and no answers. If someone had drugged Ellen, how had they gotten her to swallow the pills? She did have *some* diazepam in her system. If she only took a few, where were the rest? Who had written that prescription? And where did the Demerol come from? She added all these questions to her notebook and then flipped it shut.

Katie sighed.

She walked to the counter with her half-eaten sandwich to get it wrapped. Autopsy reports and thoughts of murderers tended to dampen the appetite.

Katie returned to her office and dumped her bag on her desk. Emmett was seeing patients. Friday afternoons were reserved for sick patients, and the weekend on-call doctor worked until they were all seen. Usually it was a short day and helped avoid calls and ER visits over the weekend.

She walked over to Emmett's hallway and waited by the nurse's station for him to exit the exam room. She knew he'd want to hear her news as soon as possible.

The door opened, and Emmett backed out of the room. "You should be feeling better by the end of the weekend," he said. "Call me if you get worse."

He turned and saw Katie standing there.

"Katie, do you have any news?"

Katie nodded and gestured down the hall toward his office. Even though most of the town would know soon, she didn't want to broadcast Nick's situation in the clinic.

They walked down the hall together, and Katie wondered if it was her imagination or if Emmett was slower and more stooped than just two days ago. She felt terrible for him and almost put her hand on his arm but stopped. If he were anything like her, any expression of sympathy would just make the whole thing even harder to bear.

He sat behind his desk and indicated the patient chair on the other side.

"I didn't get a lot of information, but I know that they are keeping him under suspicion of murder."

"Murder? Of Ellen Riley?" Emmett sat back in his chair and almost seemed to relax. "But that's ridiculous. Nick wouldn't hurt Ellen."

"He doesn't have an alibi, and there are witnesses that have seen him visiting her." Katie stopped. She didn't want to be the one to tell him about the rumors, but she had to. "There are rumors that he and Ellen were having an affair."

Emmett laughed. "Carlson must be desperate. This makes me feel much better. I thought it was about the meds. *That* would have been bad."

"Your son under suspicion for murder makes you feel better?"

"Yes. I know he didn't murder Ellen. They'll have to let him go." Emmett reached for the phone.

Katie held up her hand. "Emmett, Chief Carlson told me your alibi for that night was a church meeting."

Emmett's smile faded. "What are you asking?"

Katie took a deep breath. She couldn't let this slide. Her career might be just as much in danger as either of her partners. "Did you lie to me or to John?"

Emmett sat back in his chair and looked at Katie for a long moment. "Do you know why I offered you the job here?"

Katie felt like she had just walked in on another conversation. She looked away from him and studied the corkboard full of baby pictures. She loved this practice. And she loved working with Emmett. "I assumed it was because you thought I was a good doctor and we got along well."

Emmett nodded. "That's part of it. But there are a lot of good doctors out there." He spread his hands out on his desk. "And I get along with everyone."

Katie smiled then. "So why?"

"Because you never back down when you think you're right. I had gotten a bit bored and very set in my ways. Then you came along for your rotation and challenged every outdated diagnosis or treatment you came across. You never accepted someone else's treatment plan until you had done your own exam. I admired that."

Katie looked at her feet. She had no idea how to respond to such a compliment. They came so rarely in medical training, she didn't know what to say.

"Thank you. That means a lot coming from you," she said. She looked up then and met his eyes. "So were you with Nick or at a meeting?"

Emmett laughed until his eyes watered. "I was with Nick. There was a meeting at the church, and I hoped that whoever checked my alibi would only check to see that there was a meeting, not whether I was in attendance. I couldn't tell them about Nick—not without opening him up to investigation. I had hoped I could get him some help and shut down whatever he was doing in his pain clinic without involving the police."

"I'm glad to hear that," Katie said. And she was glad. She understood why Emmett had covered for Nick and hoped for all their sakes that they would be able to fix the problem before Nick destroyed the practice.

Emmett raised his eyebrows and glanced at the phone.

Katie nodded.

"I'll tell Debra to keep his patients on the books for next week. I'm sure it will all work out by then," Emmett said.

After his brief conversation with Debra, Emmett thanked Katie and walked back down the hall to the next exam room. There was a definite jauntiness to his stride this time. Katie was glad that he felt better even though she couldn't share his enthusiasm or certainty that Nick would be fine.

25

Katie pulled into her driveway and killed the engine. She sat in a daze, staring out the windshield at nothing in particular. She had a couple of hours before Matt was due to pick her up, but all she wanted to do at this point was figure out who killed Ellen and put it behind her.

She got out of the car and went into the house through the kitchen door.

Caleb met her there. "Katie," he said. "Thank God. I've been texting you for an hour."

Katie pulled out her phone and saw the texts. She'd turned her phone to silent and hadn't checked it. "What's wrong?" Katie asked.

"Just a bit of stellar computer work on my part."

"You texted me twenty times to brag?"

"You're going to want to see this," Caleb said.

Katie followed him into the dining room.

"I finally cracked the code to get into the locked files," Caleb said.

Katie dumped her bag on the ottoman in the living room and went to lean over his shoulder at the dining room table.

"The files each have names on them, and they're all individually locked," Caleb said. "But now that I got into the main file, the rest should be easy."

"Show me what you've got," she said.

"We talked about how one of her clients may have killed her because she knew too much about them," Caleb said.

Katie nodded.

"When I opened the main file, this is what I saw." Caleb clicked and a window popped open revealing the contents of the protected files. There were three of them: clients, taxes, and research.

"Let's start with clients," Caleb said. He clicked on that file, and a list of names popped up: Nick Hawkins, Lynn Swanson, Matt Gregor, Sandra Boules, Aaron Latimer, Jackie Munson. Katie only recognized the first three.

"Oh, I see," Katie said. Matt was one of Ellen's clients. Did he have a secret that was big enough to kill over? Could he have injected Ellen with the Demerol right there in the ER? There had been stories about renegade medical personnel using their access to harm patients.

"It's not that I thought he was a homicidal maniac, but I thought you might want to know about this before you got too involved." Caleb had been almost as devastated as Katie when Justin broke off their relationship. They had become as close as brothers—it had been one of the things she loved about Justin. Since Justin, Caleb had become more protective of Katie.

"Yeah, you're right," Katie said. "Thanks." Katie had to get a grip. This was what came of investigating. It was similar to treating patients. All the secrets came out, often ones you didn't want to know. But also the physician had to consider all possibilities until everything but the culprit was ruled out.

Caleb grunted and clicked on the research file.

Twenty or more documents filled the computer window. Caleb clicked on the first one.

"A scientific journal on color-blind genetics," Caleb said. "She was obsessed."

"What's the next one?"

"Looks like a scan of a newspaper article." He zoomed in.

There was a picture of two couples. The caption read, "Jack and Sylvia Riley with Eugene and Lily Talbot."

The next document was a birth announcement for Christopher.

After they'd opened all the documents and spent an hour reading through them, Katie still felt like she didn't know more than before they had broken into the computer.

"Can you put all this on a thumb drive for me?"

"Sure," Caleb said. He rummaged among the papers on the table and came up with a thumb drive. He stuck it into the slot on the side of the laptop and copied it.

"Thanks. I'll have to read through all the articles more carefully and see if I can figure out what she was looking for."

Caleb pushed away from the computer. "I haven't looked at the client files yet. Do you want to do that on your own?"

"Yeah, I think I should," Katie said. "Thank you, Caleb. I'll let you know what I find."

She tamped down the discomfort of snooping in Ellen's private files and clicked on one of the names she didn't recognize first. Maybe if she found something in those notes, she wouldn't have to read the files on the people she knew.

After reading about Sandra Boules's desire to be a tour guide in Italy and not a secretary at the phone company, she hovered the mouse over Matt's name. It seemed that Ellen had been doing life coaching stuff with Sandra; maybe that's all these files were about. People who just needed a little help getting their priorities straight and formulating a plan for success.

But Matt was already successful. Why would he need a life coach? And he hadn't told her he knew Ellen professionally. She checked the time. He was due in a half hour. Should she click, or should she ask him? Gabrielle's voice floated into her mind. *Everybody lies.* She didn't want to get involved with another man who had only a passing acquaintance with honesty or who had no idea what he really wanted. She clicked.

*   *   *

The doorbell startled her out of her computer trance. Crap. He was early.

Caleb zipped out of his room and went to the door. "I have to meet him before you can go out with him," he said. Katie rolled her eyes.

She heard Matt's voice at the door and jumped up to go change into something better than her clinic-day clothing.

She heard them talking but couldn't tell what they were saying. She hurriedly tossed on a wool skirt and tights, ankle boots, and a soft gray sweater. She heard them laughing and hoped Caleb hadn't trotted out some embarrassing story from childhood. She swiped on another coat of mascara and decided that would have to do.

There was a quiet knock on the door. Caleb.

"Caleb, if that's you, come in."

The door opened a crack and he slipped inside. "Matt thought I was your boyfriend." Caleb was fighting a smile and losing. "He said he heard at the hospital that you were 'living with some guy.' I said you were, but the guy was your brother. He seems cool. He asked me which online games I play. He saw the equipment and said he plays too."

Katie had to interrupt the budding bromance, or she'd never get out of the house. Just as she was about to cut into this stream of admiration, her stomach dropped. Caleb had left Matt alone in the dining room. With the computer that Katie had left open to Matt's file. She pushed past Caleb and rushed out to the dining room.

Matt was sitting in the chair that she had recently vacated. He looked up as she entered the room.

"I hope you don't mind," he said. He gestured to the computer. "This one seems to be all about me."

"Matt, I can explain," Katie said.

Matt shook his head. "No need. I know what this is. Somehow you got your hands on Ellen's files, and rather than ask me about it, you read my file."

"That's only partly true," Katie said. This was going so wrong, so fast. "You know I'm helping Beth figure out who killed her mother. I had no idea there would be a file about you on there."

"That's okay," Matt said. "I came here thinking you were living with a guy and had agreed to date me behind his back, so I guess we haven't really established trust."

"Matt, I'm sorry." And she really was. She had known that reading those files would put her in an uncomfortable spot in general. She hadn't known it would ruin things with the first guy she'd been really interested in since Justin.

"It's fine," Matt said. He headed to the door. "I'm sure you'll understand that I don't much feel like going out tonight."

Caleb came and stood behind Katie.

"It was nice to meet you, Caleb." Matt shut the door, and seconds later they heard his car roar to life and head down the street.

Caleb turned to Katie. "Katie, I'm sorry. I should have flipped the computer shut."

Katie shook her head and wiped her eyes. "It's my fault. I should have asked him before I read it." She made a weak attempt at a smile. "At least now there's nothing to distract me from the case." Katie took off her boots and slid into the seat in front of the computer.

Several hours later, her brain was filled with snippets of information. She felt like someone had dumped a complicated jigsaw puzzle out of its box and took away the picture.

A huge yawn overtook her, and she felt dizzy and blurry-eyed. She was no stranger to sleep deprivation, but usually she kept active to stay awake. She stood and stretched, feeling the tension in her shoulders as she finally unhunched.

She saved all the files back to the thumb drive and brought it with her to her room, where she undressed quickly and fell into bed. She closed her eyes and waited for sleep. And waited.

Her brain continued to try to put some of the things she'd read into perspective. Of course, she had read the Matt Gregor file and was relieved to discover that he had been seeing Ellen for career counseling. He was thinking about leaving medicine and was exploring other career options. That's why he was doing all of the locum tenens work. It paid really well, and he'd be able to take some time off in another year.

Lynn Swanson's file held no surprises either. Ellen had met her at the women's shelter where she volunteered. She described Lynn as skittish and was not confident that she would ever leave her husband. They had arranged for private counseling away from the shelter, as Lynn was worried her husband would find out what she was up to.

The biggest surprise was Nick Hawkins. He was seeing Ellen for burnout. Katie thought all physicians got burned out once in a while. It was part of the job in many ways. Caregivers of all sorts eventually got to the point where they had to learn to take care of themselves first or risk losing the ability to care for others. But true burnout was harder to shake. The emotional toll of caring for sick and dying people and the constant demands of time and emotion were often too much to bear. The protective mechanism was to put distance between oneself and the patient. And then stop seeing them as individuals. And then stop caring. Nick had endured his own difficult recovery from his motorcycle accident, and his dependence on pain medicine combined with his continuing work with chronic pain patients was taking its toll.

He hadn't been having an affair as the rumor mill claimed. He'd been trying to save his career. Katie had to figure out how to steer the police away from Nick as a suspect without requiring Emmett to give him an alibi. She would ask Beth to turn the computer over to the police. Once Chief Carlson saw that there had not been an affair, maybe he would let Nick go. She knew that neither Nick nor Emmett wanted to tell him where they had actually been, and for the time being she would respect that choice.

Her brain continued to run in circles and finally exhausted itself. Katie fell asleep and didn't dream.

26

Saturday morning came much too soon for Katie. She woke at seven when her radio blasted nineties hip-hop. She had forgotten to shut off the alarm. With the determination of a marathon trainer, she powered through and fell back to sleep. She woke again at ten, disoriented and groggy. There was no bright sunlight forcing its way past her blinds. She got up and looked outside to a gray and gloomy day. The window was still wet from the morning's rain, and yellow leaves stuck damply to the grass.

It was hard enough to get out of bed on a Saturday, but weather like that made her want to crawl back under the covers with a good book and pretend that she wasn't involved in a murder investigation. Because that's exactly what she was doing, wasn't it? She was secretly investigating a murder and keeping information from the police.

The smell of bacon seeped into the room. Caleb. He knew how to get her out of bed. She followed the delicious aroma to the kitchen, where he was just plating a Swiss cheese and mushroom omelet.

"For you, madam."

"Thank you."

"I'll give you five bites, and then I need to know what you found out."

Katie dug in. The food made her feel better. The coffee that Caleb set next to her plate brought her back to life.

She gave Caleb a brief summary of what she had discovered. She told him about the photos of Christopher's parents and another couple.

"There was a family tree showing the inheritance of color-blindness. That was probably what all the color-blind searches were for. Color-blindness is an X-linked trait. That means it passes to sons from their mothers. If a woman is a carrier, she has a fifty-fifty chance of passing it on to her son. A woman can be a carrier if her father was color-blind."

"So if the mother's father was color-blind, the child has a fifty-fifty chance of being color-blind?"

"Yes, if the child is male. If it's female, then the father would have to be color-blind as well in order to produce a color-blind daughter."

"Got it. But none of the files pointed to anyone in particular? No deep, dark secrets?"

"Not really." Katie sighed. "But Matt said something interesting the other day."

"I'm sure he did," said Caleb and waggled his eyebrows.

"Stop," Katie said. "He did. It might be the last bit of wisdom he'll ever share with me after last night. He said to follow the money."

"Well, she has that tax file in there."

Katie nodded. "I looked at it, and it seemed pretty standard. So far, I haven't found any money to follow."

"I thought Christopher was the one with all the money."

"I think that's right, but Dan and Todd had that brawl at the funeral. Beth said it was about how Christopher was running the business. I wonder if Dan felt threatened by Ellen?"

"It seems like the more we find out, the more suspects we have. I thought the whole idea was to narrow things down."

Katie nodded ruefully. "I agree. The more I look into this, the more secrets are uncovered. It's like trying to diagnose a patient with a weird presentation. The more tests you run, the more slightly off results you get until your diagnosis is all muddled up with inconsequential lab tests."

Caleb looked at her for a beat. "Yeah, that's what I meant."

Katie threw a dishcloth at him. He dodged it and escaped into the dining room. "Your turn to do the dishes!" he yelled gleefully from the safety of the other room.

* * *

Katie had cleaned up the kitchen and taken a shower. Just as she was about to open the files again on her computer to be sure she hadn't missed anything, the doorbell rang.

She left her room and went through the dining room to answer the door. Caleb was there at the table, engrossed in his own computer project.

"Don't get up," Katie said. "I'll get it."

Caleb hadn't moved, but he managed to mumble, "Mmm-kay."

Katie pulled the door open expecting a kid selling coupon books or magazines.

"Surprise!" Gabrielle said.

"Hey, come in." Katie stepped away from the doorway.

"I didn't *really* expect a call last night, but I thought I'd at least get a text or something this morning," Gabrielle said. "When I heard nothing at all, I decided to come get the scoop myself."

"Oh, you mean Matt?"

Gabrielle put her hands on her hips and scowled at Katie. "Of course, I mean Matt. How did it go?"

"I'll need some more coffee if we're going to talk about this," Katie said. "Come into the kitchen, and I'll tell you all the gory details."

"I love details," Gabrielle said. She dropped her coat and bag on the couch and waved hello to Caleb as she passed.

Katie poured two cups of coffee from the pot that Caleb had made earlier and sat at the table with Gabrielle.

"Go on then. Spill it."

Katie made a face and sighed. "You're not going to like this," she began. "There was no date. I blew it."

"What? How?"

Katie filled her in on the disaster date that never was.

"I don't think he'll ever talk to me again."

"This is pretty bad," Gabrielle agreed. "I'm not sure *I* would talk to you again."

"Thanks for the pep talk."

"But what were you thinking? Why would you read his file?"

Katie shrugged. "I wasn't thinking about *him* so much as the murder. I felt like I had to look at everything. You don't avoid checking for cancer just because you really like the patient and don't want to give them bad news."

"I guess that's true." Gabrielle drummed her fingers on the table. "You didn't really think he could be the killer did you?"

"No, not really. But it's not like I know him that well . . ."

"This is ridiculous," Gabrielle said. "You need to figure this thing out so you can go back to your life without suspecting everyone you meet."

"You're right." Katie sipped her coffee.

"What do you know so far?"

Katie rubbed her forehead and tried to put everything in reasonable order in her mind. "Ellen took, or was given, some diazepam—but not enough to kill her. She was injected with a high dose of Demerol, which *was* enough to kill her. On the night in question, Christopher may or may not have been seen at the house. *Someone* was there, but he was seen from a distance and was wearing a sweat shirt with the hood pulled up. Ellen had some clients who may have shared secrets, and she was in possession of a notebook that had been used for blackmail. Also, there were rumors she was having an affair with Nick, which puts the wife on the list of suspects. Because even if it wasn't true, if Cecily thought it was true, that's all that matters."

"This is complicated," Gabrielle said.

"And I haven't even mentioned the secondary suspects—the ones that I don't really suspect, but I have them on the list just to be thorough."

"What are you going to do?"

"I'm going to start pushing for some answers. I'll start by bullying a little old lady."

*   *   *

After lunch, Katie drove to Ellen's house and inspected the homes on either side. Mrs. Peabody had said Miss Simms's house was on the far side of the Rileys' driveway. A light-blue

bungalow was nestled among trees, bushes, and an exuber-
ant display of mums in every color on that side of the Riley's
place. There were two white wicker chairs on the small porch
and white lace curtains hanging in the front windows.

Katie figured this was the place. She parked in the street
and walked up the paved pathway to the front porch.

She knocked on the door and waited. She glanced across
the street and saw the curtain twitch in Patsy Travers's window.

Shuffling and bumping noises floated out from inside the
house.

"Who is it?"

Katie recognized Mrs. Peabody's crisp voice from the
other side of the door. It seemed she would have to deal with
both of them.

"It's Dr. LeClair," Katie said. "May I come in?"

The door swung open, and both ladies stood there looking
delighted.

"Dr. LeClair, I'm so glad you stopped by. We were just
about to have some tea and cake," Miss Simms said. She took
Katie by the hand and pulled her through the house to the
kitchen.

"Betty, let Dr. LeClair tell us why she's here," Mrs. Peabody said.

"Of course," Miss Simms said. "Just let me get her a cup."

Mrs. Peabody shook her head at Katie. Katie took it to
mean that she would have to go along with the tea party
to get a word in.

Katie sat and thanked Miss Simms for the tea.

Miss Simms bustled about, put a plate with a slice of car-
rot cake on it in front of Katie, and poured tea from a beautiful silver teapot.

Miss Simms sat after Mrs. Peabody assured her that everyone had everything they needed.

"Now what brings you here, Doctor?" Miss Simms sipped her tea.

Katie had been rapidly reworking her strategy. She berated herself for not planning that Mrs. Peabody would be there as well. The best way forward might be to just tell them the truth.

"I'm glad you're here as well, Mrs. Peabody. I wanted to talk to you both about our last visit at the clinic."

"Are Betty's labs back? Is it bad news?" Mrs. Peabody set her cup down gently and seemed to steel herself for a physical attack.

"No, I didn't take any labs. This isn't about your health. You're both as healthy as ever."

Miss Simms and Mrs. Peabody sighed, and Mrs. Peabody patted Miss Simms's hand.

Katie looked at them and held each woman's gaze.

"You each told me something last time I saw you, and I want to be sure it's okay to discuss it with both of you. You may remember we discussed Ellen Riley?"

Miss Simms looked away from Katie toward her kitchen window. Mrs. Peabody studied her cake.

"Can I discuss it with both of you?"

Miss Simms turned back to Katie and nodded. "I shouldn't have kept it from Mrs. Peabody anyway."

Mrs. Peabody looked at her friend in surprise. "Kept what from me?"

"Is it okay with you as well, Mrs. Peabody?"

She looked back at Katie and flapped her hand. "Yes, yes, okay."

Katie took a deep breath.

She turned to Miss Simms. "You mentioned that the Rileys had been fighting in the last few weeks and that it was unusual for them."

Miss Simms nodded and stole a glance at Mrs. Peabody.

Katie looked at Mrs. Peabody. "You mentioned that you saw someone enter the house that evening wearing a hoodie and sweat pants."

Miss Simms put her hand to her mouth.

"Can you see how the two of you have some very important information that you should share with the police?"

"Why didn't you tell me?" Miss Simms gasped at Mrs. Peabody.

"I had no idea you were hiding this!" Mrs. Peabody snapped back.

Both women fell silent, not looking at each other. After a few moments of uncomfortable silence, Miss Simms turned to Katie.

"Would you like more tea, dear?"

Katie took a deep breath. "I'm sorry, ladies, but I don't have time for hurt feelings here. I need to know what you saw or heard in the past few weeks. My partner is in trouble, and I don't think he had anything to do with Ellen's death."

"Emmett? He wouldn't hurt anyone," Mrs. Peabody said. "Not ever." She crossed her arms, and her look dared Katie to contradict her.

"Not Emmett. Nick," Katie said.

The two friends exchanged a glance.

"Oh, well, Nick Hawkins . . ." Miss Simms drifted off. She sipped her tea and looked out the window again.

"What does that mean?" When Katie couldn't get Miss Simms to look at her, she appealed to Mrs. Peabody.

"She just means that Emmett's boy hasn't been the same since his motorcycle accident. He used to be such a delightful person, and now he's moody and sometimes downright unfriendly."

Katie had only known Nick after his accident, and she had a hard time imagining him as "delightful."

"But you can't think that he had anything to do with Ellen Riley's death?"

Miss Simms set her teacup gently in the saucer. "We've both seen him going in to the house at odd times of day." She looked to Mrs. Peabody, who nodded. "We know there are rumors that they were having an affair, which I find very hard to believe. We thought Ellen and Christopher were very happy. I don't know about Nick and Cecily. They used to be happy, but Cecily has withdrawn from most of her activities in the last year or so. It's difficult to say what might be happening. And we don't like to gossip."

Katie swallowed the snort of laughter at that last comment and made herself cough.

Mrs. Peabody stood and whacked her on the back several times, which only made things worse. Katie held up a hand.

"I'm fine," she said. "Just had a sudden tickle in my throat."

Mrs. Peabody sat down.

"On another subject," Katie said. "I was wondering what you might remember about Christopher's parents, Jack and Sylvia."

Miss Simms shook her head. "I don't like to speak ill of the dead, Dr. LeClair."

Mrs. Peabody leaned forward. "I don't mind. She was awful!"

"What?" Mrs. Peabody reacted to the shocked look her friend gave her. "She was nosy, and pushy, and was horrible to Jack the whole time they were married."

"Really?" Katie asked. She hadn't heard this part from Patsy.

Miss Simms reluctantly nodded. "She used to find out things and then use them to get people to do what she wanted."

"Blackmail?" Katie knew the answer but didn't want to stop the ladies from sharing anything they knew.

"I don't think she ever asked for money." Miss Simms moved the cake crumbs around her plate. "It was more that she would try to influence things."

Mrs. Peabody took over the story. "If she was running for school board president, she might look into any gossip she could find on her opponent and convince them to drop out."

Miss Simms said. "I think Christopher got into some typical teenage trouble—drinking and reckless driving—and she was always able to get him out of it. The chief of police at the time must have had a few skeletons in his closet."

Katie had surmised all this from reading the notebook Beth had given her. She was more interested in what they could share about the photo Ellen had or the family tree she had drawn.

"What do you know about the Rileys and the Talbots?"

The ladies looked at each other, and Miss Simms nodded at Mrs. Peabody.

"They were very close friends, all of them." Mrs. Peabody studied her cup and saucer. "I hate to drag up old rumors."

"Please, Mrs. Peabody," Katie said. "I think it could be very important."

Mrs. Peabody sighed. "There was some tittle-tattle that Jack Riley and Lily Talbot were closer than they should have been. Jack always took a special interest in Lily's girl, Marilyn. If you'd seen her and Christopher when they were children, you would have sworn they were related."

"Do you mean Marilyn Swanson?" Katie leaned forward.

"Yes, dear," Miss Simms said. "She was a lovely girl. And so bright. It's a shame, really, that she never finished nursing school."

Katie sat back in her chair. This was what she'd suspected from all the genetics research that Ellen had been doing. But she hadn't made the connection to Marilyn. Gossip and notes on genotypes didn't prove anything, but it gave Katie a few ideas.

The mention of Marilyn reminded Katie of her initial reason for stopping by.

"Do either of you remember anything about Noah Swanson?"

"My goodness, Dr. LeClair," Miss Simms said. "You *are* bringing up all the old stories."

Miss Simms hesitated and a look passed between the two older ladies.

"Noah was always trouble. From the time he was in kindergarten, we knew he had a temper," said Miss Simms.

"I know people tried to talk Marilyn out of marrying him, but she was determined. I felt terrible when stories of ER visits and injuries made the rounds," Mrs. Peabody said.

"And then he just up and left," Miss Simms said. "Marilyn had to raise both of those boys on her own."

"I don't know the other Swanson son," Katie said.

Mrs. Peabody shook her head and smiled. "Noah was so awful that the younger son took Marilyn's maiden name. Todd Talbot is her youngest."

"Oh," Katie said. Marilyn had been married to an abusive man. Eric Swanson was her son and so was Todd Talbot. This was one of those moments when Katie most felt her outsider status. Probably everyone in town knew that Marilyn had two sons and that one of them had changed his name to Talbot. This explained Marilyn's world-weary manner; she'd been through a lot in her life. But what did it have to do with Ellen?

She turned to Miss Simms. "Let's get back to Ellen and Christopher. You're sure they were arguing more in the past few weeks?"

She nodded. "Definitely. I had never heard either one of them raise a voice to the other before."

"And you couldn't tell what they were arguing about?"

Miss Simms shook her head and crossed her arms.

Katie waited.

Miss Simms sighed and put her hands in her lap. "Only once, when they were in their backyard, I heard Ellen tell him that it was the right thing to do. Christopher said he would think about it, but it was ancient history, and he didn't want to dredge up the past and disrupt everyone's lives."

"Do you know what they were talking about?"

Both women shook their heads.

"Thank you both for telling me all of this," Katie said.

"We're happy to help you, dear," Miss Simms said, "but I do hope you'll be careful with the information. People don't always like to talk about the past."

27

Fifteen minutes later, Katie sat on the bench in the garden by the hospital. She'd asked Beth to meet her. Beth had beat here there and looked worried.

"What did you find out?" Beth asked.

"I don't have any proof, but I'm starting to think maybe Christopher *did* have something to do with your mom's death."

Beth shook her head. "I don't know, Dr. LeClair. I think he was really in love with her. They were very happy together."

"A friend said something interesting to me the other day," Katie said. "He told me to follow the money. At first I thought it meant to figure out who benefits, and that still may be the case. But what if this whole thing revolves around money?"

Beth nodded. "Okay."

"One person in this situation with a lot of money is Christopher. What if your mom found out something that threatened his business?"

"Like what?"

"I'm starting to suspect that your mom thought Christopher had a sister. She had a copy of Jack Riley's will scanned into her computer. I didn't think much of it at first, but the wording was unusual. He didn't leave his business to Christopher by name. He left it to 'any surviving children or grandchildren.'"

"Isn't that pretty standard? You want to protect unborn children in case you don't get around to making another will?"

Katie nodded. "But this will was dated twenty years ago, when Christopher was in his thirties. I doubt Jack Riley thought he'd have any more children at that point."

"I suppose that's a little strange, but is it worth killing my mother over?" Beth asked.

"I think the research she was doing about the color-blindness was because she suspected that Jack Riley had had an affair, and there was another child of his out there."

Beth's eyebrows rose. "That would cause some trouble."

"Yes, it would. I think that your mom confronted him, and he either didn't believe her or had always known and had covered it up. But if anyone started demanding DNA tests, he could lose at least half of his business."

"But Sylvia Riley only died two years ago. There wasn't any mention of another child in that will."

"Maybe she didn't know."

Beth gave Katie a skeptical look. "More likely she knew and wanted the secret to die with her."

"Did you know her?"

"I only met her once, and that was enough. She made me nervous, like she was judging every word and gesture."

"I've heard she could be . . . difficult."

"That's probably not a secret she'd write in her book. Do you know who the other child is?"

"I have an idea," Katie said. "Apparently, Jack Riley was color-blind."

"Oh, like Todd," Beth said.

Katie nodded. "It's an X-linked trait. The mother can pass it on to her children if she carries the gene. Even if she herself is not color-blind." Katie waited for her to make the connection.

"You think that Todd's mother is really Jack Riley's daughter?"

"It's a possibility."

"So that would mean Todd is his grandchild. And he should have inherited some of the business."

"Yes, if it's true."

"You think Christopher killed her to cover up the fact that Jack Riley may have had more heirs?"

Katie leaned back against the bench and looked up at the trees. "This is all supposition. But your mother was researching color-blind genetics and had some articles on Christopher's parents and the Talbots."

"Wow. If it's true, not only will Christopher lose some of the business, but so will Dan. I'd be more inclined to think Dan did it."

"Maybe, but he wasn't in town that evening as far as we know."

"Right. But Christopher was out of town too."

"That's what he says . . ."

"I don't like any of this, Dr. LeClair," Beth said. "I feel like everyone I know is a suspect. I'm not sure who to trust."

"I agree."

"I think we're going to need more than a few old newspaper articles and web searches to convince Chief Carlson to look at Christopher. They've been friends since elementary school."

"You're right," Katie said. "Let me do some digging on my own. Maybe I can get us some proof that we can take to the chief. But in the meantime, you should turn this in to the police." Katie handed the laptop to Beth.

Beth hugged it to herself and shivered. "I don't even want to think that Christopher did this."

28

The next morning, Katie woke with the urgent need to follow up on every clue immediately or at least pick up where she'd left off the night before when she had passed out at her computer. She ate some toast, packed a thermos of coffee, and left a note for Caleb.

She decided to walk to the clinic. The golden light of autumn on the changing leaves was too beautiful to rush past. The streets were deserted, as the residents were either sleeping in or at church. Postchurch activities like gardening, biking, walking, and entertaining children wouldn't start for another several hours, so she saw no one for several blocks. Mist still hung in the air and shrouded everything in a smudged pastel watercolor fog. The cooler fall sunshine was just beginning to burn off some of the haze and made the air itself sparkle.

Katie reached the back door of the clinic, fumbling with her coffee and her keys to unlock it. She quickly entered the security code on the panel, relocked the door, and went to her office. She put her jacket on the back of her chair and set the coffee mug on her desk. A twinge of paranoia had her deciding to make a quick run through the clinic to be certain she was alone.

The hallways were dim and quiet. She glanced into each exam room, flicked on every light, and finally convinced herself she was the only one in the building.

In the records room, there was one shelving unit that contained the files for deceased patients. Emmett didn't have to hang on to these records, but he said he would keep them as long as he had the room. Katie doubted he would still have records from forty years ago, but the man *did* save everything.

She had decided to look for the charts for the Rileys, Christopher's parents. If any of them had been alive, she would have felt more like she was intruding on their privacy. But under the circumstances, she felt that she was justified. Ellen's research into color-blindness had given Katie an idea. Mrs. Riley had died about two years earlier, and Katie found her chart easily. Flipping through the pages revealed no surprises. When she died, she had been seventy-eight and suffering from diabetes and hypertension. The two factors combined to cause a fatal heart attack.

She was less lucky with Jack Riley. His chart was nowhere to be found. Katie doubted that he'd gone to a different doctor. Maybe that was a chart that had been shredded? Katie pulled a chart at random that looked old. This patient had died in 1975, so there were charts at least forty years old in this section. She couldn't remember when Christopher's father had died. She thought she remembered hearing that Christopher took over the business when he was quite young.

Katie doubted that Emmett ever purged files of people who had moved away or left the practice. If he didn't pay attention, Angie would. She looked under the *S*s to see if Noah Swanson's chart was there.

It was. A slim file showing only a few visits for illnesses and one for a broken finger. There was very little information and not even an intake history.

Katie sighed and leaned against the wall. This was hopeless. Digging through old files was not going to help her solve Ellen's murder. She wasn't sure at this point what *would* help. She slipped the file back into its spot and turned out the light. She had one foot in the hallway when she heard a noise. Someone else was in the building.

"Hello?" Emmett's voice cracked.

Katie let out the breath she'd been holding.

"It's me, Emmett. I'm in the records room."

She heard his footsteps turn and head in her direction.

"Katie, what are you doing here?"

"Just catching up on some paperwork."

"I'm glad it's you," Emmett said. "When the alert came through on my phone, I didn't know whether to call the police or just come check it out myself."

"What alert?"

"Angie added this app to my phone." He held it up for Katie to see. "It lets me know whenever the alarm is shut off or reset."

"I didn't know you had that." So much for sneaking into the office.

"She just added it last week," he said. "It seemed like a good idea with everything going on . . ."

"You mean Nick?"

"When the alarm went off, I thought it might be him. The police released him on Friday night just like you said they would. They didn't have enough evidence. I rushed over here to see if I could confront him and figure out a way to help him. I'm sure being arrested hasn't helped his mental state."

"Do you think he's been taking the drugs for his personal use?"

"Not necessarily," Emmett said. "I think he's been selling some of them to finance his own habit. We found some charts that don't seem to belong to any patient in our computer. A bill is never generated, and insurance isn't used. Most of them are patients with back pain or some other chronic pain, and he gives them Vicodin or OxyContin. I suspect he pays them to fill the prescriptions for him, in either cash or drugs. The medications themselves aren't expensive, but he'd need to involve others to fill them for him. He's too well known around here to do it himself. And if he wrote narcotic scripts for himself, it would trigger an investigation by the licensing board."

So Nick had been selling medications and probably trading prescriptions in order to get people to fill prescriptions for him. Katie wondered if that made him more of a suspect in Ellen's murder or less. Matt's comment to follow the money came back to her. Maybe she and Beth were wrong. What if Nick killed Ellen because she found out about his scheme?

29

Katie was just drifting off to sleep when her phone buzzed on the nightstand. She sighed and picked it up, the glow from the screen illuminating the bed and casting weird shadows on the walls.

The readout said, "ER." Katie sat up and answered the call.

"Dr. LeClair," she said.

"Doctor, one of your patients is here in the ER. He is the assumed victim of a hit-and-run," a businesslike voice told her. "Doctor Gregor wanted me to let you know he's going to transfer him to the U of M trauma center."

"Who is the patient?"

"It's Christopher Riley."

Katie was out of bed immediately. She fought the dizziness from standing up so fast and pulled on the clothes that she had left draped over a chair.

"I'm on my way," she said.

"I don't think—"

But Katie didn't wait to hear what the nurse was going to say. She ended the call, grabbed her keys, and let herself out the side door. It was only a three-minute drive to the hospital. Katie hoped she'd get there before Christopher was transferred. There was no telling whether she'd be able to talk to him once he was in the trauma unit. She wasn't even sure if he would be able to talk. But at least she could get the full story from Matt.

The waiting room was empty again, just as it had been when she had come in a week and a half ago to see Ellen Riley. Now Ellen's husband had been the victim of a hit-and-run?

"Katie, I see you got my message," Matt said when she entered the patient area. "I figured you'd want to know."

"What happened?"

Matt led her off to one side away from the activity surrounding Christopher's gurney.

"He hasn't said much, but there was a witness who said a dark pickup truck swerved to hit him. He was walking to his car after leaving the restaurant. No one else saw anything."

"Is he stable?"

"For now. Vitals are stable, and he's breathing on his own, but he has several fractures and a severe concussion."

"You don't think we can keep him here?"

"University Hospital has a dedicated trauma unit with highly trained nurses. I think the ICU here could handle it, if we weren't nearly full and understaffed."

"Can I see him?"

Matt gestured for her to follow him, and they entered the cubicle where Christopher seemed to be resting. His face had multiple contusions and lacerations. His left eye was swollen, and he wore a neck brace. Katie assumed they'd dosed him with narcotics to help with the pain and to be sure he could be transferred without undue discomfort.

"Do you think it was an accident?" Katie whispered to Matt.

"The witness doesn't think so. She claims the truck drove right up on the curb to hit him."

"Drunk?"

"Maybe, but she claims it drove off just fine. Of course she didn't get a license plate number or a good look at the truck. It all happened so fast, and she was definitely shocked by it all."

"Who was the witness?"

"Mrs. Peterson. She was working late at the Purple Parrot. She happened to be looking out at the street when the accident happened," Matt said. "It's a good thing too. The ambulance was able to get there within a couple of minutes to stabilize him."

"Who would want both Ellen and Christopher dead?"

"So you think this is related to his wife's death?"

"I think that if they aren't related, it's a huge coincidence—maybe too big," Katie said. "I can't help thinking of it like a medical diagnosis. You try to find the one thing that will fit all the symptoms. It's more likely than a patient having two major illnesses."

"Listen to you, going all forensic on me."

Katie smiled at him and felt the ice melt a bit.

"Katie, I'm sorry about the other night. I overreacted."

Katie was already shaking her head. "No, I shouldn't have read the file without talking to you. I just got so caught up in trying to figure out who killed Ellen that nothing else mattered."

"Well, seeing Christopher tonight made me realize that this person needs to be stopped, and soon."

Katie stepped out of the cubicle and saw John Carlson standing there looking grim.

"Who do you think did this?" Katie asked.

Carlson shook his head. "I don't know. I'm going to go talk to a couple of people now. I broke up a fight between Christopher and Todd Talbot earlier tonight. I wish I'd arrested them both for disturbing the peace. At least Chris would have been safe."

"What were they fighting about?" Katie asked.

"They wouldn't say. And since all the damage was to the restaurant, I just gave them a warning and left it at that."

"There was damage to the restaurant?" Matt asked.

"Just a few tables turned over and dishes broken. It happened earlier in the evening before they opened. One of the kitchen staff called us when the argument got physical."

Beth must have told Todd about Marilyn's paternity situation. If he had confronted Christopher, it may have sparked the conflict.

"Doc, Linda told me you're still looking into Ellen's death," Carlson said. "I don't want to get a call that you're here in the ER as a patient."

Katie started to respond, but he put up his hand.

"This is serious. Trying to follow in Ellen's footsteps to see what she knew is dangerous. Whoever killed Ellen Riley apparently thought Christopher was a threat. Don't give that person an opportunity to feel threatened by you as well."

Thinking she could trick a reporter—even one that mostly worked on births, deaths, and weddings—was a mistake. Linda must have seen right through them and talked to John about it.

"You think Katie is in danger?" Matt asked. He moved closer to Katie.

"I don't know," John said, "but I have to assume that this is the same person. Which means I don't want to see anyone else hurt for digging where they don't belong."

Matt looked at Katie with a worried expression. He seemed about to say something when the nurse called him away to talk to the transfer team.

The two EMTs from the university transferred Christopher to their wheeled gurney. The nurse took the details from Matt, and the team swooped back out to the ambulance.

30

Katie drove slowly home. The streets were deserted, and only the occasional barking dog broke the silence. Her brain felt overwhelmed by all the information she had gathered in the last week. She didn't know how it all fit together or even *if* it all fit.

Ellen had been researching something and arguing with Christopher. Katie had convinced herself that Christopher had killed his wife to cover up his relationship to Marilyn. According to Beth, there was a lot of money at stake if Jack Riley had more heirs.

But Christopher's attack had her rethinking all her assumptions. Could it have been Dan, Christopher's son? Had he found out what Ellen was up to and tried to silence her? Maybe Christopher had decided to come clean about his sister and nephews. If Ellen's death and Christopher's injuries were connected, it seemed even less likely that Nick or his wife had anything to do with it. They had no reason to attack Christopher.

She climbed under the covers even though she knew she wouldn't sleep for a long time. Just as she felt herself relaxing, she heard the train in the distance. According to Matt, that meant nothing bad would happen tonight. Maybe it only worked for Matt.

An hour later, Katie got out of bed. Her brain was running in circles, and she needed to do something else to distract it from the perpetual loop it was on.

She padded into the dining room and flipped open her laptop. Even though she'd looked at everything that Caleb had found on Ellen's laptop, she felt she needed to go through it all again. If only to assure herself that she had considered everything. Why didn't Ellen have a file of notes where she spelled everything out? Or a list? If anyone looked at Katie's laptop, they would know exactly what she was working on.

She had to look at everything again from the point of view of someone who might want to get rid of both Ellen and Christopher. Katie had to admit that the first time through, she had been seeing these files from Ellen's point of view and considering why the contents had sparked a fight with Christopher. Since discovering his sister, she'd decided Christopher was guilty, so all the notes were filtered through that lens. It was an intern's mistake to make a snap diagnosis and force the symptoms to fit the illness. It was the way things got missed.

So this time, she would read through everything with an objective view. Rather than thinking "Christopher would have thought this" or "He would have wanted *that* kept a secret," she had to determine how the pieces might all fit together.

She clicked on the first file.

*   *   *

Two hours and three cups of coffee later, Katie was no closer to solving her mystery. She was jittery from the caffeine but also exhausted. She snapped the computer shut and rested her head on top.

She may have fallen asleep because the next thing she knew, she was sitting up straight in her chair. She'd heard something outside. Footsteps on the porch? She glanced at her watch: three thirty. She got up, went to the front window, and peeked outside. The streetlight had burned out. Her house and her neighbors on both sides and across the street all sat in darkness. Down the road, lights glowed dimly through the mist.

She was about to put the shade back when a shadow pulled away from the side of her house and melted into the neighbor's shrubbery.

Without thinking, Katie ran to the front door and pulled it open. She was almost off the porch before she realized how stupid this was. She had no idea who was out there, no way to protect herself, and no one knew where she was.

She backed slowly toward the door, scanning the yard and the street for any sign of movement. She stepped onto the welcome mat and felt a crumpled piece of paper under her foot. She picked it up by the corner and let it fall open.

"YOU SHOULD HAVE STAYED IN ANN ARBOR."

A shiver of cold went up her spine. She stepped inside, closed the door, and bolted it.

"What's going on?"

Katie screamed and spun around. Caleb.

She held out the paper with a shaky hand.

He took it, and she saw his jaw clench as he read.

"We'd better call Carlson," he said.

"No, he has enough to deal with tonight," Katie said. "I'll call him in the morning."

"What were you doing outside?"

Katie explained that she couldn't sleep after returning from the ER, her work on the computer, and then hearing the noise outside.

"Will Christopher be okay?"

"I think so," she said. "He's lucky, really."

"Hard to consider him lucky when he's been run over by a maniac."

"I just meant, it could have been worse." Katie walked into the living room and sat on the couch. "Whoever did this is getting desperate. To try to run him down in the middle of town doesn't seem like the action of a stone-cold killer. Ellen's death was so planned out, so careful. This was . . . I don't know . . . reactive?"

"Did you figure anything out by looking over the notes again?"

"Not really. I just wanted to look at them all without thinking that Christopher was guilty. I figure he didn't run himself down, so maybe he also didn't kill his wife."

31

Katie woke up late Monday morning and rushed out of the house, grabbing a granola bar on her way through the kitchen. She planned to drive out to Ann Arbor to see Christopher. He was technically her patient after all.

The drive to Ann Arbor took less time than finding a parking spot near University Hospital. Katie bemoaned her lack of a staff parking pass since she didn't see patients there anymore. She looped through the visitor parking garage and finally began stalking the door that exited from the hospital. She followed a stout balding man to his car and waited with her blinker on while he adjusted his seat belt, fiddled with his radio, and checked his mirrors three times.

She was certain that steam was coming out of her ears by the time she finally pulled into the spot and switched off the ignition. She sat for a moment taking deep breaths.

Katie exited her car, locked it, and went in through the visitor door.

Katie knew certain areas of the hospital like they were her own home, while others were a complete mystery. The hospital complex was vast, and she had only spent time in patient care areas. The ICU was one place she knew very well. She hit the metal plate outside the doors and walked inside as they whooshed open.

There was a different sort of air in an ICU. Katie could never put her finger on it, but the softly beeping machines, the quiet squeak of shoes on linoleum, and the sleeping patients who were fighting epic battles while unconscious always felt like an alien world to Katie.

She identified herself to the nurse behind the central desk, who pointed to a cubicle at the far end of the room. This was a good sign for Christopher. The nurses tried to position the sickest patients near the nurse's station.

"We just gave him his pain meds; you'd better hurry if you want to talk to him."

Katie walked toward the bed and was surprised to see that Christopher was awake. His right eye was swollen, with bruising on his cheek. His leg was in a cast, and he had gauze wrapped around his arm. She could tell by the way he breathed that he probably also had a fractured rib or two.

"Dr. LeClair, hello," he said in a raspy voice.

He tried to sit up, and Katie stepped forward to help him, finding the remote that worked the bed and pushing the button that would raise his head.

"Hello, Christopher," she said. "How are you doing?"

He closed his eyes. "I've been better."

Katie pulled up a visitor chair. She didn't know how long he would be able to talk, so she had to get right to the point. "Christopher, I came to check on you but also to ask you some questions."

He opened his eyes and gestured at the cup of water sitting on the tray by the bed.

Katie picked it up and held the straw out to him.

He nodded his thanks.

"Beth and I have been . . . looking into Ellen's death," Katie began. "We never thought it was suicide, and Beth knew her mother had been doing some research."

Christopher nodded. "It's true."

"What's true?"

"Marilyn Talbot is my half-sister. I've known forever, but my mother convinced me that the business would fail if I shared ownership with her," he said. He stopped talking, and Katie thought that was all he was going to say.

"My mother hated her. I realize that now. She was furious with my father for the affair and did everything she could to make Marilyn's life unpleasant. My father made me promise to watch out for her, and I did. But I should have told her the truth—especially after my mother died."

"Were you fighting with Ellen about it?"

Christopher closed his eyes. Katie waited.

"Christopher?"

"She wanted me to tell Marilyn. She wanted Todd to have more of a stake in the restaurant, and I wanted to wait. I needed to talk to the lawyers and figure out how to take care of everything."

"How did Ellen find out?"

Christopher sighed. "Some comment Beth made about Todd being color-blind triggered a memory. Ellen remembered a story my mother had told about my father's color-blind troubles. She knew it was rare and started poking around." Christopher stopped and breathed shallowly.

Katie sensed there was more and waited.

Christopher closed his eyes, and Katie worried he had fallen asleep. She pressed the button to put the head of the bed back down, and his eyes snapped open.

"She finally confronted me about it, and I told her everything. She promised to let me tell Marilyn and Todd after I had talked to the lawyers."

"Thank you for telling me," Katie said.

"I wish I'd never kept it a secret." Christopher sighed. He closed his eyes again, and this time Katie knew the medicine had taken effect. He'd be asleep for several hours.

Katie walked back out to the parking garage thinking about what Christopher had told her. She was starting to understand what Marilyn might have meant about digging up old secrets.

32

Katie called ahead to her clinic and asked them to reschedule everyone. She needed to follow up on what Christopher had told her.

"Lynn Swanson is already here," Debra said. "Should I ask her to reschedule?"

"No," Katie said. "I'll be there in five minutes, and I can see her. But reschedule the rest. Tell them I have a family emergency."

"Oh, no," Debra said. "Is your brother okay?"

"He's fine. I just need an excuse."

"Oh, gotcha," Debra said.

Katie disconnected the call and turned off the highway at the Baxter exit.

She rushed in the back door and dumped her bag and jacket on the chair. She walked toward the patient rooms and saw a chart in the bin outside of room five.

Lynn Swanson. The paperwork on top just said, "Follow-up." Inside the chart, Angie had logged the vitals and listed the chief complaint as, "Follow-up: refused to elaborate." Katie could imagine Angie's exasperation. She hated the idea of a renegade high-maintenance patient scheduling a fifteen-minute slot when they really needed forty-five minutes.

Katie knocked and opened the door.

Lynn was alone again. Katie noticed a healing bruise under her left eye. Probably three days old.

Lynn looked up as Katie entered and smiled. Her face was transformed, and the years fell away. Katie approached her and held out her hand. Lynn grasped it with both of her own.

"Dr. LeClair, thank you."

"You're welcome," Katie said. "What for?"

"The woman you referred me to has found a spot in a safe house. It's all arranged."

Katie sat on her wheeled stool by the low counter.

"That's fantastic, Lynn. I'm really happy for you."

Lynn nodded, and her eyes teared up.

"I need to make a few more arrangements, and then I'll plan to leave during Eric's poker night tonight. He never comes home before midnight, so we can be long gone by then."

"You're sure he doesn't have any idea?"

Lynn shook her head.

"I don't think so. They told me to act as normal as possible. I think I've been the same as always."

Katie wondered if Eric had noticed the new glow of relief and excitement that Katie thought was a tangible energy in the room.

Katie wrote her cell number on a card and handed it to Lynn.

"Here's my personal number if you need anything. You shouldn't take your cell phone with you. It's too easy to track someone that way."

"Yes, they told me that at the shelter. Thank you," Lynn said. "I didn't want to leave without seeing you to say good-bye. If it hadn't been for you, I don't know if I would've moved forward with this after Mrs. Riley died."

Katie briefly examined Lynn's eye. She told her how to take care of it and to watch for swelling even though she knew it would heal up just fine.

"I've had worse, as you know," Lynn said.

Katie squeezed Lynn's shoulder and nodded.

"Please let me know how it goes," Katie said.

She stepped out of the room and leaned against the wall in the hallway. She knew this was often the most dangerous time in domestic violence cases. She hoped it would go well for Lynn and her kids.

*   *   *

Katie quickly wrote her note and left the chart in her office. She hid it among a stack of medical journals. She was being paranoid, but she didn't want anyone to know what Lynn was up to until she had made her escape.

She grabbed her bag and jacket and headed out to her car.

She planned to talk to Marilyn about Christopher and whether she knew about the possibility that they were related.

She'd gotten the address from Beth and plugged it into her phone's GPS app. There were still many areas that Katie had never explored in Baxter. She followed the directions and found herself in a somewhat run-down neighborhood with small ranch houses and cottages. The yards consisted of burned-out grass, and many of the homes needed a new coat of paint.

She spotted Marilyn's address and parked just up the street. She was about to get out of her car when a blue pickup truck pulled into the driveway, and Eric Swanson climbed out. Now that she saw him from a distance like this, she recognized him as the man Marilyn had been talking to in the parking lot last week. Katie watched him go inside and then started her engine and pulled away from the curb. She'd have to try again later.

Her next stop was Todd.

She pulled up to a cute duplex that was just a couple of blocks from downtown. She knocked on the door and heard noises from deep inside the house.

Todd pulled the door open with a big smile and a fading black eye and then took a step back.

"Oh, I thought you were Beth," he said. "Come in."

Katie stepped across the threshold, and Todd closed and bolted the door behind her.

"Is Beth on her way here?" Katie asked.

"I think so. She was going to stop to pick up something for lunch."

"I wanted to talk to you about Dan Riley."

Todd rolled his eyes and slumped onto one of the armchairs in his small living room. "Okay, shoot. You probably noticed we don't really get along." He pointed to his eye.

"Yeah, I picked up on that." Katie sat on the edge of the couch.

"He's just mad because Christopher put me in charge of the Chicago restaurant."

"Is that all it is?"

"Yes, what else would it be?"

"I'm sure Beth told you about our theory that you might be related to Christopher."

Todd sighed. "I don't see what difference it will make. Of course, try to tell that to my mother."

"What do you mean?" Did Marilyn want him to claim his birthright? Did she harbor anger that it had been kept from her for so long?

"Christopher has been very generous. I own part of the restaurant here in town, and I get to run it however I choose. If I'm some kind of half-nephew, I don't think anything will change. But my mom is all worked up. She says Sylvia Riley made her feel like a loser her whole life."

"Why did Sylvia have anything to do with your mom?"

"I assume Sylvia figured out that her husband had had an affair and took it out on my mom when she was young." Todd waved his hand to encompass the whole room and maybe the whole town. "And she cleans for tons of people in town. She's done it for years. When my father left us, apparently Sylvia treated my mom like some sort of Victorian-era servant. I have no idea why my mom put up with it."

"I've heard Sylvia could be difficult."

"That's not the word I would have used."

Katie mentally checked off the question of whether Marilyn had known about her biological father. Apparently the answer was no.

"How did you get along with Ellen Riley?"

"Great. I adored her." Todd leaned forward. "Ellen's death has been horrible for everyone."

"How did she get along with Dan?"

"Well, that's another story," Todd said. "He never warmed to her. I think that Christopher's realization that Dan couldn't be trusted with the business happened right around the time he met Ellen. Dan was convinced she had turned Christopher against him. Which is ridiculous because he did enough of that on his own."

"Do you think he would have harmed her?"

Todd shook his head. "Actually, no. Dan is a bit of a bully. Like all bullies, he's really just insecure and something of a coward. Plus, Beth told me Ellen had been injected with something. Dan wouldn't know how to do that."

The doorbell rang, and Todd hopped up to answer it.

Beth came into the room carrying paper bags from Pete's sandwich shop.

"I would have picked up some for you too, Katie."

Katie stood. "No, I should be going now. You two enjoy your lunch."

Katie settled into her car and headed toward the police station. She wanted to talk to Carlson. She was starting to wonder if this paternity thing was the key. Todd may not be impressed with the news, but what about Eric? Now that Katie knew they were brothers, Eric would have just as much claim as Todd. Would Eric fight Christopher for part ownership of the business?

*   *   *

She parked down the street from the police station, climbed out, and locked the car. She was almost to the door when Cecily rushed out. Her eyes were red and her makeup smeared. She rummaged in her bag and didn't see Katie.

Katie took a few steps toward her. "Cecily? Are you okay?"

Cecily looked up in surprise. "Oh, it's you. I'm just fine—can't you tell?"

Katie took a step back. She and Cecily had always been cordial, if not friendly. But this was a different level of unfriendly.

"Can I help? What's wrong?"

"I think you've done quite enough. Why are you snooping around? You and Ellen are just the same. You can't just leave things be."

"I don't know what you're talking about," Katie said. She heard the edge to her own voice and worked to keep her temper in check. But her mind flashed to the page in Sylvia's book about Cecily's past. Did she think Katie had found out about that? Or was this somehow about Nick?

Cecily stepped closer and brought her face inches from Katie's. "I know what you're up to, and it's not going to work." She turned and stalked up the street.

Katie felt her heart racing, and her head pounded. She took deep breaths to calm down. She hadn't been threatened like that since a middle school run-in with the class bully. She didn't like the feeling.

She continued to the police station and went inside.

The same young woman was sitting at the desk as last time. Katie approached and asked if Carlson was in.

"Yup, let me find him for you." She hopped up from her seat and went to the door leading to the offices. She opened it and yelled, "Is the chief back there?"

She listened for a moment and then turned to Katie. "Okay, you can go back." She held the door wide, and Katie walked through.

John Carlson appeared from one of the offices. "Hi, Doc. Sorry about that." He tilted his head in the direction of the front. "We got a new intercom system, and no one knows how to use it yet."

He led her down the hall to his office. She sat again in the chair in front of his desk. Bubba's smiling doggy face looked down at her from the wall.

"What brings you here?" he asked. "You know I can't tell you anything about an ongoing case."

"Two things," Katie said. She slid the note that she had found on her porch across the desk. She'd sealed it in a ziplock bag.

Carlson took it out and read it. Furrows appeared between his eyebrows, and his lips compressed to a thin line. He slid the note back in the bag without comment.

"Tell me," he said.

Katie told him about not being able to sleep and going outside to find the note.

Carlson drummed his fingers on the desk and stared at the photo of Bubba.

Finally, he said, "You need to take this seriously. Why would you go outside in the middle of the night?"

Katie shrugged. "I wasn't thinking. I just wanted to see who was out there."

Carlson let out an exasperated breath. "I'll send this out to the lab for fingerprints. I still don't have the results from the first note. Promise me you'll be more careful."

Katie nodded.

Carlson pushed back from his desk. "If your second thing is questions about the case, I can't help you." He stood and gestured toward the door.

"No, I'm bringing you some information."

His eyebrows twitched up, and he sat back in his chair. "Excellent. What have you got?"

Katie told him about the likelihood that Marilyn was Christopher's half-sister. And what that would mean for Dan and Christopher.

"Interesting." He opened his ever-present notepad. "I'd never heard these rumors, but I guess it would have been more my parent's group who would have suspected. So you think Dan killed Ellen to protect his stake in the business?"

Katie sensed a thawing in the atmosphere from just a moment earlier.

"I don't know," she said. She leaned forward in her chair. "I assume Dan has an alibi?"

Carlson held her gaze for a moment. Then she saw his shoulders relax.

"He claimed he was in Chicago. And we never checked up on it—I mean he lives there, and we had no reason to suspect him. I'll get one of the guys on it, and we'll track it down."

"Also, someone told me they saw Christopher at his house that night hours before Ellen died."

Carlson smiled. "Mrs. Peabody?"

"Yes," Katie said with surprise.

"She called me the other day. Told me exactly what she thought of my policing but shared her information anyway." Carlson chuckled. "She's just as terrifying now as she was when I was in school. But Christopher is in the clear. I checked his alibi myself—he came straight from a meeting in Chicago to the hospital."

"Thank you for telling me," Katie said.

"Well, I didn't want you trying to interview the poor guy in the ICU."

"Of course not," Katie said.

33

That evening, Katie pored over her notes and followed up on some of the other people in Sylvia's book. She'd been so focused on Nick and then Christopher that she hadn't looked at some of the outlier possibilities.

There was Cecily, who Katie was currently disposed to suspect of any number of crimes. If she thought there was an affair between Ellen and Nick, would she have killed her friend? Did the friendship fizzle because Ellen had mentioned Cecily's secret past or because of Nick?

Dan was still a possibility. He had a temper and had possibly seen Ellen as a threat, but surely someone would have recognized him if he had come to town that night. And how would he have gotten Demerol?

Then Katie changed tactics and looked at the problem from the point of view of opportunity. Who had access to Demerol and access to Ellen's house?

She was back to Nick or Cecily. Either of them could have taken Demerol from the clinic, and both could have gotten into Ellen's house. She would have let them in herself.

Katie kept circling back to the hoodie-wearing stranger that Mrs. Peabody had seen. She was convinced it was Christopher because he had a key . . .

Her phone buzzed with a text message from Lynn: *I'm sorry to ask this of you, but I can't take my dog to the safe house. If I leave him behind, Eric might hurt him. He's threatened as much in the past. I know it's a lot to ask, but can you take him for a little while, just until things settle down?*

A dog in trouble was Katie's weakness.

Katie sent back a message: *Yes, I'll take him. Where's the dog? I'll come get him.*

What followed was a list of directions that seemed to wend their way into the woods. Lynn sent a photo of a small cabin: *We left Samson with my friend for the evening until you can come get him. Thank you, Doctor! I'll be in touch soon.*

Samson? She hoped it was an ironic name for a toy poodle.

* * *

Katie parked her car off to the side of the cabin on a patch of bare ground. She heard the woodsy sounds of squirrels chattering and crows cawing. The trees seemed to draw close around the small house as if protecting it from intruders. But the light was fading fast, and the shadows were deepening.

She crunched through the few leaves and stepped onto the wooden porch. Her knock echoed in the small clearing. Katie looked around nervously. The dog didn't bark.

Worried now that she was too late, she tried the door. Locked. Katie walked to the back of the cabin and peeked in the window. The place seemed deserted. Could Eric have already harmed the dog? Had he found them and taken them back home?

She wondered if there was a key hidden under a rock or on a windowsill.

Katie pulled out her phone to check the text. Could she have stumbled onto a different isolated cabin? Then she noticed that the text had come from Lynn's phone—her *old* phone. Katie had warned her not to bring her phone with her when she left.

Thinking about a hidden key reminded her of a fleeting thought she had about the key to Ellen's house. Besides Ellen, Christopher, and Beth, there was one other person who would likely have a key. She thought back over the last couple of days, and then she knew who had really sent the text.

Katie frowned. The pieces finally clicked into place. She backed quietly away from the window and turned to run to the car.

"Stop right there, Dr. LeClair." The voice was cold with just a hint of threat.

Katie stopped and turned slowly. Maybe she could bluff her way out of this.

"Marilyn, what are you doing here?"

"This is my cabin. I come here sometimes when I want to get away."

"I came out here to pick up a dog for a friend. Do you know anything about that?" Katie stayed at the bottom of the steps looking up at Marilyn. The light from inside made Marilyn no more than a silhouette, and Katie couldn't read her face.

"There's no dog here," Marilyn said. "Would you like to come in?"

Katie backed away. "No, I must have made a mistake."

"Yes, you did." Marilyn opened the door wider and pointed a hunting rifle at Katie's chest. "Come inside."

Katie cast a forlorn look at her car, but it was too far away to make a run for it. That was why Marilyn hadn't answered the door. She'd wanted to get Katie as far from the car as she could. She had no idea how good a shot Marilyn was but wasn't going to take the chance.

She walked up the steps and into the cabin. It was lit only by a couple of oil lamps on the kitchen table.

Marilyn pulled out a chair. "Give me your phone. Sit."

Katie sat and surveyed the room. They were in a barely used kitchen. If Marilyn spent any time here, she didn't do much cleaning. The table where they sat had been recently wiped, but the counters were covered in dust and food wrappers.

Marilyn gestured at the mess.

"My son likes to use this as his hunting base camp. I never could get him to clean up after himself."

Katie didn't say anything. She watched the rifle and stayed very still. She didn't want to agitate her more than she already had.

"I really liked you, Dr. LeClair. I wish you had left the Ellen Riley thing alone. What is it about you newcomers that you need to stir up trouble by looking into the past?"

"Marilyn, all Ellen discovered was that you might be related to Christopher. She suspected you had the same father."

The gun dropped and pointed toward the floor. "So it's true?"

"I don't know for sure, but it seems likely."

"When Todd told me, I was so furious with Christopher for all the years I'd tolerated his mother. All the years I was grateful to him for paying me to clean his house just so I could get by. I could run him over again, just thinking about it."

Katie didn't think she was doing a very good job of defusing the situation. She decided to give Marilyn something else to focus on. "You can take a DNA test if you want to find out for sure. Then you could sue him for your portion of the business."

"No, I don't care anymore. I just want to be sure Todd is okay."

"Todd?"

"Don't act like you don't know what I'm talking about." Marilyn glared at Katie. "Ellen Riley must have told you. She found out somehow. I heard her arguing with Christopher about how he should do the right thing. That Todd could handle it." Marilyn's eyes narrowed, and she swung the gun so it pointed right at Katie.

Katie felt her heart racing. Her mouth was dry. She had to keep Marilyn talking. Maybe she could convince her to put the gun down.

"Marilyn, how is Todd involved?"

Marilyn pulled a chair away from the table and sat down facing Katie. The gun didn't waver.

"I might as well tell you." Marilyn sighed. "I'm sure you've heard Christopher's side of the story. Even if Ellen never told you, I know you went to see him at the hospital. Besides, neither one of us is going to get out of this alive."

A chill crept down Katie's spine. *Just keep her talking*, Katie told herself. *Watch for an opportunity.*

"It was a night like any other," Marilyn began. "Eric was at a friend's house, so it was just me, Todd, and Noah. We'd finished dinner, and I was cleaning the dishes while Todd did homework at the table."

Marilyn nodded toward the table where Katie sat.

"I was nervous because Noah had been drinking. Anything could happen when he was drunk." Marilyn stopped and stared into space.

She looked back at Katie. "Anyway, Todd asked a question, and I turned to answer him. I hit a plate on the edge of the sink, and it broke." Marilyn mimed the action.

"That was all it took. Noah went ballistic. He came at me saying I was clumsy and stupid and that he wasn't made of money." She hesitated.

"I don't know why I did it. I still had the broken plate in my hand, and when he swung at me, I lifted my hand, and he sliced his arm open on the jagged edge. Blood was everywhere, and he was enraged. He launched himself at me and got his hands around my neck. I thought, *This is it; he's really going to kill me this time*. Todd was yelling at Noah to let go. Just as I started to see black dots, Noah's hands loosened, and he fell to the floor."

Katie didn't move. She didn't want to break Marilyn's trance.

"Todd stood there with the baseball bat that Noah kept by the front door. His 'antiburglar system.'" Marilyn tightened her grip on the gun. "Todd was only thirteen, just a kid."

"I'm so sorry, Marilyn," Katie said. "I didn't know."

Marilyn shrugged off the sympathy. "It was in Sylvia's book. She showed me where she had it all written out. After she died, I kept thinking, *Someone is going to find the book, and after all these years it will all come out*. But then, nothing happened. I thought maybe Sylvia had destroyed it before she died. Then one day at the house, I saw Ellen with the book. She tried to hide it, but I knew what I had seen."

"What happened to Noah?" Katie asked, but she had a feeling she already knew.

"Noah lay dead on the floor in his own blood. I didn't know what to do, so I called Christopher. We'd been close since we were kids. He was the only person I could think of who would help me and not run screaming from the house."

Marilyn stood and paced in front of Katie, far enough away that Katie didn't want to try to get the gun away from her.

"Ten minutes later he arrived. He took Noah out back and buried him while I cleaned up the blood. The three of us swore never to tell anyone. But Christopher told his mother, the worst person in the world to tell. She held it over my head until the day she died. She made it clear that with one word from her, Todd would go to prison even though he had been underage at the time. I was so glad to see that witch buried. And then, somehow, Ellen found the book. I wasn't going to live in fear of someone spilling the secret again. I had to get rid of her."

"I'm so sorry for what you went through with your husband, Marilyn," Katie said quietly. "But if Ellen knew about it, I don't think she wanted to hurt Todd. Christopher said she wanted him to acknowledge Todd as his nephew and to give him part of the business. I have the book now. You and Todd are not in it, but there is a page missing. Either Sylvia destroyed it or Ellen did."

"What?" Marilyn turned to face Katie.

Katie shifted in her seat, trying to gauge whether she could knock the gun out of Marilyn's hand.

Marilyn's eyes grew wide, and she set the gun down on the floor next to her. "What have I done?"

Katie stood and reached for the gun just as the back door flew open. Marilyn stood to face whoever was there. Katie's eyes widened in surprise, and she ran for the front door.

"Don't move, Doc." The voice was deep and raspy, and Katie knew who it had to be.

Katie turned slowly to face Eric Swanson.

"Eric, put the gun down," said Marilyn.

Eric shook his head. "Sit down, Doc. You too, Ma."

"Quit messing around," Marilyn said. "That thing is loaded." But she sat next to Katie at the kitchen table.

A crooked smile spread over Eric's face. "I'm glad you weren't bluffing. Imagine my surprise when I followed the GPS on Lynn's phone out to the cabin. I didn't think she'd be stupid enough to try to hide here. And I was right."

"Mr. Swanson, please put the gun down. I'm sure you don't want to hurt anyone."

Eric spun and leveled the gun at Katie. "I've been trying to get you to back off for weeks. I left those notes. I warned you. I thought once that meddling Ellen Riley was dead that Lynn would settle down. Little did I know it was my own dear mother who killed her." He winked at Marilyn. "Thanks, Ma. I could always count on you, right? And then you started in with Lynn, telling her to leave me."

"Eric—" Marilyn began.

"No. I'm not listening to you anymore. You have Lynn's phone, which means you must have helped her get away. How could you do that?" His eyes became red and watery. "She took the kids, Ma."

Marilyn stood and took a step toward Eric. She put out her hand, but just as she was about to touch him, he raised the gun and pulled the trigger.

34

Katie watched in horror as Marilyn crumpled and fell to the ground.

Katie took the opportunity to launch herself at Eric. She knocked the rifle out of his hand and slammed him into the cabinet. His surprise only lasted a moment, and then Katie felt him spin her around so her back was against the wall. His hands circled her neck and squeezed.

"Why didn't you just mind your own business?" Eric's face was an inch from her own, and she saw the fury in his eyes.

She knew she only had a few moments before she passed out. Her breaths were raspy, and she felt panic set in. Her hands were on his, trying to pry them off. She dug her nails in, hard, and felt his grip loosen. She put her hands on his shoulders and used the one trick she knew. She brought her knee up and into his groin and pushed him away at the same time.

Eric fell and curled himself into a ball. Katie grabbed the gun off the floor and pointed it at Eric. She eased over to

Marilyn, keeping an eye on Eric the whole time. Marilyn was breathing shallowly and winced when Katie touched her.

She looked around the kitchen for her phone and saw it on the counter next to the sink. Still watching Eric, she side-stepped to the counter and picked it up. When the emergency operator answered, she told her to send an ambulance and the police.

"Address?" the operator asked.

"I don't know. It's in the woods off route twenty-nine. It's Marilyn Swanson's cabin."

"The old Swanson place?"

"Yes, I think so."

"I'll have someone there in less than ten minutes. Stay with me on the line until they get there."

Katie wanted to help Marilyn. She could at least assess how bad things were and maybe stabilize her, but she didn't want to give Eric an opportunity to get away. He began to sit up, and Katie stepped forward and slammed the butt of the gun into his lower back. She hoped that it would reactivate his injury enough to keep him down until the police arrived.

She heard the voice on the phone talking. "What happened? Are you still there?"

Katie put the phone to her ear. "I'm fine, but I need to check this patient—I'm going to put the phone down."

Katie set the phone on speaker and set it next to Marilyn. She kept one eye on Eric, but he had curled into a ball again and wasn't moving.

She carefully rolled Marilyn onto her back and saw that the bullet had entered her right shoulder. Katie grabbed a dish towel off the table and pressed it to the wound. Marilyn moaned.

"Shh. You're going to be fine," Katie said. "Help is on the way."

Then she heard the sirens in the distance.

*　　*　　*

John Carlson was the first one through the door. He rushed to Katie's side.

"I'm fine, but Marilyn's been shot."

John looked at Katie carefully, and his eyes cut to the gun at her side.

"I didn't do it," she said. She gestured at Eric, who was trying to sit up again.

Carlson went to him and pulled him roughly to his feet. Eric cried out and grabbed at his back. Katie thought about telling Carlson to be careful but decided against it.

Carlson turned Eric over to Sean Gallagher, who had followed him into the room, and stepped outside to direct the EMTs.

Katie's hands were shaking and covered in blood when she finally stood up and let the paramedics do their job. She went to the filthy sink and ran water over her hands until it stayed clear. She wiped them dry on her jeans as Carlson put his arm around her shoulders and led her outside to his cruiser. She suddenly felt very cold as the shock settled in. John grabbed a blanket from his trunk, and she pulled it tightly around herself as she watched the stretcher come out of the house and get loaded into the ambulance.

The trees lit up alternately red and blue. Katie closed her eyes, but she could still see the changing of colors.

Finally, she heard the ambulance siren start up and disappear into the distance.

35

The tiny police station was packed when Katie walked in, still holding the blanket tight around her shoulders.

Sean and Chief Carlson had brought Eric through the back door to the interview room. The chief groaned audibly when he came out to the reception area to talk to Katie.

It seemed half the town was there. Katie and Caleb sat in chairs along the wall, and Katie fended off questions from Beth and Todd. Apparently Debra had called everyone she could think of when Sean got the emergency call about Katie and a shooting. Matt had been in the ER finishing his shift when he heard that a gunshot wound was on its way. He'd raced to the police station when he'd heard that Marilyn was the victim and Katie was with Carlson. Matt sat on the other side of Katie looking worried. Emmett and Nick stood with Linda Carlson and Debra. They all turned to the chief when he came through the door.

"I need everyone to go home now," he said. He held his hands up when the questions began. "I don't have any information yet."

Caleb had already jumped up and was dragging Katie toward the door.

"Wait," the chief said. "Not you. I need Dr. LeClair and her . . . friends to stay."

"We're *all* her friends," Emmett said.

Katie looked at him and fought the tears that had sprung to her eyes.

"No, just those friends," the chief said. He pointed to Matt and Caleb. Katie had told the chief that she, Matt, and Caleb had still been investigating on their own. He had not been pleased.

Grumbling ensued from the others, but they eventually left after extracting promises from Katie to call when she could.

The chief stood in front of the three of them and glared.

"Who is going to tell me how Katie ended up out in the woods with Marilyn and Eric and a loaded gun?"

"I went out there to rescue a dog," Katie said.

"I didn't see a dog," Carlson said.

"There wasn't one," Katie said. "I was tricked."

"Tricked how?" Carlson crossed his arms.

"I got a text from Lynn Swanson saying she needed me to watch her dog for her."

Carlson narrowed his eyes at her. "Do you always run a pet boarding service for your patients?"

"No." Katie dragged out the word to show her irritation with his snarky attitude. "She had gone into hiding at a women's shelter to get away from Eric. She said she was worried he would hurt the dog. You know how I feel about dogs in need." Katie knew it was emotional blackmail, but she didn't shy away from reminding John about his precious Bubba.

Carlson's voice softened. "Yes, I do know." He turned to Matt and Caleb. "You two wait here. I need to talk to Dr. LeClair alone."

Chief Carlson brought her back to his office. She nodded at the now familiar pictures of Bubba.

He gestured to the chair in front of his desk. "Do you want some terrible coffee?"

Katie shook her head.

Carlson sat in his brown leather desk chair and pulled a legal pad out of a drawer.

"Okay, shoot."

Katie told him the whole story. About her suspicions that Ellen had discovered something that led to her death, about the color-blindness research, and how she had guessed that Marilyn and Christopher were related. She didn't mention the computer or Caleb's assistance. She'd save that for another time if it became necessary.

She told him again about Lynn and her escape from Eric and how Katie ended up going out to the cabin alone, thinking she was helping Lynn by rescuing a dog.

And then, she had to tell him about Marilyn's husband and his death.

The chief took notes throughout. His pen only faltered when she described Todd hitting his father with a baseball bat to protect his mother.

"We'll have to dig up the yard out there and see if she's telling the truth," the chief said. "That's enough for tonight. This gives me a whole list of questions for Marilyn and Eric. As far as you know, Lynn is safely away with her kids?"

Katie nodded.

"Okay, I'll let Caleb take you home. I've got a long night ahead of me."

They walked out to the reception area again. Matt and Caleb stood as they came through the door.

Matt took a step toward Katie. "I was so worried when I heard that an ambulance was coming to the ER with a shooting victim."

Katie smiled and walked toward him. He put his arms around her, and they stood like that for a long moment.

Caleb sat back down and pulled out his phone. He feigned absorption in the small screen.

Matt pulled away to look at her. "I thought it was you who had been shot. Once I found out from the EMTs that you were fine, I came straight here to try to get some information."

"As you can see, I'm fine." Katie's voice shook, betraying the lie.

"I'd like to keep it that way," Matt said. And then he kissed her. It wasn't a gentle, tentative first kiss. It was an I've-wanted-to-do-this-forever-and-I'm-glad-you're-not-dead kiss. Katie felt warm and jittery and bubbly all at the same time.

Chief Carlson cleared his throat in an embarrassed but pointed way.

Katie and Matt broke apart and smiled at each other.

Matt nodded at the chief. "We'll take her home."

36

A month later, Katie and Matt bumped over a rutted pumpkin patch in a wooden wagon. Matt had claimed it was a necessary part of living in Michigan. Everyone went to the apple orchard and the pumpkin patch in the fall.

The grapevine had been overloaded when Baxter heard about what'd happened out at Marilyn's cabin.

There had been one final twist in the whole saga of Noah Swanson's death. They'd unearthed a skeleton with injuries on the back of the head *and* the front. Christopher had admitted that he had seen Noah move before he buried him and had hit him with the shovel "to be sure he wouldn't hurt Marilyn again."

Marilyn had admitted to killing Ellen Riley. She thought Ellen was threatening to reveal that Todd had killed his father. She'd filled the diazepam prescription with a stolen prescription pad and had taken the Demerol and syringe from the clinic. She'd hoped to make it look enough like suicide to fool the police.

The chief had his hands full figuring out whom to charge with what. Marilyn was charged with the murder of Ellen Riley and the hit-and-run of Christopher. Eric was charged for shooting his mother and assaulting Katie. And Christopher was likely to be charged with murder in Noah Swanson's death. The chief said he had a really good lawyer.

Matt put his arm around Katie, and she snuggled closer in the crisp air.

"You said you had some news for me," Matt said.

Katie turned to look him in the eye.

"We might be looking for a locums doc for the next six months or so," she said.

Matt's eyebrows rose. "Is Emmett finally retiring?"

"No, Nick needs to take some time off," Katie said. "The night Ellen died, he was at a Narcotics Anonymous meeting. Emmett found him a very exclusive rehab center. He'll have to go through a board review after he gets out, and we'll see what his situation is then."

"That's very interesting," Matt said. He pulled her closer. "What's the policy on interoffice dating over there?"

Acknowledgments

First, thanks go to you, Reader, for ignoring your phone, computer, tablet, TV, and other distractions to spend a few hours with these characters.

Thank you to the incredible crew at Crooked Lane Books: Matt Martz for believing in this book. Anne Brewer for making it so much better than it was. Jenny Chen for shepherding it through the publication process. And Melanie Sun for the beautiful cover design.

Thank you to my agent, Sharon Bowers, for helping me to continue doing what I love.

As always, a huge debt of gratitude goes out to the amazing writer friends who encourage, support, and inspire this literary journey: Wendy Delsol, Kimberly Stuart, Kali Van-Baale, and Carol Spaulding-Kruse.

And thanks to Steve, Jake, and Ellie for everything else.

Read an excerpt from

DO NO HARM

the next

DR. KATIE LECLAIR MYSTERY

by *DAWN EASTMAN*

available soon in hardcover from
Crooked Lane Books

NEW YORK

1

Not yet, but soon. He felt it like a shimmer in the air.

He stood by the window, peering out from behind the drawn curtains, flicking ash from his cigarette into an empty cat food tin resting on the table nearby. His nose wrinkled at the smell. Should have rinsed it out first. Another in a long list of should haves.

The cat, possibly attracted by the odor, skulked into the room. It weaved through his ankles, leaving long white hairs behind on his jeans, and meowed imperiously. He leaned down to pet it and it skittered away. The cat had moved in during his ten-year absence from his childhood home, and it saw *him* as the intruder.

He stood and fumbled for the lamp. Clicking it off, he squinted into the dim evening light. Darkness arrived earlier than when he'd first returned home a month ago. Then, it had seemed that summer would linger forever, and that he had his whole life ahead of him once again.

He clicked a beaded bracelet through the fingers of his left hand, bringing the cigarette to his lips with his right. Drawing deeply, he listened to the quiet crackle of the tobacco as it burned. He'd promised himself all those days, weeks, years in prison that he would appreciate the little things when he got out. Like a peaceful smoke in his own house, a clear blue sky, and the freedom to go anywhere. But on this evening, as the light faded and the streetlights flickered on (except for the one near his house—broken three weeks ago and still not repaired), he watched with the twitchy anxiety of prey waiting to be found.

He heard his mother's heavy tread in the kitchen and quickly stubbed out the cigarette.

"Eugene," she said quietly. A slight quiver in her voice gave away her concern, and he tensed with guilt. "Are they out there again?"

He shook his head. "Not yet."

She took several more steps into the room. "We have to do something. You have to go to the police."

He spun from the window, feeling anger replace the self-loathing. It felt better, more powerful, even if it was directed at the only person who had ever been kind to him.

"I'm not going to the police." He clenched his fists and turned back to the window. "Do you think they care?"

He'd dutifully reported the first acts of vandalism. GO AWAY spray-painted in red on the garage door had been hard to deny. After the officers had taken his statement, they'd said they'd look into it. Nothing had changed. He'd quietly painted over the letters and waited. Next was a classic: a bag of dog shit on the porch. Then, a rock thrown through the front window. Finally, a snarky map slipped under a dead bird on the hood of his car. The map had dark red arrows showing all the ways out of Baxter, Michigan.

Just as he drew breath to apologize for snapping at his mother, he heard it. A scraping sound outside. Someone sneaking along the side of the house. Before he had time to think, he ran outside to confront the intruder.

2

D r. Katie LeClair was running late. As usual. She stepped out of room one—a baby with colic whose mother was at the end of her rope—and glanced morosely at the line of plastic green flags that greeted her. Each one signified a patient who was ready to be seen and had probably been waiting longer than Katie would have liked.

She'd been working with Emmett Hawkins and his son, Nick, at the Baxter Family Medicine office since the previous summer when she'd finished her residency. Baxter was about twenty minutes west of Ann Arbor, and Katie had spent some time at the clinic during her training. She loved the way Emmett practiced an old-fashioned kind of medicine. The pace was slower and the pay was lower than Katie could have found in a bigger city, but she had found it to be the perfect fit for her.

She moved to the next room and pulled the file from the plastic bin affixed to the door. The file was thin. Katie flipped it open, hoping it wasn't a new patient wanting a physical.

That would push her into the rescheduling zone and she hated to do that.

She released a sigh when she saw it was only a suture removal. She read the brief intake information. *Eugene Lowe: 30 years old, 5' 10", 140 pounds, blood pressure 124/82.* The patient had been to the ER a week earlier. She noted Matt Gregor's signature at the bottom of the ER note.

She knocked and entered the room. The clinic building was old and the decor had not been updated in years. Someone had decorated in the eighties or nineties, which meant all the rooms had wallpaper borders running along the edge of the ceiling. Her patient had been put in the "kid" room, which had a brightly colored train border. The man sat hunched in the patient chair. He held a bracelet of light-pink beads in his hand and ran it through his fingers like a rosary. His dark hair was thinning on top, which didn't help disguise the large ears that stuck out from the sides of his head. He wore big round eyeglasses that covered the top third of his face. Thick black eyebrows almost met in the middle, and Steri-Strips covering a long cut over his left temple accessorized the lenses. Yellow-and-purple bruising betrayed a healing black eye.

Holding out her hand, she said, "Hello, I'm Dr. LeClair."

He reached up and took her hand lightly, not meeting her eyes. "Eugene Lowe."

Katie sat in the wheeled stool by the low counter. She opened the file and pretended to read its meager contents. Something about his demeanor and the healing bruises had set off alarm bells. She wanted to question him, but he seemed skittish, as if he would bolt any minute. "It looks like you need to get rid of some stitches." Katie flipped the file closed and turned back toward him. "Have you had any problems with the wound?"

He shook his head and studied his shoes. The beads clicked through his fingers.

"This won't hurt nearly as much as getting them put in. It just feels like a slight pinch."

He nodded.

Katie sighed inwardly. He wasn't much of a talker, and it made her feel like a camp counselor trying to jolly the shy kid into having fun. But she didn't need to get his whole story today. That was one of the things she loved about family medicine. There was time to get to know the patient.

She stood and gestured at the exam table. "Do you want to lie down on the exam table, or sit there?"

"I won't faint on you," he said. "I'll sit here."

Kate pulled the metal tray on wheels over to where he sat. She used sterile gauze and saline to wet the Steri-Strips and loosen the scab.

"What happened?" she asked. She pulled up on the knot of a suture and slipped the scissors underneath.

"I ran into a door."

Katie glanced quickly at his face. No one ran into a door and got this kind of injury.

"I haven't seen you here before. Did you just move to town?" Katie tugged a suture free and placed it on the tray.

"You could say that," he said. "I grew up here, but I just got back recently." He'd stopped clicking the beads and held his hands clasped tightly together—was he worried about the stitches or about her questions?

Katie had removed the first two sutures and tried to distract him by keeping him talking.

"Where were you living?"

"Jackson Prison."

Her hands hesitated, and he glanced up at her.

"They didn't tell you?"

"No," Katie said. She moved on to the next suture, not meeting his eyes. His guarded manner began to make sense.

He laughed bitterly. "You must be the only person in town who doesn't know."

"I'm new here myself, so sometimes I'm out of the loop on the gossip." That was an understatement. She felt like she was always playing catch-up. Katie pulled the last stitch free and set down her instruments.

She put a regular bandage over the cut and slid the tray away. "You may have a bit of a scar there. It should fade in time."

"Most things do," he said. He began fidgeting with the bracelet once more.

Katie placed a hand lightly on his shoulder. "Mr. Lowe, I'm not sure what kind of health care you received in prison, but if you'd like to come back for a physical or if you need anything else, I'd be glad to see you."

The beads stilled again. Eugene Lowe looked Katie in the eye and held out his hand. "Thank you." This time his grip was firm and warm.

Katie moved to the next exam room in line and pulled out the file. She smiled. Miss Simms was one of her favorites.

She knocked once and opened the door. Miss Simms was in the paisley-border room, Katie's least favorite. Katie was surprised to see Mrs. Peabody sitting in the guest chair while Miss Simms sat on the exam table.

"Hello," Katie said. She extended her hand to Miss Simms. She was a small woman with silver hair pulled up into a bun and the rounded physique of someone who enjoyed sweets. "It's good to see you up and about."

Mrs. Peabody made an indistinct noise, and Katie turned and shook her hand as well. Tall and thin, Mrs. Peabody wore her hair short and spiky with a pink streak on the right side. Both women were in their eighties. They wore velour tracksuits and brightly colored running shoes. Mrs. Peabody's tracksuit was the exact pink of her hair streak.

"I'm surprised to see you together today," Katie said. Usually the ladies made appointments at the same time but took separate exam rooms so they could fill Katie in more thoroughly on their concerns for each other.

"Well, I didn't need to be seen today," said Mrs. Peabody. "But I wanted to be sure Miss Simms didn't try to convince you she's totally recovered." She lowered her voice, as if it would make a difference in the tiny room. "You know how she is."

"Agnes, I'm sitting right here and I can hear you," Miss Simms said. "Honestly . . ." She shook her head and rolled her eyes at Katie. Katie suppressed a grin, feeling like she was in a room with a teenager and her mother rather than two retired teachers.

Two weeks earlier, the ladies had been driving their Vespas just outside of town to enjoy the fall colors when Miss Simms had hit a rock and tumbled off the scooter. Fortunately, she had been going only about ten miles an hour at the time and had escaped the accident with a few scrapes and a sprained wrist. Considering her age, Katie was grateful the accident hadn't been worse.

"How are you doing?" Katie asked.

Miss Simms sniffed and sat a bit straighter on the table. "I'm doing much better now." She held her wrist out for Katie to examine.

The swelling was gone, as was most of the bruising. She had good movement in the joint.

"Are you still wearing the brace?" Katie asked.

"Yes," said Miss Simms.

"No," said Mrs. Peabody.

Katie stepped away from Miss Simms so she could look at both women at the same time. "Which is it?"

Miss Simms sighed. "It gets in the way. My knitting production is down and we're heading into the holidays." She shot a glance at Mrs. Peabody. "*And* I don't think it helps."

Mrs. Peabody gestured at Miss Simms as if she were Exhibit A in a court case. "I told her to keep it on until you say it's okay, but will she listen? No."

"I think if you're to the point where it gets in the way and you don't have pain, you can probably stop wearing it." Katie addressed herself to Miss Simms. "We don't want the joint to get stiff or for you to lose strength in that hand."

Miss Simms smiled and shot an I-told-you-so look at Mrs. Peabody. Mrs. Peabody crossed her arms and looked away.

Miss Simms leaned closer to Katie. "Dr. LeClair, I hope you don't mind me asking, but did I see Eugene Lowe in the waiting room earlier?"

Katie thought that if anyone else had asked her that question, she would have said, "I don't know, did you?" But that would have been like kicking a puppy.

"It was," Katie said. "Do you know him?"

Both women nodded vehemently. "We both taught him in our classes," Mrs. Peabody said.

"I think it was just before I retired, maybe a year or two," Miss Simms said. "And then, of course, there was all that trouble with him during his senior year."

Mrs. Peabody nodded. "He was such a sweet boy. I couldn't believe it when he went to prison."

"He told me he's just been released," Katie said. "Why was he in prison?"

"Oh, my dear, of course you wouldn't know," said Miss Simms. "We forget that not everyone has been here forever. He was convicted of murder."

3

"**M**urder?" Katie said. Katie knew very well that murderers could hide in plain sight. That lesson had been brought home six weeks ago when a patient's presumed suicide had turned out to be murder. But when Eugene had said he had been in prison, she'd assumed tax fraud, or maybe he was a hacker or an identity thief. Murder had not entered her mind.

"Yes, dear," said Miss Simms. "We were all just as shocked as you. It was around this time of year."

"Halloween," said Mrs. Peabody.

Miss Simms nodded. "It must have been twelve or so years ago. He was found standing over the body of a dead girl."

A quiet tap sounded at the door. Katie's signal to wrap things up. There were some patients that could take up the whole clinic time if you let them. Katie and her nurse had a little code to move things along if necessary. She glanced at her watch.

"I'd really like to hear more about this," Katie said. "Can I stop by this week sometime?"

"Oh, yes. That would be lovely," said Miss Simms.

Mrs. Peabody nodded. "You know we have tea every day at five. You should stop by then."

"I'll do that," said Katie. She handed the clinic paperwork to Miss Simms along with a sheet on post-sprain care. "Be sure to take it slowly with your wrist and let me know if you have any trouble."

Mrs. Peabody snatched the instructions from Miss Simms and tucked them into her large straw tote bag. "I'll keep an eye on her, Doctor." She leveled a beady-eyed stare at Miss Simms, who pretended not to notice.

The rest of the clinic proceeded in a blur of coughs, colds, aches, and injuries. Katie finally made it back to her office at six o'clock and slumped into her desk chair. She tugged Eugene's chart out from the bottom of the stack and took out the ER discharge note. Matt was on the schedule to work that day as well, and since she hadn't seen him all afternoon, she assumed he'd been just as busy as she had. Midautumn was always a crazy time with all the back-to-school viruses, yard work injuries, and early influenza cases.

When Matt Gregor had first begun working with the practice, Katie had worried that it would negatively affect their new relationship. But, so far, they had been so busy it was almost as if they didn't work together at all. Matt spent part of his time in his father's internal medicine practice and did locum tenens shifts to fill the extra hours. It was like being a temp doctor. Physicians could fill in at clinics, ERs, or hospitals where they were short-staffed due to illness, vacations, or unfilled positions. Matt claimed to love the freedom and variety of his arrangement. He was filling in in Katie's office while her other partner, Nick Hawkins, was away dealing with personal issues.

Just over a month ago, Katie had solved a murder involving one of her patients and uncovered her partner's addiction to pain medicine. Nick had jeopardized the practice, and Katie was still not sure if she could forgive him for that, or for the stress he had inflicted on his father, Katie's mentor, Emmett Hawkins.

Katie got up, grabbed the ER note, and went in search of Matt.

She found him in the next hall over just coming out of a patient room. He was tall with dark hair that fell onto his forehead. His strong features and intense brown eyes made him classically handsome. But Katie loved his warm smile and the scar on his chin from a bike accident as a boy. Katie continued to be amazed at the way her pulse increased whenever she caught sight of him. He broke into a dazzling smile when he saw her.

"That's my last one," he said, and crooked his thumb at the door. "Are you finished?"

Katie nodded and followed him to his office. All of Nick's things were still there, waiting, but at least the desk had been cleared so Matt could work.

He dumped his stack of charts on the corner of the desk, peeked out the door, and pulled her into an embrace, which led to a long kiss that only ended when they heard footsteps in the hall. They broke apart and assumed casual poses.

Angie Moon, the office manager and nurse, peered around the door frame. She was a small woman with straight dark hair and thick bangs. A little older than Katie, Angie had helped Katie get used to the rhythms and routines of the clinic. She knew absolutely everything that happened in the clinic. By the way Angie's eyes sparkled, Katie suspected she and Matt weren't fooling her.

"I'm off; see you both tomorrow," she said.

"Thanks, Angie," they said in unison.

Katie took a step back and held out Eugene's ER discharge paper to Matt. He looked at her curiously and took it.

"Yeah, I remember him. Skinny with big ears?"

"That's him. I took his sutures out today," Katie said. "Nice work, by the way; it looks like he won't have much of a scar."

"Good. He had quite a laceration."

"That's what I wanted to ask you about. Did he tell you what happened?"

Matt glanced at the ceiling, thinking. "I think he said he fell while running, although it didn't seem like that's what happened. He had the beginnings of a black eye, but no scrapes on his hands or knees like you might expect with a fall."

Katie nodded. "Hmm. He told me he walked into a door."

Matt shook his head. "Not unless it was a really sharp door."

"Did you know he just got out of prison?"

"I heard something about that." Matt tugged on his ear and focused on his pile of charts. "But I'd think he'd be better off now. He doesn't look like the kind of guy that would survive prison very well."

Katie pressed her lips together. "Maybe. Unless he has more enemies on this side of the prison gates. I can't put my finger on it, but there's something off about him."

Matt pulled his jacket from the back of his desk chair and slung an arm over Katie's shoulder. "Are you interested in dinner at Riley's?"

Katie shook her head. "I have my Gabrielle dinner tonight."

"Oh, right. Forgot," Matt said. He gave her shoulder a squeeze and pulled his jacket on. "Maybe tomorrow?"

"Sounds good."